Graham's Resolution

Book 2

The Cascade Preppers

By
A. R. Shaw

Liberty Lake, Washington

D1713949

Dedicated to my father,

Amos R. Barber

Thank you, Dad, for giving me the writing gene.

Table of Contents

1 The Trail between the Trees 7

2 Daily Routines 17

3 His Best Girl 31

4 Addy at Heart 35

5 Skinning Wolves 47

6 Going on the Hunt 53

7 A Call In 59

8 Hunting 63

9 Whiteout 71

10 Precautions 75

11 A Sleep Over 85

12 Mark Takes a Walk 89

13 Frayed Ends 95

14 Tended 101

15 Not This Time 109

16 Decided Chance 117

17 A Quick Trip 121

18 The Carnation Boy 129

19 Manning Media 133

20 Marcy Moves 143

21 McCann 151

22 Good and Bad 155

23 The Caretaker 169

24 Story Time 173

25 Night Drive 181

26 Fire 183

27 The Return 193

28 Alarms 199

29 Missing 201

30 Found 207

31 Unforsaken 219

32 Tracker 225

33 Intervention 231

34 Coming to Terms 233

35 The Return of Sam 237

36 Repairs 239

37 The Fall 243

38 A Chance 247

39 Hope 253

40 Aid 255

41 Like a Promise 261

42 Dawn 265

43 The Last Candidate 267

44 The Birth of Spring 271

About the Author 275

Acknowledgments 277

The early winter sky was cast in a vibrant lavender that led to piercing blue above the horizon. It was as cold as hell is hot, if one can imagine the heat of hell as freezing. Graham pulled in the weighted line, hand over hand. He wrapped the twine from hand to elbow while staring down the murky blue ice hole of the frozen lake. The brown trout came squirming its way up the ice tunnel toward him to meet its fate.

Sam reached out and grabbed the greedy guy that currently hung midair. Removing the hook from its mouth, he dropped the frigid fish into a pail with its brothers. Sam and Graham were going for quantity over size when fishing in the shallow waters beneath the ice, but the chore of getting enough to feed everyone in their group had taken a little longer than usual this morning. In a matter of minutes the sky had gone from the deep blue, with a moon encircled in a fine mist to daylight so intense that eye protection was needed. Despite the warmth of the sunlight, extra layers of fur were still a necessity.

Once they'd caught enough for everyone's breakfast, they silently gathered their gear to make their way back up the trail to camp. Like any two men who'd worked the same routine, they would perform their job without uttering a single word with regard to the task. "Get your nose out of there, Sheriff," Graham gently warned the dog in a worn, low voice as he caught him peering into the bucket. "You'll get your share." He patted the dog's head, tousling his fur, and picked up their morning haul. Sam came up behind him with the other lines after he'd covered the ice holes with spare plywood to keep them from freezing over too much.

"Ready?" Sam asked.

"Yeah."

They crunched along the reliable crust as their boots echoed in the vast open until they met the trail between the trees. Mark had recently finished clearing the paths from that night's continuous onslaught of snow.

As they walked up into the clearing, Bang, dressed in his snow gear from head to toe, tossed scraps to the chickens as they scampered all around him, eager for the meager delicacies. Sheriff ran up ahead to help out his young friend. Amused that the dog didn't understand why they kept the birds caged, nor why he wasn't allowed to visit with them inside the coop, Graham laughed. The hens often ran away and rudely, collectively, scurried to the other end of their enclosure when Sheriff came to greet them each morning.

Graham called out to Bang, "Make sure you give them fresh water."

"I always do," Bang replied, looking put out by the unnecessary reminder, but then his expression changed. "Mark told me to tell you Ennis isn't up yet."

"All right, thanks. I'll give him a hand." Graham and Sam walked in silence past the front of the cabin. Sam seemed to be pondering something, which wasn't unusual for the man. One could spend the entire day with him and, other than a nod or an occasional word, he wouldn't say much, but Graham always suspected Sam was either thinking ahead or mourning the separation from his daughter Addy. Whether he'd ever let another in on his thoughts was anyone's guess, so it surprised Graham when Sam spoke up.

"You know, Ennis won't see another winter. You might want to be prepared for that, Graham."

Graham spoke softly. "Yeah, I've pretty much figured that out. We're losing him a little each day. He rarely talks, but when he does, it's always warnings. Like, he's trying to give us as much as he can before he goes." Graham stopped midstride and scuffed his boot into the ice, sending crystals a few feet forward. "I'm thankful we've had him for as long as we have."

Sam clapped him on the back. He liked Ennis too. The old man had even shown Sam a thing or two about carving the little wooden figurines he made for Addy, the daughter he could see and hear but never again touch. If a man taught you something useful in life, he was a keeper in Sam's book. Too bad they had to witness Ennis fade away so soon after coming to love and respect him so much.

"Hey, I'll clean the trout and gear. You go ahead and help Tala with Ennis," Sam said.

"Thanks, Sam." Graham handed off the gear to him, then noticed Sheriff trotting behind Sam in high hopes of a fish head or two. The dog easily shifted his daytime alliances based on who had the better treats. This morning Sam was the man, but by nightfall he'd no doubt shift his loyalty back to Macy.

Graham walked back toward the cabin, took the stairs two at a time, and thudded onto the porch. The cabin door swung open. Tala greeted him with a fretful expression.

"There you are! I need your help; he's not doing well," she said. The worry lines on her forehead became clenched as she fought back tears. Graham reached for her. "Shhh, don't worry," he said, soothing her as best he could. Not often one for anxiety, Tala had proven herself to be levelheaded, more so than most of the women Graham had ever encountered. Everyone silently predicted and dreaded the upcoming loss of Ennis. Yet, Tala's evident anxiety worried Graham and made him fear the end was near.

"Mark and I tried to help him up, but he said he'd wait for you. Sometimes I think he doesn't recognize us."

"I'll go check on him. Has he eaten or drunk anything yet?"

"I brought him some water earlier. I don't think he's had any yet." Then, lowering her voice even more, she whispered, "Graham, what are we going to do? He's getting worse every day, and he's avoiding water and other drinks. I think he's got an infection, and he doesn't want us to catch on to how much pain he's in."

"We've been lucky to have him this long," Graham said and pulled her toward him. She looked pale. He caressed the side of her face with the back of his hand. Looking into her eyes, he saw a flash of fear and wondered what scared her. Before he could ask, his attention was diverted by footsteps behind him. Macy stepped out of the bathroom, getting a clear view of their embrace.

"Can't you guys do that somewhere else?" she said, stomping with frustration out the door.

Graham and Tala both laughed. "Poor girl," Tala said, returning to the subject of the ailing old man. "I think Ennis needs antibiotics and phenazopyridine hydrochloride."

"Phenazo-what?" Graham asked.

"Phenazopyridine. Numbs the urinary tract. Don't ask me how I know. The antibiotics we have, but none of the other. I hate to think of him in constant pain."

Graham nodded. Hugging her close, he kissed her on the forehead, then released her. "Let's keep him as comfortable as we can until we know for sure."

Tala closed her eyes and nodded, unleashing quiet streams down her cheeks.

Graham took off his coat and he left her there. His shadow preceded him toward the bunkroom, gliding across the golden gleams of the formidably cold morning light as it spilled onto the worn, weathered flooring.

He strolled into the bunkroom to find Ennis asleep on his side; still and quiet, snoring with a whistling Graham had become accustomed to over the last few months. He straightened the covers a little and felt the old man's forehead for any trace of fever. Finding none, he left him alone to rest and closed the bunkroom door behind him to keep out the noise of the living, going about their morning routines.

"He's sound asleep right now," he whispered to Tala, not wanting to break the peace within the cabin. Best to keep things quiet for a little while longer before the others returned. "After breakfast, I'll try again. When's your next call into Clarisse? Maybe she can give us some pointers."

"We're scheduled to talk tomorrow afternoon." Tala still looked tense and, as Graham peered into her brown eyes, he saw something more concerning in there, in fact, on further inspection, she looked quite pale for someone with her American Indian heritage and skin tone. "Are you sick?"

"I'm fine. Just a little worried."

Tala quickly went off into the kitchen to get things prepared for breakfast. Graham wanted to press her for a better answer, but the door opened. Sam entered, with the kids and Sheriff in tow. Graham and Tala hardly ever had a moment of privacy, living in such close quarters with four kids, two additional adults, and Sheriff.

Sam handed the cleaned fish off to Tala for her to make quick work of pan-frying them; they were all starving from the morning tasks. While everyone else cleaned up and set the table, Graham reloaded the woodstove to fend off the persistent cold that seeped through the cracks in the old cabin.

Soon the sounds and aroma of fried fish fillets held promise for hunger, and a familiar line formed by the bathroom door to clean up before breakfast. Just as quickly, they finished their meal of cornmeal pan-fried trout, creamy grits, and biscuits without much conversation beyond the uttered gratitude. To keep their rations plentiful they didn't eat a formal lunch, so they'd learned to eat well at breakfast and dinner. If they were starving in between from the hard labor their days demanded, they partook of the extra baked goods Tala kept available.

Graham finished eating and looked up, expecting to meet eyes with Tala, as usual, but she purposely looked down as if in deep thought. He knew she was worried about Ennis, but he missed her usual cheerfulness. She seemed unnaturally quiet this morning. "Good breakfast, Tala," He said. "Thanks."

She glanced up at him and flashed a small smile, then went back to contemplating her meal, barely eating anything at all. He was about to ask her more when Sam piped up. Since Sam didn't waste words, Graham gave the man his full attention, while Tala and the rest of the gang began to clear the table.

"Hey, Graham, before you go…" Sam leaned one elbow on the table. "I want to propose another hunt. Mark and Marcy want to go out this time." He gestured toward the two teens, who scuttled out the door to stand their watch.

The noticeable pause after his statement told Sam that Graham had some reservations. "I don't know," Graham finally said. "I haven't seen a winter as cold as this in several years."

Sam knew that was true. The outside temperatures had ranged in the low single digits these last few weeks. It was February now, and they all yearned for warmer weather. As if the earth itself mourned the massive loss of human life, Mother Nature expressed her grief with a desolate landscape, draped in white. Still, Sam tried to convince Graham it was necessary to go out in the deep of winter yet again. "We need more meat to preserve for later, and the two kids should come along. They need to learn how to safely go on their own hunt next year."

Graham looked thoughtful, and Sam waited. He and Graham needed to teach them things for their own survival. In this life they now lived, one never knew if they'd see the next sharp cold days of winter, let alone the hopeful blooms of the coming spring.

Experience told Sam this hunt would be the last of the season before things got too muddy and dangerous to travel far enough to make the expedition worth it. He hoped Graham would see it his way.

"Can you wait another week?" Tala asked, breaking up the uncomfortable silence. "Maybe the temperature won't be so cold by then."

"If we wait any longer, things will start to thaw and the environment will be worse. Camping in wet snow is no fun, and it's much more dangerous hiking through the mountain passes, risking slides. This is the last safe time to go till later in the season. I wouldn't offer to take them out if conditions were too dangerous."

"Of course not, Sam. I think taking them out when things are at their worst is probably a beneficial learning opportunity for them. Marcy, for one, hasn't asked to go on a hunt until now, and this will be a good chance to improve her survival skills."

"Well, she might have ulterior motives." Tala voiced her suspicions with significant, feminine perception.

"There won't be any of *that*." Graham pulled a tired hand down his whiskered face. "If you go, just make sure the lovebirds stay busy." He sighed. "I don't know how much longer we can keep Marcy and Mark apart though. All of a sudden, I've been strapped with two teenage daughters, and they're driving me insane."

Tala darted a quick glance at him and then flicked it toward Sam as she leaned against the kitchen counter.

Graham caught on at once. "I'm sorry, Sam. Feel free to give me a swift kick."

Sam raised his hands up as if to physically keep the apology at bay. Yes, his pain at being separated from his own daughter was still raw, but sympathy didn't help ease it.

"Graham, I've accepted the way things are, for now. She's fine, and I still get to visit and talk to her. I can't be with her but, she's healthy and well cared for. Being apart from her kills me, but Clarisse said she'd keep researching a cure for the virus. I can only hope that one day she'll come up with something that will cure all of us. In the meantime, I'm stuck with you guys. No offense." Despite the way

Sam had worded it, Graham knew he still felt a certain resentment toward the carriers. The consequence of his sacrifice even strained relationships between them and the preppers at times.

Tala smiled. "No offense taken at all; we're happy you're here with us. We only wish the circumstances were different." Graham's nod of agreement looked as genuine to Sam as his contrition at having spoken carelessly.

Sam huffed out a breath that could have covered a sob. Even he wasn't sure which directions his emotions might go. "Me too. Even after months of this, the pain is still as strong as the day I left her behind with the preppers. I feel like a divorced parent, and Dalton's got custody of her. I love the guy, but hate him too. Does that make sense?"

"It makes a *lot* of sense," Tala assured him.

Though Graham and Tala had always encouraged him to talk about the situation, Sam seldom did. When he'd first arrived to live with them, he was too grief stricken to utter a single word out loud for fear he would release more than he could handle. Instead of gut-wrenching weeping, he kept to himself. He would leave early in the morning to hike through the woods. No one asked him what he was doing with his time. He'd overheard some of the kids ask questions, and when Graham told them to give him some time to deal with his torment, he knew the other man understood. The pain Sam endured was a living hell. Once—only once—Graham had commended him for not taking his anguish out on him and his little group of carriers. Sam knew he certainly felt guilt over the situation and wished there was something they could do to alleviate the circumstances.

The weight of Sam's grief sometimes came close to overwhelming him, but out there among the stoic trees, desolate mountains, and endless snow, he'd finally come to accept what he couldn't change.

Now that he carried the China virus, he had had no choice but to join Graham's camp. At least he still spoke with his daughter Addy over the radio, and every few days Dalton would bring her to the Skagit River rendezvous spot where, at a safe distance, Sam could lay his eyes on her. Somehow things had normalized, or at least worked in the only way possible given their situation.

It took time, but Sam adapted. Every day at dinnertime a place had been set for him at the table whether he was around the cabin or not. He always returned to settle in with them for the night, and then, slowly he began sticking around more and taking part in their daily lives. Now he felt like part of the family.

"I hear Addy has been spending a lot of time with Clarisse lately." Tala said. "We talk on the radio at least once a week. She enjoys having Addy in the lab, where she's taught her how to identify different elements through the microscope. She's even found a lab coat to fit her."

A prideful smile crept over Sam's face. "Dalton told me Addy would rather spend her time with Clarisse in the lab than at the day school. Said you gave her some tips on teaching Addy advanced math?" Sam asked.

"I did. I think this is the best arrangement for her. She's very shy, from what I hear. If she were to stay in the school with the other kids, she wouldn't progress as much as if Clarisse taught her. Clarisse is kind of a loner anyway. This arrangement is suitable for both of them."

"Dalton said Clarisse still blames herself somehow," Graham said. "She rarely leaves the quarantine building and sends the guard back to camp so she can sleep in her lab."

"What happened wasn't her fault. It wasn't anyone's fault. What happened *happened*. I'm a carrier now. At least I didn't die," Sam said in practiced resignation, then tried to change the subject. "So we're good with the three-day hunt? I can take the two lovebirds tomorrow?"

"Yeah, at least Macy can catch a break from their antics for a few days. She's getting pretty fed up, and she's armed. It worries me, man," Graham said, joking.

"All right, I'll get them geared up," Sam said and rose from the table.

"And I'll pack up the food supply," Tala said.

Each morning in this desolate life after death they rose and began the day's never-ending tasks together, each going their own way as cogs in a wheel; without one the others soon tired, and this jeopardized the whole bunch.

Graham went to put another log on the fire in an attempt to chase the persistent chill away. Afterward, he checked on Ennis once more, and found him sitting up and leaning against his pillow, whittling a potential arrow and dropping wood shavings on the blanket in front of him without a care. Noticing how Ennis shivered, Graham became concerned with him handling the sharp blade against the soft wood with his hands trembling so.

"Are you cold?" Graham asked him, but not only did he not acknowledge the question, he stared ahead and blindly slashed at the wooden arrow. Graham placed his hand on Ennis's shoulder, getting his attention. At first, his eyes looked as if he saw only a stranger but, after a second beat, a spark of knowing flashed. "Are you cold?" Graham repeated, trying not to startle him with a blade in his hand.

Ennis stopped and lowered the arrow and knife to his lap, as if he needed a moment to ascertain whether or not the shaking meant the cold had overtaken him or if the constant, burning pain caused the trembling. "No," came his words gravely and slow.

"Do you want to go sit in the living room by the fire? I'll help you."

"I can do it, but you can help." Ennis's old gnarled hands closed his knife with care, as they'd done countless times in his long life. Graham blew a silent breath of relief. He didn't want to hurt the older man's pride by taking the blade away from him. He peeled the littered blanket up and away and held out his arms to help Ennis up.

"I gotta go," Ennis said. So Graham helped him slowly shuffle his way to the bathroom. Reluctant to leave him alone, he stood close by after Ennis motioned for him to close the door. Graham left him to have his own way. *Hell, I won't want anyone to help me go when I'm an old man, either.* Still, Graham waited by the door. As a second thought, Graham peered around the corner to check if Ennis had drunk the glass of water offered to him earlier. The glass stood full to the rim on the nightstand. *Oh crap.* With the man shivering and not drinking, Graham began to worry he might be not only sick but also dehydrated. *He's probably got a bladder infection.*

Standing there adjacent to the clean and shiny kitchen, Graham noticed that Tala had already taken off to the greenhouse to work on the spring seedlings. *Is she avoiding me?* She loved spending time out in the greenhouse—they all did. The hopeful sprouts represented, somehow, a promised achievement, a milestone at long last. If only the damn snow would melt and go away for good, allowing them to line out the new garden and get things ready. The sooner, the better. They needed to enjoy a triumph in survival.

The greenhouse they'd found on one of their many scavenging hunts stood resurrected between the cabin and the lake entrance as a welcome addition and a harbinger of good things to come. Tala, so excited when they showed up with the deconstructed load, divided her day job between the care and keeping of the cabin, food preparation, and seed starting. She'd spent several days scrubbing down and sanitizing the inside of the building, piece by piece. Once the guys cleared the snow from a large enough area to erect the greenhouse, everyone pitched in to put the contraption back together like some giant jigsaw puzzle.

Now she used every possible spare container to start the seedlings, and, as his mother had taught him each spring back in Issaquah, Graham scavenged newspaper from the abandoned homes to craft spherical pots.

They set up tables with scavenged grow lights, and Tala emphatically threatened anyone who even considered touching the emerging tender sprouts. Mold and bacteria posed the greatest threats, and she kept as watchful an eye over the plants as she did her newly acquired family.

Graham chuckled to himself as he thought of Tala threatening Sheriff for sniffing at the seedlings the first and only time. She'd shaken her head at the beloved dog and pointed her finger at him. Sheriff had tilted his head to one side, perplexed by her peculiar actions. His big brown eyes conveyed his concern to Graham. *Has she lost her mind?* She'd made her point over the plants, though, and now Sheriff didn't even get close to the tables.

These days no one acknowledged the scars Tala had suffered at the hands of her two horrible kidnappers. Graham had happily cut the cast off her leg after Clarisse pronounced the bone healed enough. They made a grand production of cast-break day, turning it into a celebration of sorts; they needed all the celebrations, both minute and grand. Tala limped about gingerly for a week or two, and Graham helped her stretch out her calf muscles, but soon she walked perfectly fine on her own. Her outside scars had healed well.

But Graham growled to himself when his mind drifted to the thought of Tala's inside scars. In truth, she'd lucked out with the incident and refused to admit—to him or anyone else—the terror he knew she'd felt. If it hadn't been for Dalton's and Rick's invasive tactics, Tala's fate would have been much worse. Regretting Sam's fate beat out the fact that he didn't die of the virus and instead became a carrier. His suffering from being separated from his daughter because of this sacrifice was hard to bear.

Graham's mind drifted now. He and Tala had become close, in some ways closer than he and his wife had ever been, because of their recently shared circumstances. Tala's sudden distance told him something bothered her, something beyond Ennis's deteriorating condition. Her silence worried him because he knew her well enough to come easily to the conclusion that, for some reason, she now kept something from him—something important.

Ennis turned the knob of the door, signaling Graham to open it for him. The old man had neglected to tuck in his shirttails, like he usually did, but he had no one to impress these days. They all looked more unkempt as the winter wore on. Ennis seemed exhausted from this little journey to the bathroom. He leaned on Graham's arm.

"Do you want to sit by the fire?" Graham asked again. The old man's frail hands continued to shake, and the draft seeping through the cracks had them all wearing double layers.

"Yeah, I'll sit in there." It was good to hear a bit of strength in his gravelly voice. "Where's my girl?"

Happy for the first real sign of clarity, Graham asked, "You mean Macy?"

"Yeah, Macy. Where's she at?"

"She's coming. Don't worry, she'll be here soon." Graham guided him to the rocker by the woodstove in the living room. He settled Ennis down into the chair and grabbed the blanket draped over the back, tucking it around him. He added another log to the fire, then poked at the embers a bit, sending sparks flying within the enameled cast iron hold. After he had closed the latch, he asked Ennis, "Are you in any pain?"

"Nah, I'm all right."

Graham doubted this; he'd seen Ennis become punier over the passing weeks. He wished he had a cure to keep the old man with them longer, especially for Macy's sake. She'd become especially close to Ennis in recent months and would often read to him in the evenings after dinner from the various books Graham managed to scavenge. Macy would finish one chapter each evening, and shortly after, Ennis would rise and Graham would help him to his bunk for the night.

In the early morning Sam rose first and would assist Ennis into his chair by the fire and set him up with his coffee before heading out for the day. They'd all come to love Ennis so much, and Graham feared his inevitable death would be a real blow to the group.

They both looked up as Tala came through the front door, closing it quickly to preserve the warmth inside the cabin. Her earlier frown lines disappeared suddenly at the sight of Ennis up and about, and she flashed a thankful smile toward Graham. It removed all his doubts about secrets being kept.

"Good morning, Ennis. You ready for coffee?" Tala removed her outerwear and quickly reached down to hug the old man.

"No. You two gotta stop fussin' over me," Ennis said.

"We're not fussing. We're trying to care for you. You'd do the same for us," Graham told him.

"No, I would not! You're too much trouble to fuss over," Ennis said to fluster them. He seemed proud of himself for the dig and laughed out loud.

Tala smiled at Graham and murmured, "At least he still cracks jokes." Out of the old man's sight, Graham shook his head.

"I'll bring your coffee in a minute," Tala said, raising her voice a bit so he could hear her. She bent down to kiss him. Graham motioned for her to leave them alone to talk, in an effort to preserve Ennis's dignity.

"I could use some banana bread," Ennis called after her. "I miss banana bread." He held out both of his old gnarled hands, shaking as he formed a rectangle shape.

"I doubt we'll have any bananas around here for a long time," Graham said. He felt the old man's head for any sign of fever again. "In all seriousness, Ennis, you have a fever. I think you're in pain and keeping it to yourself. You're also not drinking anything. Do you have an infection?"

The old man huffed and looked down into his lap. "I do not want you to waste your medicine on me. I'm on my way out, Graham. Them kids, Tala, they might need them more—later. They do not make them anymore, you know that?"

The admission shocked and angered Graham. "How long's this been going on, Ennis? Hell, we can get more meds. Yeah, they don't make them anymore but there are sure as hell more supplies nearby. You cannot sacrifice yourself like this for us. *Jesus*, Ennis." He reached for the old man's face again, but Ennis tried to bat his hand away. "No, Ennis, knock it off, man. Are you even going? You know what I mean." He tried to whisper it.

"No, not much. Hurts to go," he admitted.

"God dammit! Tala, get him some water and the antibiotics," he yelled, ignoring Ennis's protests as he rose to take what Tala brought in.

She handed him the water glass and meds. "Go easy on him, please, or he'll shut down altogether. We do not have any painkillers for this and these antibiotics will take a few days to work."

"The old doc's house probably has those pain meds," Graham said as he handed the two capsules to the stubborn old man along with the water. "Take these and drink this," he ordered, then remembered Tala's words of caution. "Please."

Ennis accepted them both, looked up at Graham, and said stubbornly, "You're not the boss of me." He shook his head, but he took the medicine all the same. While he drank, Graham told him, "I am your boss right now, and that's okay. We'll trade, and you can be the boss of me later."

Graham looked behind him as Macy came in with cold rosy cheeks, "Tala, I'm ready to call in. Any news to report?"

"Yeah, tell them Sam, Mark, and Marcy are leaving in the morning on our last hunt for mule deer this season," Tala said. Graham was grateful she didn't mention Ennis's condition; best they keep it to themselves for the time being.

"All right, Macy said, rolling her eyes. "Not having them around for a while will be nice." She went into the bunkroom and sat at the table set up with the radio to the prepper camp. Communicating daily became her routine chore now—to make a check and relay news each morning.

Macy depressed the microphone's button. "Hi, Rick, Macy here," she said.

"No, no, no, you're doing the entry all wrong," Rick said.

"Why do I have to use the Twin Two call sign? *You* don't use a call sign," Macy complained emphatically.

"Rick *is* my call sign. I don't make up the rules, I just enforce them," he said, kidding her with the old cliché.

"Fine. Twin Two here," Macy said with as much mustered sarcasm as the occasion called for.

"Much better," Rick said. "Whatcha got this morning?"

"All is well. Sam, Mark, and Marcy are leaving on a three-day hunt, going north for mule deer tomorrow morning," she said.

"Okay, sounds good. We'll be free of the north exit by 0800. All is quiet here, except we're having a banjo tournament. We discovered there really is a Bigfoot, and we're having a pizza party. Sorry, you guys aren't invited," he said teasing her.

Macy didn't bite; she used her deadpan voice instead. "I'll share the good news. Have a spectacular day, Rick; Twin Two out," she said, barely acknowledging Rick's exit call before she hung up.

Macy often found Rick exasperating. Why they still went by what she considered an expired procedure mystified her. She liked that term, *expired procedure,* and always used it in references to school, politics, and braces. Only 2 percent of the population still alive meant the chance of an unknown tapping into their radio frequency was highly unlikely. Still, she enjoyed having a camp job that gave her an important responsibility, and she'd volunteered for it willingly. After the call ended, she wrote in the log, noting the time and response, leaving out the banter part, and went back into the kitchen to check in with Tala.

"I'm headed out for watch now," Macy said as she passed through, only to find Tala leaning over the sink, with her eyes closed, and breathing deeply. "Are you okay?" Macy asked, alarmed.

Tala quickly put her hand up behind her to ward Macy off. "I'm fine. I'm fine. I think I didn't get enough sleep, is all."

"Yeah, I heard you up early this morning. Did you eat something that was past its prime?"

"No, I don't think so. I'll be fine, go ahead to guard duty."

"Okay," Macy muttered, still concerned. She hadn't seen Tala this way before. Anyone coming down with an illness concerned them all. Naturally, fearing sickness after the pandemic came easily. For now Macy let her suspicions go, but she vowed to herself to keep an extra eye on Tala all the same.

On her way to gear up for the outdoors, Macy stopped to see Ennis. He gazed up at her, and when she smiled at him he reached up and patted her on the arm as if to affirm her existence, but no words trailed behind the effort. He absently returned his attention to the blaze of the woodstove, as Macy readjusted the blanket around him and donned her jacket, which Sam had lined with wolf fur to keep her warmed through in this prolonged, frigid winter. She holstered her pistol and slung her bow and quiver around her back.

She kissed him on the cheek. "Bye, mister."

Ennis peered up into her blue eyes again. "Yep. You be careful, girl. Keep your ears open, your eyes steady, and trust your instincts. Always trust your instincts out there. They'll save your life."

"I will, Ennis." She patted him, and he held her hand a moment too long. She smiled at him and pulled away.

~ ~ ~

Macy had to blink to let her eyes adjust to the bright morning light reflecting off the snow. The quick rhythm of Bang shoveling a trail to the chicken coop with his little shovel greeted her as she put on her gloves. Graham tinkered under the hood of the Scout, topping off fluids for the hunting party. "We're up, Bang," she shouted. "Guard duty!"

"Did you call in?" Graham asked.

"Yes, Graham. It's all good."

"Did he ask about the cameras again?"

"No, I think he's given up on that one."

"Last time I talked to him, he brought the subject up and griped about the injustice. I told him to take it up with Sam. Rick's not often without something to say," Graham chuckled, lowering the hood with a *clank*.

"Too bad. I can't believe they spied on us for so long."

"Well, it's a good thing, considering what happened."

"He still insists I use Twin Two," Macy said dryly.

Graham laughed out loud while Bang ran up to Macy, ready to go on duty.

"Any eggs yet?" she asked Bang.

"Nope, not yet. I think the weather is still too cold for them."

Macy handed him a hand warmer Tala had made with rice sewn into little flannel bags warmed in the oven right alongside breakfast. She kept them by the door in the morning so the watchers' hands wouldn't freeze. Macy put one in each of Bang's pockets and helped him to zip up his jacket.

"I get the lake today," she told him with a smile.

"I know. See ya," Bang said, and skipped away toward the driveway with Sheriff giving chase behind him. The lakeside provided more entertainment with wildlife than did driveway duty.

Macy waved at Graham, who waved back as she walked down the shoveled trail to the lake. The snow crunched and compressed beneath her boots as she walked. She squinted her eyes at the overwhelming brightness, the sun reflecting off the white snow in the clearing. Down the trail and in the shade, the temperature dropped further. Rick had an outside camera on her, though she'd forgotten exactly where, and she waved a greeting blindly toward its general area. It was all in the name of security, but having eyes everywhere still gave Macy the creeps. She didn't like always being spied on.

Hearing her twin, Marcy, stirring in the deer blind, she buffered herself for the possible quarrel she had come to expect these days.

"You're late again," Marcy accused.

"I am not. Get off your high horse, Marcy. I just got here."

"Remember, girls—no arguing!" Graham's voice came over the handheld radio, warning them both.

Marcy thrust the radio into her sister's hand. "You started it."

"Stop doing this, Marcy. I don't want to clean out the waste box again, do you?" Macy whispered sternly while holding the radio muffled against her jacket.

Marcy stomped off up the trail without another word, and Macy wondered why her sister had a need to drive a wedge of discontent between them every chance she got. She huffed out a breath, then braced her boot toe on the first step of the deer stand as she climbed up into position. She checked the perimeter with the binoculars they kept in the stand. Other than a small gray deer trying to sip from the frozen shoreline to the west of the lake, isolation reigned. She called in her report to Graham, knowing he would be expecting it on time. Afterward, she sat back and reflected on her troubled relationship with her twin.

Happy that Marcy would be gone for a few days, Macy couldn't understand her sister took every opportunity to needle her about something, anything. They were turning sixteen next month, and Tala planned to make a real cake for them—*if* one of the chickens laid an egg. Macy scoffed at herself. Last year at this time, she'd selfishly begged her mom and dad for an iPod, and now she looked forward to a chicken laying an egg so a simple cake might commemorate her and her sister's day of birth. They had lived on, despite the fall. So much had changed in only a few months.

A tear slid down her cheek anyway. She missed her mom and dad more than anything. She'd almost trade Marcy for either one of them right now. *Almost.*

The honking of approaching geese alerted Macy before she could see them, circling around and landing on the frozen lake. "Noisy birds," she said to herself. They reminded her of SeaTac Airport, where the planes would arc around as they lined up to come in for a landing; that seemed so distant now.

Her melancholy was broken by a gray shape darting out from the opposite end of the lake, chasing one of the waterfowl and sliding on the ice. Her heartbeat hastened until she felt the pounding even in her slim wrists. She drew icy air sharply into her lungs, depressed the microphone on the radio, and repeated in an intentionally calm voice three times, the way Rick had trained her, "Wolf on the lake, wolf on the lake, wolf on the lake."

Almost instantly, Graham, Sam, and Mark charged down the trail. Always armed and ready, the men were a formidable crew in any contingency. A wolf or bear sighting always meant serious business: the potential for meat and fur.

As Macy watched, two more of the dark animals raced onto the ice, but she didn't even try to aim at the creatures with her pistol or bow. The three men rushed past her and got into position. The three wolves were within sight, and if there wasn't a potential for a good hunt, the scene would have been comical: the wolves slipped and slid on the ice as the geese easily flapped and flew away.

Graham aimed and shot one wolf, dropping it quickly; the others aimed for the two fleeing toward the tree line. The remaining geese took flight in a rush as the booming gunfire resounded.

Mark took down his mark, but Sam didn't, and everyone sucked in a breath at this rare miss as the lone wolf took off. Still, they counted themselves lucky to have nabbed two.

"Good job, Macy girl," Graham said while the other two men went out to retrieve the kills. "It's a good thing I got the truck ready for the trip this morning. Looks like I'll be skinning in the greenhouse the rest of the day."

Graham had learned to skin animals from his father, but Sam had taught him several new tips and tricks for preserving the pelts so nothing was wasted. Everything would eventually be made into warm coats, blankets, or mittens. Macy knew Graham didn't enjoy the tedious skinning process any more than he or the rest of them had enjoyed the rift that processing the kills caused between Tala and Sam.

Graham mused over how, even now, the great wolf debate raged on. Thankfully they'd all came to an agreement over their first debate. Sam wisely never wasted anything from various hunts of deer or even bear. Tala, always accommodating, dried and preserved all cuts of game. However, when it came to wolf, she put her foot down. Tala's Indian heritage held her back from eating wolf meat. She refused to even handle the meat or the pelts since her traditions forbid consumption of wolf flesh.

Her grandparents had taught her this traditional taboo. Though she couldn't explain why, she said the ritual had something to do with the animal's soul. Sam agreed, instead of poking fun at her as she expected. Each of them held something sacred, and this was hers. After all, *Tala* meant "wolf."

The prospect of starvation had changed things, though, so they had made a contingency compromise: they would forgo eating the meat unless starvation became a factor. If or when food became short, all bets were off, and Graham said he'd personally make smoked wolf sausage if Tala didn't want to handle the kills herself. So, for now, they consumed all food except wolf meat.

Tala, typically easygoing and sensible, had surprised them when she'd adamantly spoken up about her aversion to the meat. But they'd all listened, and they granted her this one; Tala made few demands.

Even Sam admitted later that he'd never liked the taste of the gamey meat. Wolf meat tasted surprisingly too much like chicken, and it felt too close to eating your own dog. Since they all loved and admired Sheriff, eating wolf would be a particular turnoff.

For now Graham surveyed the ice as the guys slid the gray wolves to shore. Mark dropped his and ran up the trail to grab a sled, huffing and puffing, his breath in clouds.

At the same time, Tala's voice crackled over the radio clipped to Graham's belt, telling him she called in the disturbance to the preppers' camp so they wouldn't worry over hearing the commotion coming from their direction. "Thanks, babe," he said.

Sheriff came up to inspect Mark's kill, sniffing the large wolf, then trotting on to sniff the next one, only four feet away.

"Macy, can you call in to Tala and have her radio Rick? I need a child visitation tonight before dark please. I'll be gone for a few days, so I'd like to lay eyes on Addy before we head out," Sam asked.

"Sure, Sam. I should have requested the visit earlier." Macy relayed the message right away.

"I'll help you get these hung before I head out," Sam said to Graham.

Graham shook his head. "No need. Macy and I can handle it. She has muscles. You go spend time with Addy before you go."

"I just want to see her for a moment or two," Sam said.

Soon the sound of Mark and the sled dragging behind him drew closer. The boy did everything in fast motion these days. They were amazed at how well he had fully recovered from his unfortunate experience with the preppers. Though they'd had their reasons, it had been tough on the kid. When they'd first found him, he was a wreck, and now the young man could outdo both Graham and Sam at most any task.

"All right, let's get these up to the greenhouse," Graham said.

"I've got to finish packing," Sam said. He headed back to camp, closely followed by Graham and Mark dragging the sled with the two wolves piled on it.

Macy waved good-bye to them as they trudged back up the trail. Again she lifted her binoculars and checked all corners in her view and, after a moment, listened again to the lonely silence wafting across the frozen lake before her.

"All right, let's try this again," Graham said, "you two hold him by the shoulders and, on my count of three, we'll heave him upward, and I'll slide his"—he took a breath and wiped the sweat from his brow with his shirtsleeve—"back leg onto the hook. Ready?" Another deep breath. "One, two, *heave.*"

As Graham lifted the tail end of the wolf, Macy and Bang attempted to heft the rest of the weight high enough for Graham to slip one back leg over the hook by the sliced opening between the bone and tendon.

Graham's arms and shoulders shook from the effort of maintaining a steady hold on the animal. Macy and Bang grunted right along with him as they hoisted the animal into position. Triumphantly, Graham pulled the catch through the slice, and they slowly let go of the weight, releasing the breaths they'd held during the task.

"Whew, big guy! He must weigh close to a hundred and fifty pounds," Graham panted.

Bang laughed. "He's as big as you!"

Sam walked into the greenhouse, "Hey, I said I'd give you a hand with that." He strode to the smaller wolf, still lying on the sled, and lifted one back leg, shoving his thumb through the skin at the right place between tendon and bone. Then, he pulled the hook down, while at the same time hoisting the leg up. He slipped the hook through the slot in the animal's leg and hauled it aloft. He struggled a little, but his long sinewy muscles, accustomed to this type of work, proved their worth, and he let out a steady breath; it was nothing compared to Graham's exertion.

"How the heck did you do that?" Graham asked incredulously while Macy and Bang laughed.

Sam, never one to show up another man, said simply, "This one weighs less. I'm off to visit Addy. Be back later."

~ ~ ~

Sam busted through the layered snow, breaking a new path. It had snowed since the last time he'd traveled the trail to where the Skagit River bordered the prepper camp. The sun hung lower with midafternoon, behind the evergreen treetops, though you couldn't tell through the darkness of the thick forest; it might as well be late evening. Sam came closer to the rendezvous spot, thinking how the tinkling sound of the frozen river would soon become a roar as the spring snowmelt came from high in the Cascades. He walked into the clearing and brushed the weightless sugar snow off the boulder that he'd come to use as a waiting stool.

He fished the latest carving out of his jacket pocket and sat. This one was a gray wolf, like the one he'd shot at today and missed. He took out his knife and made a few detailed curving cuts along the chest of the animal to highlight the wolf's furry mane. Finally he scraped the soft wood smooth with the edge of the blade to finish the carving off.

Pretty soon his girl wended her way through the long, desiccated brush with Clarisse right beside her. Addy waved, her face lighting up when she spotted him. "Hi, Daddy!" she hollered across the river distance to Sam.

"Hi, darlin'!" Sam yelled back. How he masked his pain remained a mystery to him, but he was still glad he had the strength to shield her from the wretchedness within himself.

"Look at my hair, Daddy," Addy said and pulled her knit hat off. Sam's heart sank at the sight. His dismay must have showed because Clarisse turned the child to show him the back of her head.

"She wanted to try my hairstyle!" Clarisse shouted. "She still has all her beautiful long hair, Sam."

"It's beautiful, baby."

He remembered many evenings watching his little girl sitting on her mother's lap as she pulled the boar bristle hairbrush through her locks, singing a lyrical tune. He missed brushing Addy's hair himself, like he'd done after her mother's death, smelling the sweetness of her, rosy cheeked in clean pajamas fresh after her bath. Missing Addy and her mother kept him in a state of constant agony. "Thank you, Clarisse, for watching out for her," he said.

"Oh, no problem, Sam. We get along quite well." Clarisse hugged the girl to her side.

"I brought you a new one, Addy," he said, getting ready to toss the wolf carving overhand to the pine trunk, as always.

Clarisse took a baggie out of her pocket and handed it to Addy, who ran over to retrieve the figurine. There was little risk she would contract the virus from something Sam had handled, but they guarded against it anyway.

"Thank you, Daddy! It's beautiful," Addy said, examining the wolf carving through the plastic of the bag.

"You're welcome," Sam said, "Addy, I have to go on a hunt for a few days, but I'll be back soon, okay?"

"Okay, Daddy." She frowned as a thought crossed her mind. "But you will come back, right?"

"Yes, Addy. I'll always come back to you. I won't ever leave you, baby."

"Daddy, I miss you," Addy said loud enough for Sam to catch the disappointment in her voice, over the expanse; more of a confused question than a statement. She didn't understand their circumstances. How could she, when even he walked around in a half-life, constantly bargaining for any remedy in silence?

"I miss you more, sweetheart." Sam's own voice fractured. "I won't be gone more than three days. Draw me pictures, okay?"

"Okay, I will. I love you, Daddy. Be careful on your hunt," Addy said, waving her little left hand while she held the beloved wood carving to her chest with the right. She blew her dad a kiss over the void, and Sam caught it and sent another back to her, not at all worried how foolish the ritual might seem to Clarisse.

"Bye, Clarisse," Sam said, but he suspected she didn't trust her voice to say it back. She simply waved good-bye to Sam, as he visually guarded them, watching them walk back into the forest and out of sight.

Sam's heartache made him tremble. "Dammit," he said under his breath as he placed both hands above his knees and doubled over, facing the snowy ground below.

The merciless sorrow infiltrated his soul with an agony as incessant as he imagined a crucifixion must produce. He awoke each morning and met the day filled with the knowledge of where he was, and why, and what he'd left behind, then carried the same pain with him into sleep. Sometimes his visits with Addy sustained him enough to subsist, but others, like this one, left him feeling like a prisoner, powerless to protect himself and his daughter from the madness.

"I will never leave you," Sam whispered the vow. He took his time getting back to Graham's camp.

Clarisse held Addy's hand as they walked back to camp. "How about you and I go to the mess hall and grab dinner before they eat all the barbecue TVP chicken?" Clarisse suggested in an attempt to break Addy's glum silence. Most people in camp liked the chicken flavored textured vegetable protein, and it usually went fast. The girl hadn't said much, and Clarisse sensed the wheels turning as Addy's young mind sought a solution to the problem. She was that kind of child, and Clarisse sympathized, but too much reasoning and plotting could lead her into trouble. If Addy was working on a way to be with her father, Clarisse would need to head her off at the pass, to keep her safe in spite of herself. Addy was looking for a solution instead of thinking about chicken TVP.

"Clarisse, Dad stays away from me so I don't get the virus. But can't you figure out a way for me to get it, so I can go stay with him? I think he's lonely." In genuine concern, little lines etched on her forehead.

Clarisse knelt down by the child's side on the snowy path. "Sweetheart, every spare moment I'm working on this." She tucked a wayward strand of the girl's locks behind her ear. "Nothing would make me happier than you and your dad being back together, but I can't give you the virus. Do you understand that if you get it, you might die?"

"Daddy didn't. He got better."

"Most people don't. If I let you die, your daddy would be very, very unhappy. I know he's unhappy now, and you are too, but you're both alive and can see each other, talk to each other. You just can't touch, because it's dangerous to you. I promise you I'm working hard to find a vaccine, but I don't know if it's even possible. Please understand, I'm trying everything I can, but I don't want you to get your hopes up, dear." She hugged the girl again, as much to hide her own anguish over the situation as to comfort Addy.

"Now, come on, let's go get dinner, and you can show Dalton your new animal."

~ ~ ~

The guard buzzed Clarisse and Addy into the main camp, and they made their way over to the mess tent where the preppers caught up with one another toward the day's end. Dalton waited with open arms to greet the girl. Addy didn't run into his embrace like she would her father's, but leaned into him for a long hug, frowning.

Right off Dalton sensed melancholy in both Clarisse and Addy. He shot Clarisse a questioning look. She smiled sadly and shrugged in answer, as if to say, *What else can we expect from this situation but a sad little girl?*

"Hey, Addy, what did your dad make you this time?" Dalton asked. Addy held up the baggie displaying the wolf carving. When her sad brown eyes met his, he said, "Wow, I like how the fluffy tail came out. He's getting better and better at carving. Do you want to show the boys?"

She shook her head and pulled the baggie closer to her chest. Her reaction, and the reason for it, brought a hard lump to Dalton's throat. He wrapped her up in his arms again, trying to dispel the feelings of unwantedness, unwelcome in his family, that he was pretty sure she held; he lifted her and sat her on his knees on one of the dining table benches.

Clarisse went to get Addy's dinner. Dalton smiled as he watched her. Being a picky eater herself, Clarisse would select Addy's meal with care. The child always wanted things simple on her plate, predictable, exactly as she did with other things in life—facts laid bare, not dressed up, no trying to make something of it that it wasn't.

Just like Kim, Dalton thought as he stood to set Addy down on a bench to await her food. He went to get his own dinner. The line was longer now, moving slowly, but he was in no hurry. As he stood waiting for his turn to be served, he thought about how his wife had reacted to the idea of caring for Addy.

~ ~ ~

Without ever really trying, Kim had quickly given up even the pretense of trying to communicate with the girl, and the whole situation had put a strain on their marriage. In public, Kim said the things she should have, but in private she remained stone cold to the task. She had her boys to prove her capable of motherly love. This devastated, quiet little girl with great but unspoken neediness was too foreign to her; *beneath her*, she said.

She excused herself to Dalton by telling him of all the time and effort she'd spent trying unsuccessfully to reach the girl, and revealed regretfully that they just "never clicked" despite her efforts. As Kim would say to anyone who asked about the situation, "I just don't *get* her," as if Addy were the one at fault.

One day Kim had discovered Addy hiding in the latrine during school hours. She yelled at the despondent little girl, who'd escaped there to cry in privacy; the other kids always made fun of her for crying.

Later that night Dalton found Addy up in the dark of night, packing her own backpack to leave camp. Something had to give, or the girl would end up hurting herself. He argued with his wife to accept her because he owed this debt to Sam. He couldn't understand why Kim held such animosity toward the orphaned girl; it made no sense to him. How could she be so hard as to let a harmless child sense she wasn't wanted? Besides, what other options were there?

That same day, he later learned, Kim had made a rare appearance at the quarantine building expressly to speak with Clarisse. Kim had concluded that, of all the females in the camp, Clarisse—another person she didn't *get*—would have the best chance of becoming a guardian for Addy. As Kim explained it to Dalton that evening in bed after a quiet but intense session of lovemaking, Addy was just like the antisocial, brainy, outcast doctor, only in a younger form. Pawning the girl off on Clarisse was the best way. End of all the troubles; end of story.

That night Dalton stroked the soft, pale skin of her exposed hip. She lay on her side, curves highlighted by the glow of a flickering lantern. Kim knew her value and always used it to her advantage. She whispered sweetly, "Dalton, about Sam's kid. She does not belong with us. She doesn't fit in. She'll have to go."

He lifted his hand, stopped the caressing. Kim turned to face the wall, obviously uncaring what his opinion might be on the subject. She always left him to view the good parts instead of her flaws. The lantern light danced on the exposed crack of her bare ass, her lower back, the dipping curve of her waist, her slender shoulder. He loved her even though he feared her inner soul contained nothing more than frost.

"Go?" he echoed, turning her back to face him. Her expression was guileless. "Go *where*?"

"Clarisse will take her. I've already fixed it. You'll see I'm right; it's for the best." Again, she turned her back, pulled the covers over her shoulder and burrowed into the covers.

Dalton lay staring at his wife's form for a long time. Then, without a word, he rose from their double camp cot. He pulled his mottled green camo pants up over his naked hips. His dog tags jangled away from his chest as he bent over, slipped on his boots, and lifted the lantern. As he left their tented room, he peered in on his boys' partition, watching their little chests rise and fall. He turned again to the next section and sought out Addy's form, only to catch her up on her knees at the end of her cot gazing up through the small plastic window at the moon. She detected his presence as he stood silently looking at her. She half turned. "Do you think Clarisse will like me?"

It disturbed him that Addy had heard. He and Kim had learned to be quiet in lovemaking as well as in private discussions. Not wanting to address Addy's question he said, "Why aren't you sleeping, sweetheart? It's late." The moonlight cast a glow on her profile.

"Not sleepy." Addy fingered the fabric of her nightgown, pleating the hem, squeezing it tightly then smoothing it out. She looked at him. "Can Daddy see the moon, too?"

Dalton swallowed hard. "Yes. Yes, he can." He pulled a chair over to her so he could gaze upon the moonlight too, both of them in on this wondrous event; Addy turned back to face the bright orb with something of a smile on her crimson lips. The full, bright moon obviated the need for the lantern he held.

After turning the wick down, he said, "You're never far from your daddy. He can see the same moon you do—the very same. Now try to sleep, sweet girl. I'll stay right here with you." He held the covers open so she could snuggle down beneath. After tucking Addy in, he patted her back. Closing her eyes, she held the contented smile. Placing a light kiss on her temple, Dalton sat back in the chair next to her bed and gazed at the moonlight.

Kim's attitude toward Addy wasn't going to change. Dalton knew that, though he didn't like it. But if it had to be done, it was best to get it done at once. As the sun rose, its light replacing the moon's, he waited for the sleeping child to stir. She blinked up at him, bringing an automatic, if reluctant, curve to his lips. He didn't feel particularly happy. He felt as if he was betraying Sam as well as Addy.

"Good morning, dove." He brought a finger to his lips. "Let's go for a walk," he whispered. He'd already gathered her knapsack as she lay sleeping through the wee hours and he sat sleepless, thinking. Slinging the pack over his shoulder, he reached for Addy. She smiled, he knew she knew. She stood barefoot on her cot while he wrapped her up in the blanket, keeping her warmth to go out into the cold.

At the crack of dawn in the prepper camp, few wanted to meet the day so early. Clarisse was one of those, rarely spotted coming and going from the quarantine building, if she left it at all. That would have to change, Dalton knew.

Keeping Addy warm in his arms, he buzzed the gate and nodded to the sentry. Addy smiled a hello. The hush of the cold morning had her snuggling closer in, tucking her legs up close, leaning against Dalton's chest.

"S'okay, Addy. I'm taking you to Clarisse. To stay with her from now on. Do you understand?"

She nodded.

"She will take good care of you. I'll visit every day, sweetheart." He tightened his arm around her. He tried his best to keep the pain and resentment out of his voice.

"Clarisse is lonely too. I like her," Addy whispered.

"I do too," Dalton said as his boots crunched on the snow-covered gravel. Then Addy pointed up with a small finger. Swooshing wings beat the air in near silence. He stopped and they both looked upward at the gray morning sky to see geese flying in V formation—flocking toward the lake, Dalton guessed, near Graham's camp.

Dalton smiled at Addy, and her at him, sharing another special event. They reached the quarantine building in a happier mood, having enjoyed the sight of creatures parting air, still prevalent and unchanged despite the catastrophe that had befallen the world.

Dalton, still carrying the girl, nodded to the security guard who buzzed him in.

"She's in the lab."

"Thanks."

Clarisse looked up as he entered the room. She met his gaze before the child's. "Hi," she said, putting on a bright smile for Addy's sake. "You two are out bright and early this morning. Come on in. Addy, I'm so glad you're here," she added, dispelling Dalton's doubts in that instant. "I hear you're going to be my new lab assistant."

He put the girl down. The blanket fell about her bare feet. Her flannel nightgown hung down. Her brown hair stuck out, wild and unkempt as Addy embraced Clarisse's waist.

Dalton watched for it, for the acceptance of this precious girl. On reflex, Clarisse hugged her back and pulled her hand over the girl's tangled locks. She glanced quickly at Dalton, and he got the silent message she sent. She knew Dalton needed her to *love* the child, not just keep her. But she would have without question, without him needing her to. To Clarisse, Addy was a gift, never a question.

She knelt down to Addy's level and smiled brightly. "Let's get you cleaned up and fed."

"Do we have to go back to camp to eat?" Addy asked.

"Nope. I have enough snacks here," Clarisse replied.

Clarisse adored her already.

Clarisse reached for Addy's backpack. Dalton forgot he'd borne the weight of it all the way from his tent, as he had the child. He'd also carried a much greater weight, the one in his heart. It lifted as he watched the scene play out.

"Thank you, Dalton, for bringing Addy to me," Clarisse said.

He knew she meant it, knew for certain she saw the child as a gift, not a burden.

Dalton swallowed and bent down to bid Addy good-bye. He held her soft hands, and she leaned into him. "I'll visit with you at dinner tonight, Miss Addy."

She kissed him lightly on his roughened cheek, a sweet little brush. "Thank you for bringing me to Clarisse, Dalton." He kissed her on the forehead and stood. Addy placed her hand inside Clarisse's, and they waved good-bye to him.

As Dalton turned to head down the hall his heart ripped, but he knew Addy was where she needed to be. When he arrived back in the camp, he let Kim know he'd done it for the child's sake, not for hers.

Some time before, Dalton had expressed his concern to Clarisse about her spending nights alone in the quarantine building instead of within the prepper camp compound. But this arrangement killed two birds with one stone: Clarisse and Addy would come back each evening so that they would be in the safe confines of Clarisse's sleeping quarters and within the boundaries of the prepper camp. She was wanted, and both she and Clarisse were safe at night. Dalton felt like he'd failed the child, but he knew he'd still get to visit Addy every day.

~ ~ ~

Clarisse's passing by him as he neared the serving table brought Dalton back to the present. He smiled at her as she walked past, a smile she returned. He was glad he'd made two people happy. Well, three, if he included his wife, though that fact was a mere by-product.

Clarisse brought Addy's tray to her. While the others were having barbecue TVP chicken over rice, Clarisse opted to bring Addy her rice dressed with faux butter spread and a dash of salt and pepper, knowing the girl would not care for the rich barbecue sauce mixed in. She spooned a little of the main course on the side along with her reconstituted mixed vegetables. A slice of homemade bread and canned mandarin oranges rounded out the meal.

Clarisse always made a point of effort to converse with Kim at dinner now in an effort to ease the tension. She liked to think Kim had felt overwhelmed by all her diverse tasks in the camp and had acted in Addy's best interest. While she knew it had been against Dalton's wishes for Addy to move in with her, she had no complaints. Addy made her life complete. Well, almost.

As she went back for her own tray, Clarisse made a point of complimenting Kim on her cooking skills. "I don't know how you do it. You've managed to make something different every evening, giving everyone something to look forward to." Though she said it with effort and a forced smile, she hoped Kim would believe she meant it. In truth, Clarisse didn't care much for the woman. She felt Kim didn't appreciate her own husband and acted as the camp socialite, but she kept that slight contempt to herself, all the same.

"Well, we all have our jobs. I'm thankful I can bring a smile to most folks," Kim said in her singsong drawl with a little dig toward Addy. Then, as if she remembered a question for Clarisse, or perhaps just wanted to keep a dialogue going with her for Dalton's sake, she said, "Clarisse? Tammy and I were working in the greenhouse, and we had a question about cross-pollinating. Tammy says that you cannot plant pumpkins next to other squash but, I remembered planting them next to zucchini without any problems. Do you know what she's talking about?"

"It's a bit tricky," Clarisse informed her. "Pumpkins can cross with other squash, and different kinds of squash can cross with each other. But you will not see the results in the crop that year; you'll still get what you planted. It's the *seeds inside the fruits* that are affected, so if you take those seeds and plant them the following year the fruits you get then will be a cross. Sometimes they're quite strange looking—exotic—but often they're inedible. So if you intend to save the seeds for the next year's crop, which obviously you do in our circumstances, then you want to keep them separate to avoid cross-pollination."

"Okay, we're starting some of the seedlings now and planning the garden layout at the same time."

Clarisse said, "That's good news. We're all very excited about eating fresh vegetables. Let me know if you need any help. I'm sure Addy would love to work in the greenhouse," she added, then immediately regretted her words.

"That's a great idea." Kim lit up like a Christmas tree at the prospect. "We should get all the children involved. We'll have a sign-up sheet!"

At the mere mention of a sign-up sheet Clarisse smiled and nodded, figuring that was all she could take. She backed away with her tray, nodding and smiling until she thought it might be safe enough to turn around and escape. She sat next to Addy, feeling as though she'd completed her quota of required socializing for the day and then some.

Clarisse watched as Addy finished her rice and worked on her oranges, giggling and listening as Dalton retold the story about how her dad had snuck up behind a moose so quietly last fall that the massive beast jumped when it realized a human had come that close. "Just like a scared cat." The little girl laughed at the thought of her dad besting a moose. In Addy's mind, there wasn't a thing her dad couldn't do.

Clarisse watched as Addy climbed onto Dalton's lap and nestled into his arms while begging for another story about her dad. She ached to keep that happiness on the girl's face. When Addy turned to tell one of the other children that what Dalton said about her dad "was so true," Clarisse met Dalton's eyes and mouthed, *Thank you*.

He smiled and mouthed back, *Anytime*.

The inside of the greenhouse smelled of the loamy peat starter mix they used to encourage the new seeds to germinate. Graham associated the strong odor with the Easter holiday and with digging graves. More disconcerting was having the two memories mesh together—chocolate bunnies with pastel bowties and factory-produced yellow marshmallow chicks next to visions of him covering his father's face with dirt. Every time he set foot in the building these pictures flashed before his eyes, but that's the way it was. He would shake his head and exhale at the absurdity of his reactions. The others had similar triggers to past memories, both good and bad; you never knew what would prompt a reaction to the old in this new world.

He and Sam had erected two temporary posts for the purposes of hanging kills, to bleed them in the greenhouse. This temporary arrangement was agreed upon by the greenhouse boss—namely, Tala. They'd reserved enough space in the front to hang two kills at a time. As long as they promised not to disturb the greenery, Tala wouldn't deprive them of coffee.

Skinning for actual taxidermy purposes would take a lot more attention to detail than their needs called for. They only wanted the most intact fur from the beasts, so Graham didn't bother skinning out the paws or the head, which would take him an additional two to four hours sitting on an overturned bucket with a spotlight and visions of brightly colored jellybeans and pastel Easter eggs to contend with. He ran the small sharp skinning knife down the inside of the wolf's paw up to the inside elbow and then up the inside shoulder, with the blade tip right under the skin. Then he made similar cuts for the other limbs, after first using a lateral cut to start pulling the hide back. Afterward he ran the sharp blade from the inside back leg, up to and around the anus.

Next he sat on the bucket and scraped back any tendons or tough tissue patches as he pulled the skin down toward the skull. Skinning wolves meant stinky work, but once you got the hang of the task, you ignored the musk and pushed forward. Some of the silly visions dispersed as the odor took over.

When he got to the line around the neck he continued to finish out the forelegs. The tedious task would take most of the evening to complete both beasts, but, if not done properly, the hair would fall out of the hide. If that happened, all the effort and benefit of the task would be lost.

Graham had learned the skinning process from his dad many years ago, never realizing he would come to depend on the skill. So now, when he picked up the knife, memories flooded in a rush. Each time grew easier, and now he appreciated the memories even though, in the beginning, they nearly drove him mad.

With several building projects planned once the warm weather took hold, he'd hoped to add two more bedrooms onto the cabin; one for him and Tala and one for the twins to share. Afterward he and Sam would begin working on a better barn structure. They wanted to get a hold of a few beef and dairy cows to help supplement their diet, and possibly start a small herd.

He was nearly down to the tail when Marcy came through the entrance, bearing a welcome cup of hot coffee.

"Hey, Tala said you needed this," she said, presenting the steaming cup.

So far they'd managed to find coffee out on their scavenging trips, but Graham dreaded the day the coffee ran out.

"Give me a second," he said as he stood up, put the knife away, and removed his gloves. As he pulled the fingers of the glove off one by one, he came to the conclusion that Marcy didn't usually come around bearing gifts, and Graham suspected more to the delivery than mere coffee.

Marcy settled the warm cup in his cold hands.

"So, are you packed up for the hunt?" he asked her, knowing he'd better lead the conversation.

"Yeah, I'm ready." She lingered, passively studying the raw flesh with barely the tip of her finger.

"You cleaned your gun?"

"Yes. As you showed me, Graham."

She rolled her eyes, strolled away from the kill, and wandered behind Graham toward the seedling tables. He remembered his father telling a neighbor once, "You always have to stay at least one step ahead of teenagers to keep them from killing themselves." *Great advice, if you weren't already three steps behind them to begin with,* Graham thought.

She wanted something. Hope thickened the air they breathed. He took another sip of his coffee and vowed he wouldn't make it easy for her.

"So, what were you and Macy starting to argue about earlier?"

"Nothing, Graham." This wasn't going the way she wanted it to, and he was glad for that. "I just thought she ran behind, but we worked it out. Like you told us to," she added.

"Good. You two are sisters, and for the life of me, I can't figure out what the heck you'd have to argue about. You're the luckiest set of carrier siblings here. In fact, you're the only set of carrier siblings I know of, so far, so be thankful." He wondered what else he could yammer on about to keep her true intentions at bay.

"The only other carrier blood relatives we're familiar with are Dalton and Mark. They're cousins and, of course, Dalton isn't a carrier," he rambled on. He wasn't ready for the conversation he knew she was coming to talk about. The longer he held her off, the better.

She rolled her eyes finally and said, "I know, Graham! I'll talk to you later," and then stomped back to the cabin.

Graham took another sip and couldn't help but chuckle. This parenting thing was a pain in the ass, with fifteen- going on sixteen-year-old twin girls. At least he'd managed to hold her off one more time.

After mooning eyes at one another for months now, he suspected she and Mark were getting closer each day, but Graham and Tala felt they needed to wait at least another two years. At only sixteen going on seventeen, Mark had a lot to learn before he became a husband.

Ennis looked at it differently; he'd lived in an era when early marriage was commonplace, and to see fifteen-year-olds married off wasn't unusual. He argued that these were strange times, and if they were committed to one another, then that was fine with him. Graham and Tala decided Mark and Marcy could wait until she was at least eighteen. This would give them enough time to teach the two as much as they could.

Pregnancy presented another problem altogether. Clarisse warned them all about the possible risk of the virus affecting a fetus and mother. So far, none of the prepper community had become pregnant, so Clarisse hadn't been faced with the issue head-on. Graham and Tala took precautions on the few times they managed to be intimate, purely because they were scared of the outcome. Tala had already miscarried once, and Graham wasn't about to put her through that again since there was no assurance that a child would make it to term. There was no way of knowing the virus's effects until afterward.

Graham finished his cup, pulled on his gloves, and went back to work. By the time he pulled the second hide free, the sun had long deserted him, and he had managed by spotlight alone. A moment later, Tala called him in for supper. "Give me a little more time to put this on the frame. I'll be in soon," he called to her.

Stretching the hides over the frames didn't take him long to complete, especially with his stomach growling after a hard day's work.

Early the next morning Sam woke Mark, who in turn roused Marcy. Everyone spoke in hushed tones to keep from waking the sleeping ones.

After dressing quickly, Marcy gazed over at her sister's sleeping form. She contemplated saying good-bye, but somehow her pride kept her from giving into the urge. She didn't want to be only Macy's twin sister anymore. She thought of herself as more than just someone's sister. In Mark's eyes she was more than that; with him, Marcy—for the first time in her life—became separate from Macy. *Finally*, she thought.

Marcy met Tala in the small kitchen, lit only by the kerosene lantern they used in the dark to help conserve the solar-powered electricity, where they packed the food the hunting trio would need. Tala gave Marcy a hug, and then a well-meant warning: "Marcy, listen to Sam and Mark. Keep yourself safe, and don't take any *risks*." There was an emphasis on the word *risks*; Tala was hoping to get a point across to the girl.

"I won't," Marcy said with an incredulous smile. "I'm not a baby. Honestly, you guys treat me like I'm a fragile child."

"Marcy, we're all fragile right now," Tala said. "Please, mind Sam and don't give him any trouble," she repeated.

"I won't," Marcy promised, remembering how "not fragile" meant "whole," and to become less than whole, or dead, happened too easily now. Sifting through the events that had led them to this spot became harder as the months passed by. Trying to keep the right memories in place and let the others slip away, while at the same time trying to grow up, was a continuous task.

Mark and Sam met Graham out by the Scout, which was already idling, and helped them load the equipment. When Sam went in to grab another load, Graham pulled Mark to the side and issued a warning, not unlike the one Tala had given Marcy. "Mark, listen to everything Sam tells you to do, and don't let Marcy take advantage of you."

Mark began a mock coughing. He hadn't expected Graham to come right out with it in this way.

Graham smiled while Mark recovered, and with a grin Mark said, "Graham, Marcy and I have an understanding. I promised you I wouldn't let her 'take advantage of me,' as you put it, until she's eighteen. I plan to keep that promise, but only until then."

"If anyone else said that to me, I'd strangle him, but Mark, you're just as important to me as she is. I'll even give you away on your wedding day, as long as you keep your promise," Graham said, still smiling. "In all seriousness, you guys listen to Sam, and be careful." He hugged the young man.

Sam, Marcy, and Tala came out, followed by Sheriff, who came to see what the commotion was at this early hour. Sam got behind the steering wheel and Marcy climbed in the backseat, claiming she hoped she could get a little more sleep as they drove.

The sky began to hint at a purple hazy sunrise. With Tala at Graham's side, they waved good-bye as family members would when leaving on a long journey. And that is what they'd become over this time — a family of sorts.

As the engine noise dissipated in the cold morning silence, Graham led Tala back into the cabin, and Sheriff decided he wasn't ready for this day either, so he trotted along inside as well and camped beside the warmth of the woodstove instead of returning to Macy's bed.

Graham halted Tala in the living room and contemplated "taking advantage" of her in the semiprivacy of the quiet early hour, but Macy or Bang would, more than likely, wander in. *I can't wait for spring building*, he thought. He settled for wrapping her up in his arms and falling back to sleep on the couch instead. She still looked pale to him, and he questioned her insistence that nothing was wrong.

~ ~ ~

No more than an hour later, Graham woke and reached over to stroke Tala's long dark hair as she lay sleeping on his chest. Sensing something out of place, Graham opened his eyes to find Ennis sitting in his rocking chair, staring blankly at the flames inside the woodstove. Graham hadn't heard him come into the room.

"We're not supposed to be here," the old man muttered to himself or to a ghost; Graham didn't know.

Not wanting to wake Tala, Graham lay still and observed Ennis for a while. If he could figure out his curious behavior, he might be able to help him. It worried him that he'd walked the distance by himself from the bunkroom. Somehow, in Graham's mind, the longer the old man was spared for them, the safer they'd all be. He just hoped he'd learned as much as he needed to from Ennis and, at the same time, hoped Ennis realized how much they'd all come to love and appreciate him.

"Storm brewin' an' we's in for some trouble, now," Ennis muttered, nodding his head up and down. This time the old man looked directly at Graham.

"What trouble, Ennis?" Graham whispered. He knew Tala would wake, but he didn't want to startle her.

"Them, over the river," Ennis said and gestured with a raise of his hand toward the prepper camp.

The old man's eyes wept. Graham didn't know if old men's eyes just did that or if Ennis meant the tears. "The preppers are in for trouble?" Graham asked him. He could understand where Ennis would come to this conclusion since the death sentence of H5N1 still loomed over everything and everyone.

"Yeah, they're in for some trouble," Ennis repeated, nodding again, then returned his milky stare to the woodstove's lingering flames. Eventually he nodded off slumping, his head lolling over toward one shoulder.

When Graham had first come across Ennis here in the cabin, the old guy frequently tossed out some eerie phrases. Some people might have thought they were premonitions, but at the time, Graham suspected the old man was putting on a show for them. Now, with Ennis slowly slipping away from them, the unfathomable warnings had returned. As before, Graham took them as the mere wanderings of a tired mind.

Tala rose from her comfortable position and sat up, smiling at Graham. "Did we have an audience?" she asked.

"For a while. He's fallen back to sleep, I think," Graham whispered. Pulling herself away, she went to check on Ennis. He had drooled on himself, so she retrieved a clean rag and gently wiped his face. After touching his cold hands, she decided he needed a blanket. Graham handed her the one they shared, and as she tucked it around him, she looked up, frowning. "Something's wrong, Graham. He doesn't seem right."

Graham stretched his tall frame and widened his eyes in an effort to wake up, having had too little sleep lately. "Yeah, he mumbled something about a storm brewing and the preppers being in trouble," Graham said.

"I'll be talking to Clarisse today. Maybe she can give us some tips to help his pain," she said concerned. Graham saw fright in Tala's eyes, and he reached out to hold her. "He was just a gift for a short time, but we both know he won't be with us for much longer. We were lucky to have him to begin with."

A scuffling sound came from Sheriff. He was having his "chase the squirrel" dream again. Both of his front and back legs moved as he lay on his side in front of the woodstove with an occasional grunt exerted toward the hunt. With this distraction, both Graham and Tala relaxed a little.

"I hope he gets it this time," Graham mused, and Tala laughed quietly.

"Me too, poor guy," Tala said and slipped away to make the first pot of coffee of the day, patting Ennis's shoulder along the way.

"Has he taken in fluids in the last twenty-four hours?" Clarisse asked after Tala relayed their concerns over Ennis.

"Yes, he had a glass of water, but not much more. He had a little fish and grits this morning, and biscuits and gravy for dinner last night," Tala explained.

"Has he used the facilities?" Clarisse asked tactfully.

"Um, he goes in the bathroom, but I don't think he's passing much, if any. He's admitted to being in some pain. We've given him antibiotics, but we don't have the numbing pain meds for this. Do you think there's some locally?" Tala said.

Asking for pain meds from the preppers would be no use since they probably didn't have enough to spare. Instead Tala hoped to be able to find them somewhere in town.

"The antibiotics won't kick in for a few days. The elderly seldom show urinary tract pain symptoms unless the infection is quite severe, so the fact he's in pain concerns me. He's admitted to being in pain, he's running a fever, and is probably holding back. Yes, I believe he needs phenazopyridine and cranberry juice, which will limit the amount of bacteria able to adhere to the bladder wall. You can also give him a hot water bottle to ease the pain. An anti-inflammatory would help a little. If you found the numbing meds, that would be best. I hate for him to suffer from the pain for so long."

"Clarisse, my grandmother used a tea of sage and bearberry for urinary tract infections. Every time she fed me the stuff as a girl, I'd gag. I never thought I'd revert back to the old days, but do you think the medicinal teas would be safe to use?"

"Both ingredients contain proven scientific antiviral properties, so yes. If you get a hold of clean, dried ingredients, then use them. As time goes on, I believe we'll need all of your grandmother's medicinal recipes. Try to remember them, and write them down. All the major med producers are gone these days." She added, "I wish I could give you the meds, but our supply is very limited, and there are a lot of us here. The rules are, unfortunately, the rules, and I have to abide by them. Graham may need to run into town. I'm sure the meds would be at the old doc's house. I'm sorry, I wish I could be of more help."

"I want to do something for him to make him more comfortable. Last night his fever seemed to cause him some delusions, and he warned us trouble was coming to the prepper camp. Of course, he also keeps asking me for banana bread. I wish I could make some for him as a treat." Tala laughed, but began to cry at the same time.

Clarisse tried to comfort her. "Aw, Tala, you guys gave him a life to live, a life with purpose. At least he hasn't been wasting away in a nursing facility. Don't feel bad."

"I know. It's just that we've all come to love him in such a short time. He's a part of us here. Even Sam will sit with him for hours, talking on occasion and whittling little animals for Addy. How is she, by the way?"

"She's better, and with Dalton right now. It breaks my heart that she can't be with Sam. I've got an experimental vaccine in the works, but it's not tested yet. Unlike all the others before, this one shows some promise. I'll be able to determine whether or not it will be useful soon, but I don't want to get her hopes up. I know the separation is hard on Sam, but for a seven-year-old-girl to be indefinitely kept away from her own father has to be worse."

Tala heard tears clog Clarisse's voice too.

"Well, for now, she's loved and cared for, and Sam is doing okay here. We know the situation with the cameras upset Rick, but I think it gave Sam a little release on his anger to take them all down. Seeing him do that, Macy thought he was crazy until he explained to her we were all on camera," Tala said.

"Yeah, Rick's that kind of guy. He cares deeply and has a scorched-earth mentality when it comes to those he cares about, but no regard to personal privacy," Clarisse explained. "He'd rather forgo some liberties to be safe."

"He sure has Macy trained on the radio," Tala said, then remembered a personal question she'd meant to ask Clarisse earlier. "Hey, before you go, I wanted your advice on our young romance here."

"They're not doing that already, are they?" Clarisse asked.

"Um, I don't think so, but I want Marcy to be safe when the time comes," Tala said.

"Well, coupling is perfectly normal for human nature during a crisis. Couples pair up and mate out of a need to procreate. The term is *biological imperative*. But I'd be concerned about the effects of the virus on a fetus. I'm not certain if a pregnancy would carry to term. At birth, will the fetus be born with immunity or a half chance at immunity? Or will the baby be born without any immunity? There are many unanswered questions. So let's think about putting her on birth control for now as a precaution."

Tala was quiet for a moment, and Clarisse thought perhaps they'd lost the connection. But then Tala said, with some concern, "She's only fifteen."

"Yes, precisely. In fact, both girls are fifteen. They're at a young but reproductive age, which means if they, by chance, run into the wrong fellow, the consequences would be terrible for them. I'd like to recommend you pull the pill packets out of the med kit we sent back with you. I added several, enough for you and the girls for at least three years. I also included quite a few pregnancy test kits. Hopefully we will not need those for a while. Good luck getting Macy to take them. She seems like my kind of gal." Clarisse chuckled.

Inadvertently Clarisse had already answered one of Tala's pressing questions. She was relieved she didn't have to try and weasel a fake question for her deepest concern.

"Yeah, but I think if I explained the consequences to her, she might be willing to take them. She's a sensible sort," Tala said.

"Well, you've got your hands full, that's for sure. I've just had a sweet seven-year-old girl fall into my lap, and I'm loving every minute of the time she's with me. She's given me a greater purpose."

"The twins can be a challenge at times, but more than anything the bickering between them bugs us," Tala said.

"Yes. That is them, pulling away from one another and becoming individuals. That's normal at this age. The behavior will pass in time. Just make sure they don't get physically combative with one another." Clarisse chuckled again.

"There are days . . ." Tala said, now laughing. She was about to come clean with her friend, right there, but was too reticent to admit her suspicion out loud just yet. Instead, she let the conversation end and said, "Well, I've got to run now. Good luck with Addy."

"Oh, thank you. Let me know how the pill goes with the girls. I'll call in next week and see how the introduction went. Bye for now; Clarisse out."

"Tala out."

Tala sat there, a bit stunned, knowing the thing she had to do and afraid of the confrontation. The unknown and possible risks to an unborn child lingered in her mind. She stared out the window of the bunkroom, watching the way the snow blew from one direction to another. The trees were swaying in a heavier breeze than before, and she knew what Ennis warned was true: there was a storm coming.

8 Hunting

Sam pulled the Scout into a draw between the snow-loaded trees on an old logging road. The condition of the cypress boughs indicated the path hadn't been used in recent years. He crept along so slowly he'd lose the race to a slug, then came to a stop and put the truck noiselessly into park. To quiet the innocuous jingle of keys as he turned off the ignition, he cupped them in this fist. This would be the first spot they'd try for a few hours, and then later, farther down the snow-covered highway if they found nothing here. He and Graham had had good luck in this area the last time they'd tried. He told Mark and Marcy to disembark without a sound, and they made less than a click closing their doors. Sam did everything mute.

Going to the back of the truck, he lifted the gate, which used to have a little hydraulic hinge. He'd dismantled that on an earlier trip because it made a sound he didn't want scaring off the game. One by one, he pulled out the rifles—a bolt action .30-06, a seven-millimeter magnum with thirty inch barrels of various brands, scavenged at various times in the past months. The two teens were giggling at the side of the truck. Before they had an opportunity to get louder, Sam admonished them in a deep, hushed warning. "Knock it off, or you'll scare them all away. They're listening to you. They're keener than you, and you'll starve; and your babies will starve too unless you learn to be more clever than them."

That got their attention.

Sam handed them their gear and repeated, "Remember the rules—don't get smelled; make sure you're downwind at all times. Don't get heard; take ten-second steps. Always keep the wind in your face, Marcy. Got it?" He directed his question mostly at her, since he had already taught Mark much of the hunting lore.

"Wind in the face, check." Marcy repeated in a whisper, "but the ten-second steps look pretty stupid."

"If you want to eat, ten-second steps are worth it," Mark reminded her.

Sam pulled out several sets of snowshoes that he and Graham had made; they were a necessity in this terrain. He'd always used the commercial aluminum-framed variety, available at any sporting goods store, but as they'd learned time and again, tricks and crafts long forgotten now needed to be relearned. One day there would be no foraging for things like snowshoes; they'd all be gone. Graham's father had taught him the art of willow drying and weaving the pliable strips into snowshoe form when he was a boy. Sam and Graham had spent many evenings by the fire this winter weaving and teaching the kids this lost craft. Now Sam, Marcy, and Mark pulled the straps over their hiking boots and took a few steps to make sure the snowshoes were on tight.

Next, Sam checked the wind direction by lifting the end of his gun barrel into the air. The thread tied to the end of his gun floated up and slightly behind them. *Perfect*, he thought, and hoped the breeze would maintain that direction. They'd make their way down a narrow valley surrounded by tall Chuckanut sandstone cliffs.

For Marcy, walking with snowshoes took some getting used to; she found the waddling gait awkward, but she soon got used to the longer and wider steps needed to keep balance and move efficiently. With her rifle slung over her shoulder and her pistol strapped to her chest she was ready for action.

She'd hoped to get a deer to prove to Mark she was capable of hunting and helping him in the event that someday they started off on their own; she wanted to prove she was strong enough to live alone with him. So far, of the two girls Macy had proven herself the stronger hunter, the better defender, and more worthy at almost everything. She would not be outdone by her twin.

Sam broke into her thoughts. "Let's not waste time, guys. I'll lead in. Marcy, you stay between me and Mark. Remember, no noise, and follow my lead once we get into the clearing. I'll signal for you two to head out separately. Remember each other's location. I do not want any accidents. Long, slow, ten-second steps, then stillness; be observant. If the coast is clear, keep your eyes peeled, and wait for a clean shot. Once you shoot they'll scatter, and that will be the end of the hunt here for the rest of us. Any questions before we start?"

Marcy and Mark shook their heads. Marcy's excitement level grew. *Let the hunt begin.*

They made their way down the draw with the wind in their faces and slowly crept into the clearing of a snow-covered valley where spiked sprigs of native grasses held bravest and strong through many layers of snow. This is where the deer would come: their hunger would bring them to these few remaining grasses.

Sam turned and motioned with his left hand to his chin, up and down. Marcy remembered that meant for each of them to move at a different angle. This way the three of them each took a separate route into the valley. In their camouflage gear they headed forward at a slow, careful pace. So as not to alert the deer's sense of movement, never did two of them take their ten-second pace at the same time. All three moved forward with the keenly heightened sense of a hunter.

The snow made the hush of the valley nearly unbearable to Marcy. Her breath vaporized in front of her and then trailed backward. She perceived most strongly the beat of her own heart pounding in her chest. Her steps were clean and guided. She looked to Mark, a few yards away, for encouragement; he nodded gently in approval as she finished bringing her foot down slowly and without a sound. Next it was his turn to move. Her eyes scanned the valley, the hidden dark brush against the contrasting white, looking for any hint of brown or movement of a tail or twitch of an ear.

Getting used to wearing the gear was difficult; Marcy thought Sam had gone a little too far with his requirements for hunting. She wasn't allowed to use scented soaps, deodorant, or anything even remotely perfumed; even lip balm and lotion were forbidden. Not only that, but Sam claimed the deer could detect the color blue, so she was forced to wear brown canvas pants. They weren't nearly as soft as her worn denim jeans, and her left upper thigh itched terribly as she stood still, resisting the urge to scratch. She didn't want to be the cause of a lost hunt by triggering the prey to scatter.

In her peripheral vision, Marcy saw Sam make this careful move. Mark nodded slightly again, signaling her to begin her next step. She'd already planned to maneuver around a clump of desiccated brush that would separate her farther from the group. As she began the careful process of lifting her right leg, she saw a twitch far out to her left side and froze.

Macy's heart began to pound even faster. She knew this was it. Turning her head very slightly toward Mark she could see that his mouth was a tight thin line, and he tipped his head down to encourage her to take the shot.

Both terrified and intent, she glided her eyes ever so slightly toward her target. A doe with warm brown eyes stood with her head down, munching her way through the sparse grass, and her breath snorted out in little whips about her. The doe was beautiful, yet Marcy knew what she must do.

She swallowed and slowly brought her rifle down into position. Her hands shook from both the adrenaline rush and the regret racing through her veins. She sighted the deer, aiming for her heart, hoping to end it as painlessly as possible, not wanting to cause her to suffer. She knew Mark was getting impatient with the time she was taking. Before she let too much regret take her over, she pulled the trigger with measured determination. All erupted around her.

Unseen birds took flight, and hidden deer startled well before she heard the explosion erupt near her ear, sending it ringing.

In horror, she saw the doe leap with a graceful motion as the bullet hit its side, but then it fell to a heap on the frozen ground. What once was beautiful now was gone, and Marcy fell to her knees, heedless of the idea of cautious motion, profoundly weeping for herself and the doe.

Mark took paces to comfort her. "You did what was needed, Marcy. Remember what Graham says: *don't regret.*"

Macy nodded, wiping away her tears.

Sam passed by them on his way to the doe, then stooped to survey her kill. "Good girl, Marcy. It's a clean shot."

Marcy chalked it up as a lucky first strike. If anything, she hadn't wanted it to suffer and thus to force her into tracking it down to finish it off; she'd been warned beforehand that might be necessary. This way she'd proved she could do it once, and cleanly.

Feeling the cold sting of snow melting into the knees of her pants, she rose and Mark led her to the downed deer, holding her gently by the hand. She held her other hand over her mouth and nose, hoping to stifle her emotions. Her chest still shook as she breathed in and her throat locked.

The brown doe's eyes were open as if she were still alive. Marcy wanted the doe to think she had made her free and wished she could believe the doe's soul was in a peaceful spring green meadow.

She knelt down next to Sam and removed her glove. As a mule deer, the doe was larger than a whitetail, and her ears were so large they looked out of proportion to her head. Underneath her neck was a lighter patch of fur. Marcy ran her fingers from there down her sleek neck, fading to grayish brown. "I'm so sorry," she whispered, tears still streaming.

Sam patted her on the back.

"I'm sorry I'm upset. It's just harder than I thought," she tried to explain.

"It shows you're human, Marcy. A kill should never be wasted. You've done a good thing here. You've provided meat to stave off hunger for our family this winter." He patted her again. "Why don't you stand back this time and watch how to field dress? Mark will do most of it."

She gladly stepped back several paces, being careful not to trip over her snowshoes while Mark took out a Ziploc bag and a shoestring. He stood over the deer as Marcy watched with her arms crossed over her chest. He seemed to be contemplating something. "Marcy, you're not going to hold this against me, right?"

"Field dressing the deer? No, of course not."

Mark blew a sigh of relief. "Okay, I just wanted to make sure before I started."

Sam chuckled at the exchange.

"Go ahead," she reassured Mark, wiping her tears away. She wanted him to see she could be strong.

Blood already seeped down from the chest wound into the surrounding snow, turning white to scarlet. A little also trickled out of the doe's mouth.

Mark readied the tip of his knife, stood on the doe's leg with his back to her head, and rested the right hoof on his right knee. He bent down and pulled up on the doe's teat, lifting the fur and skin away from the insides. He slid the tip below the skin and sliced her down through the belly, being extra careful not to nick any of the intestines.

As he came to the rear, he reached in and closed off the bowel with the shoestring. He cut around the anus on the outside, then tipped the guts out of the deer's cavity by running his hand through the warm mass. Steam rose, and again, Marcy cupped her mouth and nose; nothing smelled, but the bloody sight alarmed her. Mark then separated the liver and the heart and placed them into the Ziploc bag. The rest of the guts would be a treat for any animals nearby—a steaming present for them to enjoy.

He handed the bag off to Marcy, who held it and felt the warmth of the animal through the plastic.

After Mark hoisted the doe over his shoulders, Sam said, "Great job, crew. Let's move on."

They headed back to the truck, this time taking fluid steps with the snowshoes on. As the two men headed out in front of her, Marcy stopped before they left the valley and looked back across the snowy meadow where now the pristine whiteness was stained by a scarlet mound in the distance. The cold wind changed direction and blew the grass stalks south, chilling her. She blinked back falling snowflakes. What was once peaceful now seemed foreboding.

Hitting the windshield faster than the wipers kept up, the snowfall came down like a cascading tatted drape. Sam, nearly unable to get a glimpse through the veil, cursed the storm. He knew it wouldn't let up anytime soon. The tires struggled through the deepening snow, though the Scout was in four-wheel drive.

"We're going to have to stop," Mark concluded.

Sam nodded. They had no other choice. Since they'd left the first hunting spot, the weather had grown increasingly bad. Not only that, the wind was picking up past a howl. Yesterday morning's clear sky had given no warning of these formidable conditions to come. They'd have to find a place out of the freezing temperatures and hole up through the storm.

"Yeah, I'm trying to drive over to that house there. Can you make out the structure now?" Sam said, pointing.

"Barely." Mark leaned forward to gain a better view through the vertical blanket of snow.

"At least we won't freeze to death inside," Sam said as he headed down to where he hoped the driveway led to the farmhouse, which sat in the middle of an open snow-covered field.

Marcy had fallen asleep after shooting her first kill. In the mirror, Sam saw a flicker of motion as she sat up.

"What's wrong?" she asked.

Sam glanced at Mark, saw him clench his jaw and draw in his eyebrows, frowning as if in contemplation of how much to reveal to her. He nodded to the youth. They were in this together. All of them. Marcy had a right to know.

Mark still tried to downplay the danger. "We've hit a little snowstorm," he said. "We're going to hide out until the blizzard passes, in a house down here."

Mark glanced briefly at Sam as if to say, *She doesn't need the full extent of this.* Though he didn't fully agree, Sam gave him a subtle nod. He'd probably have done the same thing if it was his wife involved; momentarily it caused him to think back to the time before she died.

Marcy sat up and immediately looked out—all around, front to back, side to side. The view out each window of the Scout was completely opaque. The snow crunching below the tires was audible even over the vicious sound of the wind against the side of the truck, shaking the vehicle from side to side with a terrible force. From the worried look on her face, Sam knew Mark's calling it "a little snowstorm" hadn't really fooled Marcy.

"What if we can't get to the house?" He heard her breathing rasp in and out, too quickly. *Was Marcy claustrophobic?*

"Don't worry, girl. We'll be fine in the truck," Sam said. "A bit colder, but fine." The temperature dropped quickly, and he knew they'd have a hard time staying warm in the truck cab, but Mark's idea of soft-pedaling the danger might not be so wrong. Marcy didn't need to be aware of the precariousness of their situation yet.

The harshness of the season made no sense. As the pandemic affected human life, so too did the weather seem hell-bent on damning the earth.

"Are we going to be able to drive over there?" Marcy asked.

Sam leaned into the windshield, trying to maneuver in the direction of the house. At the same time he fought unpredictable wind gusts blowing him first one way and then the other, banking the truck rudely to either side. "Too early to say yet," he replied after an anxious moment that lingered too long.

As he got even closer, the snow seemed to increase even more, if that were possible. "I'm worried about running into a ditch," he said. "Mark, open your door and see if you can detect anything, like an indentation where a drainage ditch might be. I think we're on the driveway, but I can't tell."

Mark opened his door about five inches, but just then the wind shifted and blew an opaque stream of snow into the cab. That blinded Sam even more and he hollered, "Okay, shut the door!"

Mark slammed it, straining hard against the wind. "I can't tell. Everything is so white. I've never seen winter conditions this bad. I've lived in this area all my life."

Sam saw an expression of terror on Marcy's face as she leaned forward from the backseat, between him and Mark. "It's okay," he told her. "We'll be fine. Once we get into that house, we'll start a fire and warm up." They sat silently, listening to the raging storm with eerie contemplation as the truck crept along.

"I thought you said this would be the last *safe* time to go on a hunt," Marcy said, her tone accusatory.

"Marcy!" Mark snapped. "The weather is not Sam's fault."

"It's all right, Mark," Sam said. "She's just scared."

As he said the words meant to calm the both of them, the truck slid and then dipped down on the driver's side. After letting up off the gas, Sam put his foot on the brake. He stopped and tried reverse, hoping to gain some traction but, it was no use. He gave the gas pedal a tentative push, but the wheel only spun, then the whole tire dipped down into an invisible gully. He knew not to try again; it would risked digging the truck's tires in deeper.

After turning off the engine and shifting into park, he cut the headlights. "No sense in draining the battery. Mark, hand me the spotlight," Sam said in the pitch dark as blasts of wind rocked the truck. They could only sit, a captive audience to the weather's tantrum.

Mark got the battery-powered spotlight going, but all it did was reflect its light back against the snow. However hard Sam tried, he couldn't make out a damn thing ahead of them. The last time he'd glimpsed the house, he'd guessed they were about a quarter of a mile away, but now it couldn't be more than a hundred feet in the distance. Yet there was no way he trusted walking that far without the risk of getting lost in the snow and freezing temperatures and missing their salvation all together.

"Well, hell," Sam said, when nothing better came to mind. He shut off the spotlight, and the three of them let the sound of the wind settle around them for a time.

"We can't even spot the house from here?" Marcy asked.

"Barely, but I don't know if we should risk taking a chance on foot in these conditions," Sam said.

"Do we have more rope?" Mark asked.

"Yeah. I know what you're thinkin,' but I'm not so sure blindly going out there, even tethered with a rope, is a good idea right now," Sam warned.

"Look. I can run a line from the truck and make my way to the house. If I can't find the house, I'll just walk back," Mark argued. By this time the howling wind had picked up even more and they were nearly shouting to one another, to be heard.

"Let's wait a while. The storm might die down some," Sam advised; he silently cursed himself, knowing they were now stuck in a snowstorm. He looked out his side window into the blizzard and thought of Addy and his promise to her—knowing, no matter what the cost, he would keep his word.

After signing off the radio, Tala checked on Ennis. His heavy lids blinked as he stared into the woodstove, and his expression bore the look of pained frustration. In any event, he hadn't moved much. She knelt down beside him and felt his shins, to make sure he wasn't getting too much radiant heat from the fire. When he noticed her, she smiled at him in response.

"Are you in terrible pain? Would you like to go lie down, sleep a little and let the meds work?"

He nodded, so she helped him up and guided him into the bunkroom and told him when to sit down as she backed him into the bunk mattress. He did so willingly, like a child being led by his mother, and chuckled at her attentiveness. Then she helped him lie down and covered him up with his blanket, then added another one since the bunkroom felt cold and drafty. He looked up at her with worry in his eyes. He whispered, "Whatever is bothering you, missy, trust Graham to do the right thing with your worries." His eyelids fluttered closed. She suspected he might be worn out from fighting the pain for so long. He couldn't possibly know what troubled her, and she shut the bunkroom door to let him rest.

When her tears started to fall, she brushed them away and hurried into the bathroom to find the medical kit she and Clarisse had talked about earlier. She willed each step closer by consolation and a little bit of self-bargaining. The med kit from the preppers included almost everything they needed except for the one thing Ennis needed.

After first putting aside a large tome of medication definitions Graham had found somewhere on his journey here, she pulled the kit out from under the sink. It was an olive drab nylon backpack that strapped on at a moment's notice if they needed to bug out. She brushed over the various paper-wrapped bandages, pain medication packs, vials of ointment, and prefilled Epi pens until she found the packets of birth control pills rubber-banded together toward the back. She took out two one-month packs for the girls and set them on the counter. Then she looked for the pregnancy test wands.

She hadn't told Clarisse what she suspected. The given advice would be to terminate, because they just weren't sure what would happen to a new life.

She and Clarisse had talked openly about most things over the past several months, but Tala just couldn't part with this suspicion—not yet. Her cycle hadn't regulated since her miscarriage. It had come and gone, but never regulated as in normal times. Stress made cycles irregular, but a late period coupled with morning nausea reminded her of her previous pregnancy and the devastating loss.

She had been taking the pills Clarisse gave to her, but she had also been intimate with Graham on more than one occasion. She loved him, and they needed each other, especially now.

Her hand brushed over a few paper-wrapped sticks standing upright. She read the black military lettering and pulled one out. As she held the test kit before her, the package vibrated as her hands trembled. The answers and implications were within reach; all the decisions she'd have to face, flashed before her. With a small window of privacy, with only Ennis resting in the cabin, she thought now would be the best time to go ahead and get the procedure over with so she'd know for sure. She quickly zipped up the medical kit and returned it to its place under the sink.

She closed the door quietly, tore open the test kit and began the procedure, remembering the first time she'd gone through this routine. All the while, she couldn't keep her hands from shaking with fear of the results. "Please no, please no," she chanted to herself over and over, quietly sobbing. She finally pulled the wand up, braving a peek . . . and now she knew. No more waiting. No more uncertainty.

The pit of her stomach tightened, and her widened eyes flooded with tears from shock of the affirmation. Both happy and horrified, as she began to allow herself to sob, a loud commotion sounded from the living room. She quickly pocketed the supplies into her gray cable sweater and wiped away the tears as Bang's small footsteps came toward the bathroom door.

He had nearly bumped into her as he rounded the corner with reddened cheeks and freezing, chapped hands. His ear-to-ear grin told her he'd been having fun with Graham and Macy outside. Their loud talking and boisterous mood cut through her desperation, the fear she'd created for herself there in the small bathroom as she contemplated the possibility of a new life in their midst, and the equally frightening possibility of having to end it.

"You guys sound happy," she heard herself say.

"Graham raced me to the door, but he tripped and fell," Bang said.

"I didn't fall. Macy shoved me," Graham defended himself, making Macy laugh maniacally and chase him.

Graham, continuing the game, turned on Macy. She emitted a piercing scream and ran in mock terror for the door. He caught up to her in easy strides.

When Tala came around the corner again and raised one eyebrow at them, pointed her motherly finger toward the bunkroom door, and raised her finger to her lips, Graham sat Macy on her feet, and they both stifled their mirth and sobered up.

What an amazing father Graham has become to these children. What a wonderful one he'd be to mine—if either of us dares let it be born.

Macy brushed past Tala and barged into the bathroom, pushing Bang out of the way so she could wash up too, while Tala went into the kitchen and stirred the dinner while she tried to remain calm.

Tonight they were having a scavenged can of potato and corned beef hash that Tala combined to make into a creamy potato chowder by adding reconstituted milk. With just enough to feed the five of them, this would be a welcome change. Looking into the pot of creamy soup made Tala wanted to flee, but she pushed through the nausea and tried to act normal until she could come up with a plan or at least until she had some time to think about what she would tell Graham. He would want to save her and discard the child out of fear of losing them both. They'd discussed the dilemma in a "what-if" manner a time or two, but hadn't yet been forced to deal with the reality.

While the kids set the table for dinner, Tala whispered to Graham, "We need to talk tonight, after the kids are in bed."

Graham said nothing, but the expression on his face signaled his apprehension. She patted his cheek and smiled, hoping he'd smile back; those sharp-eyed kids would notice he was worried.

While Tala dished up the food, Graham went into the bunkroom to rouse Ennis for dinner. He returned to report that the old man didn't want to wake up.

"Let's leave him alone then; I only put him down to rest a few minutes ago," Tala said. "Maybe the antibiotics will do their thing better if he's resting."

Graham nodded agreement. "I can always take him a cup of soup later."

With only four gathered around the table for the first time, Tala realized how attached they'd become to one another. The cabin was too quiet with the others gone. The family atmosphere she knew Graham had come to accept after his initial resistance had become official. Perhaps that was the best thing for them after all.

In an effort to break the quiet, she asked Graham, "Wolves skinned?"

"Yes, and bodies already disposed of."

"Good. If I can get away tomorrow, I'll help with the scraping," she offered.

With her attention to detail, she'd proven herself an expert at getting even the tiniest of particles lifted off the skins, but the idea of the project wasn't appealing to her in her current condition.

"Can we talk about something else at the table, please?" Macy requested.

"Sure, how was school today?" Graham asked.

"Oh, that's funny. You're such a comedian," Macy said back while Bang sat there laughing as little boys do, filling the cabin with a merry amusement that almost made Tala forget the anguish to come.

Even though she dreaded Graham's reaction to the news about her surprise, she enjoyed every minute of their happy circumstances at the moment. If Ennis were not ill, the current condition of their lives would finally make sense. Even with the death of man, they had to find joy and peace in their existence, or there was no point in going on at all.

After they had cleaned up, Graham heard Ennis stirring, so he took him a mug of the thick soup and a glass of cranberry juice.

"Hey, think you can eat a little?" he asked as he opened the door. He turned on the bedside lamp and slid a chair close beside Ennis.

"Yeah, I think I might. Where's them kids?"

Graham helped him sit up and had propped another pillow behind him.

"They're taking care of the chickens, and Tala's in the greenhouse."

"Good. Listen, before you start feeding me against my will, we need to talk about somethin' I've been thinkin' on."

"Take a drink first, Ennis," Graham said, handing him the cranberry juice.

"I hate this stuff."

"Drink it anyway."

Ennis glared at him while he took a sip with mock hatred.

"You give any thought to going back this spring?"

"Going back to Seattle?"

"Yeah. Take a truck. Pick up more supplies to bring back here. You need more ammunition for defense and hunting, and we need to know what's going on out there. A scouting trip would tell us a lot."

Graham handed him the soup and leaned back in his chair, thinking. "I've thought about going back. Problem is, someone could follow me back here, and I'd expose our camp—and the prepper's camp. I don't want to put us in any jeopardy. And what if something happens to me?"

"You gotta do something, Graham. You think these kids are going to stay put? We need to find out how things have gotten out there. These little homes here have already been scavenged by our two camps. Sure, we have enough food for now, but the ammo is running short already."

Graham nodded. "You're not telling me anything I don't already stay up at night worried about, Ennis."

"I know you want to stay here and garden, and hunt, but I'm tellin' you, Graham, turning into a hippie is not enough."

"What do you mean by that?"

"Don't ignore the outside. These kids are going out there at some point. If you're not preparing them for the dangers they'll need to survive out there, you might as well bury 'em now. The preppers are good folks right now, but they're using us for their own protection. Nothin' wrong with that, but what happens when they run low of supplies too?"

"They're not like that. Dalton risked a lot, and paid a lot, to help us the last time. Too much in fact."

"Graham, when you need to feed your own child, you'd kill your own brother for his food. Don't make the mistake of trustin' them too much. I'm saying, you need to think long-term now, and you need to see what's out there. What dangers exist by other men."

Graham took a big breath and let air out slowly. Though he didn't believe the preppers would ever turn on them, he couldn't ignore the warnings. "I'll think about it, Ennis."

After Ennis had finished off his meal, Graham bullied him into going back to the bathroom. The effort was painful for the old man, but he needed him to recover. Afterward, Graham heard the snoring sounds he'd come to get used to, indicating Ennis was fast asleep.

With the others down for the night, Graham tended the woodstove as he tried to build an emotional barrier for whatever Tala might convey. She curled her legs under herself while she waited for him on the couch. He approached her slowly with only the firelight gleaming, his feelings of dread increasing with each moment he delayed.

Tala knew Graham was procrastinating as she watched him putter around. Determinedly, she willed away the coming tears and waited for him to be ready for her news, then broached the first of the two subjects she wished she could avoid.

Carefully she began with Clarisse's recommendations regarding the girls, to get it out of the way. She told him why she and Clarisse both agreed it was a good idea for them to be put on the pill. Of course, as Tala suspected, Graham didn't take it too well.

"No way!" he said after Tala explained the situation twice. "They're only *fifteen*!"

"Graham, what if something happens to them? What if Marcy and Mark take their affections too far? Or, God forbid, someone attacks one of them. It's a simple solution." She realized the irony of her own statement.

That was enough to get him to think seriously about the recommendation, considering what had almost happened to Tala the previous fall.

He leaned forward and rubbed his beard. "Yeah," he said finally. "Maybe you and Clarisse are right at that. I remember how difficult the loss was for you to recover from when you miscarried."

She met his gaze, remembering. That was how he found her here. She could have died from complications and they'd never been sure if the miscarriage was due to the stress of the pandemic or if the fetus contracted the virus within and died from it.

"That would be horrible for them. We'd have to give them the medical abortion pills. There's some at the doctor's house. I saw them there but left them. I didn't think we'd need them." He took a deep breath. "Okay, I can see how putting them on the pill makes sense for Marcy but I do not think Macy would be willing to take them, nor do I think she should be forced into taking them. I'm not holding her down for that and good luck to anyone who tries." Tala didn't think he was joking.

"The decision should be hers," Graham continued. "So yeah, I think you're right. Let's do it, but I'm going to pick up the other pills and bring them here tomorrow when I go into town to find the painkillers for Ennis. Just so we have them. Just in case," he said with a sigh. "So, is that the problem that's been weighing you down, babe? Worrying about how I'd react to the idea?" He leaned back and pulled her to him, cradling her against his chest.

Tala's pulse quickened and panic set in as she realized he saw termination as the only possible solution to pregnancy. She tried to relax, knowing she couldn't tell him her secret now, knowing what his immediate response would be. She willed herself to calm down further and melted against his hard chest so Graham wouldn't suspect there was more.

"Okay, let's talk to them both about the option when Marcy gets back," Tala said.

"Oh no. This was your idea, and it's *your* department," Graham said, making the sign of the cross. "They're girls, you're a girl; and therefore talking to them about this stuff is your job."

"You are the bravest man I know, and yet you can't face girl issues?" Tala mocked him, trying on a smile. She shook her head, hoping she was masking her true feelings.

"Hey, I would if I had to, but you're here and so it falls to you. When Bang starts to have boy issues when he's older, I will handle it. You won't have to explain the urges, et cetera. I think that's fair," Graham reasoned.

Tala played along, and let out a breath, agreeing with the arrangement. Neither of them had ever been a parent before the pandemic, and they were winging this thing, at best. Though Tala knew those days were numbered—at least for her.

Clarisse had been through this so many times before; disappointment after devastating disappointment had become the norm. This time, however, a shred of hope proved the answers to her research. The girls played in the hallway and their laughter echoed into her office. Their voices distracted her work, but in a good way until the disorderly fracas came from the main door as Rick and Steven entered the building.

Out of defeat, she gave up any further efforts in her observation through a microscope and directed her attention to the men who'd arrived.

"What's up, guys?" she managed to say without any annoyance in her greeting.

"There's a storm coming. Rick and I got the generator set up for you in case the power goes out. I'll set up a rope line to camp, in case the snow gets as bad as we think."

"Oh, thanks. I had no idea the weather was getting worse," she said, glancing down at Addy on the floor in the doorway. "I guess I should probably quit now, then, and get us back to camp." She hoped her reluctance to leave her work didn't show. She never stopped marveling at how quickly she'd come to think of Addy as her own child, and the girl's safety demanded Clarisse put her first—even ahead of research.

On his knees, Rick, always up for anything juvenile, joined in the girls' game of jacks. As if he understood, he said, "Why don't I take Addy back with Bethany? She can spend the night with us too. That way you can work as long as you like."

Clarisse eyed Addy. "Would you like to spend the night with Bethany? The decision is totally up to you. Or I can pack up right now and we can go if you'd like."

Rick's daughter Bethany, was about the same age and the only other child Addy had formed a friendly bond with. She was much more outgoing, but she enjoyed Addy's company in small visits.

"Oh, please stay the night," Bethany begged.

Addy paused a moment and, casting a look to Clarisse that said she wasn't too sure about the arrangement, said, "Okay."

Rick apparently caught on to the look and tried to persuade her. "We'll make the night fun, Addy; I'll set up a movie, and we can make popcorn, like in the old days."

Clarisse added, "If you're okay with staying the night, I'll check in on you first thing in the morning."

"You'll be fine out here, by yourself?" Addy asked Clarisse. At times she seemed much too mature for a seven-year-old, but under the circumstances, it was probably understandable for a child who had essentially lost both parents to worry about the one sure substitute she had.

"Of course. You don't need to worry about me, Addy."

With a smile Addy ran over to embrace Clarisse. The child smelled of crayons and soap as she held her close, and Clarisse wondered why she had never thought to become a mother before. She wouldn't trade the experience for anything now and knew she'd do anything for Addy to keep her safe from harm. *What a liability a child is to a mother.* She certainly loved the girl, and knew Addy loved her in return. The emotion tugged at her heart even more.

Overjoyed at the prospect of a playmate staying with her the whole night, Bethany cheered.

To the kids, something as simple as a sleepover must have been like stepping back into the past, a reminder of something they'd done in the days before the end of school, before the escape from their neighborhoods, before they left family and friends behind, and before quarantine.

"Okay, girls, let's get your coats on," Rick said as he corralled them toward the door.

When they were out of earshot, Steven said, "The Quarantine Queen has become a mommy? When did that happen?"

Clarisse smiled at him and swiveled around in her office chair ignoring him. She knew he was ribbing her, but in a kind way. "Who could help but love that little girl?" was the only thing she would allow herself to say for fear she would start to cry.

Steven patted her on the back and said, "Don't stay too late. I'll set up the line, just in case, on my way out. The snow's already coming down steadily, and the sky is starting to look ugly out there."

She heard the wind creaking the metal siding as it came in hard gusts. It was starting to howl, and she knew what Steven said was true.

"Thank you. I'll be fine here."

With the whole evening ahead of her, Clarisse felt recharged in her efforts to make sure the data was true. She returned to her work, knowing she had a promise to keep, and she would work on it for as long as it took.

12 Mark Takes a Walk

Sam knew a young man needed to prove himself in life. After waiting through the snowstorm a while longer, as the temperature continued to drop, he decided now would be the best time for Mark to make a break for the house. The temperature could drop again in the next hour, but how much they had no way of knowing. He would lead a guide rope over to the house about eighty yards in front of their position.

"All right, kid, let's get this done; the storm is getting worse, not better. I don't think waiting it out will do us any good." Sam shivered a bit. Mark climbed back into the rear of the truck to retrieve the two-hundred-foot length of nylon line.

"You're going to let him go out there alone?" Marcy protested when she caught on to the plan. The idea scared her. It scared Sam, too, but not as much as trying to keep the kids alive in the truck all night and for however much longer the storm might last, but he didn't answer her plea.

Instead, he cautioned Mark, "Tie one end to the bumper. Take the spotlight. Keep your eyes open and go in as straight a line as you can. If you get to the end and find you're in open space, get your ass back here. Don't screw around with this, and whatever you do, don't leave the rope. Tie the line off to the first thing you can find when you reach the end, and follow it back here. If you leave the line, you're toast. I won't be able to find you in time before the cold has its way with you. Do you hear me?" Sam he stared deeply into Mark's eyes to let the young man realize he was dead serious and to make sure Mark understood the gravity of the situation.

"I got it, Sam."

Sam nodded and did a once-over of Mark's gear. The boy might need another hat. He took off his own wolf fur–lined hat and shoved it over the knit one already on Mark's head. "We can't have your ears freezing off; Marcy might not think you're too pretty without ears." Mark clipped the spotlight handle to his belt loop and looped the rope bundle over his right shoulder.

"Pay the line out slowly. Try not to let it hang up on bushes or anything."

Mark nodded, his face sober.

"All right. Take the line and tie it off to the front bumper and head out."

"Wait!" Marcy yelled. Mark was getting ready to leave way too fast when she realized he wasn't going to say good-bye to her. She pulled herself up and reached over the seat. Sam turned away to give them some privacy, while Marcy planted a kiss on Mark's lips.

"I'll be fine, Marcy." He sounded a little embarrassed. "I'll be right back."

Mark stepped out of the truck and shut the door quickly. The first sound that registered, besides the howling wind, was his own boots crunching into the deep snow, followed closely by the persistent wind that whipped snow viciously from one direction into the next. The changing directions created confusion; he was glad he already knew where he should head.

He heaved the coiled rope line again and walked quickly to the front of the Scout. The swirly snow made the simple expedition difficult; it was hard to see even a foot in front of his own face. He knew it was late in the evening, but because of the darkness the time might as well have been midnight, with the blackness beyond the fluttering white. He held his left hand against the cold metal of the frozen truck to help keep his position as he stepped blindly, one foot in front of the next. Once he found the bumper, he quickly wiped away the accumulated snow and tied off one end of the looped rope and tapped the hood twice, indicating he was on his way to the house, somewhere in the whiteout beyond their vision. Temporarily blinded by the headlights, he began to break a path ahead of him while unfurling the line.

Marcy and Sam felt the vibrations as Mark tied off the rope, even though the unceasing gusts increased in their erratic cadence. When Mark tapped the hood twice, Marcy took a deep breath while Sam pulled out a small flashlight and checked his watch, then started counting the minutes. For a short time the spotlight beam remained visible, but soon the swirling whiteness enveloped even Mark's light, leaving only the surrounding darkness.

Soon the darkness and awkward silence took over between the two occupants left in the cab of the truck. The quiet tension was too much for Marcy. "Sam, I'm sorry I yelled at you earlier."

"It's okay, Marcy, don't give it another thought." Sam drew his words out slow, to calm her nerves, and patted her gloved hand as she gripped the back of the seat near his shoulder. He kept his eyes scanning the windshield, but beyond the gleam of the headlights flaring back from the whiteout, nothing else was visible.

Then the silence took over again. Except for the occasional sound of a slight vibration tremor, Sam couldn't tell where Mark might be as he strung out the line. He figured the boy had about two more minutes before he encountered the house, which Sam guessed was about eighty or so feet from the truck. The rope was just over two hundred feet, so there should be plenty of slack, he guessed.

Then the sound stopped. Marcy let out her breath believing that Mark had successfully found something to tie onto. The violent squall seemed to increase even more in intensity, and she was glad he was on his way back now.

Sam tried to picture what Mark was doing, and he knew by experience that the boy would probably double-time it back to the truck once he completed his task. The problem was, the task was taking way too long. Sam didn't let on in the ensuing silence that he was beginning to worry, but he was. He would give Mark another few minutes. Maybe something reasonable had happened, but Sam couldn't think of what it might have been to take this long. *Unless he let go of the damn rope*, Sam thought and sat up, suddenly ready to take action.

He tried not to scare the girl, but if something had happened out there in these temperatures, he had precious little time to find the young man before frostbite would set in, causing injury. Then the killing hypothermia would come.

"Marcy, darlin', he's taking a little too long."

"No. No, he's fine, he's coming right back. He said he'd be right back." She sounded as if she was trying to convince herself as much as Sam.

Sam put his hand over hers again, resting on the back of his seat. "I'm going out for him now."

"No, don't leave me here by myself, Sam," she protested.

He didn't have time for this, and he sure as hell didn't like whiny girls. "Climb over here," he said, but she didn't move. "Get up here right now, God dammit! Honk the horn three times, and then wait to a count of ten, and repeat the sequence three more times. Keep repeating that. Do you understand me?" he said in a cold, deliberate tone to get through to her.

"Yes," she said, scowling at him.

"Good girl. I'll go get him, and I'll be right back. Do not lose your head, Marcy, and whatever you do, do not leave this truck."

"I won't. I'm scared, but I'm not stupid!" she yelled.

Good. Mad, she'd be less likely to curl up in a corner and give in.

He stepped out into the snow, narrowing his eyes, searching for the glimmer of Mark's flashlight, for his shadowy form to appear before him.

He found the line tied to the bumper and headed out, sure he'd find the boy at any moment.

He did not.

13 Frayed Ends

Sam didn't have his hat, but he couldn't worry about freezing ears at a time like this. Ice started to collect into his dark mustache and around his long eyelashes, threatening to clog his vision almost immediately. He held his arm up in defense of the soft onslaught and grasped the line, following it as he trudged forward, nearly blind. He yelled out several times, "Mark! Mark! Where are you?"

After a few steps, he cupped one hand around his mouth to formulate a loud yell again. As he let out the accumulated energy, Marcy began the honking routine, eliminating his effort to yell and startling him at the same time. Sam shook his head after his ears stopped ringing but strained his vision all the same for any sign of the boy.

He detected nothing but white as he squinted to keep the flakes out of his eyes. He held the line and trudged farther ahead, keeping the small flashlight by his side. To his dismay, the rope didn't hold tension as he went on, leading him to come to a frustrating conclusion: Mark hadn't tied the lifeline off, nor did he have a hold of the line. "God dammit!" Sam said to no one but the wind.

Out of fear he quickened his pace, hoping to find the kid sooner. Behind him Marcy begin the honking series again, and Sam strained to find any sign of footprints, but with the blowing snow, he couldn't detect anything.

When the sequence started again, the sound came sooner than ten seconds. Afraid the girl might lose her wits soon, he hoped to hell she had the sense to stay within the safety of the truck if she lost them.

Double-timing ahead, he hoped to find Mark but what he found instead sent his heart plummeting; the frayed end of the rope line. "Mark! Mark! Where the hell are you?" He squatted down to examine the snow for any signs of tracks. He finally detected a low depression in the snow, but it led farther on into frozen nothingness.

Not a footprint, but something larger. He tried to discern any reason the boy would have left the rope line. Perhaps a house mere feet away, or a light—anything that would make him ignore the warnings Sam had issued.

Sam turned back toward Marcy, who was blasting again too soon. At least he knew she was still in the truck. "I shouldn't have left her there," he said as he contemplated searching farther into the unknown or heading back to the truck. That was when he sensed someone nearby. The whisper of a presence of someone else taking up space nearby and nothing more. He began to turn around hoping to find Mark coming toward him, but what happened next took him by surprise. He only glanced for a second before the impact connected with the base of his skull, laying him out on the snow, stunned. He tried to get up, but was struck again and then again until he no longer saw white but only darkness. He felt his body being dragged seconds later, and blacked out altogether.

~ ~ ~

A distant and nagging sound pushed through the veil. The disruption came in threes and sometimes fours; then the series started all over again. *Who's making that damn noise?* The pounding pain in the back of Sam's head didn't help matters. Then he started to recall what had taken place and the panicked need to open his eyes set in, but confusion clouded his mind. The effort to fall into the silent abyss tempted him. Only his promise to Addy gave him any encouragement to climb out.

Finally he convinced himself to try to open his eyes a slit, though the effort hurt like hell. A ragged figure turned to face him: an older woman with a wild head of hair, long and silver-gray, stood over him. Her crazed eyes were of the lightest green, almost golden in color. Without ever hearing her speak, he held no doubt they were all in grave danger now.

He tried to move his head, but even the smallest effort sent pain rocketing through him. His arms were bound as well as his legs. What happened next he couldn't anticipate. She surveyed him with those strange eyes, watching every movement he made as he regained consciousness.

"What are you doing here? Who sent you?" she said as she crossed her arms in front of her, revealing a long butcher knife in one hand.

Sam licked his chapped lips as he realized his hands and feet were bound, yet shaking from the cold. He lay in a puddle of water on a cold wood floor, littered with debris. The base of a wooden dining room chair sat dismantled before the stone fireplace, along with a disembodied accordion lampshade, appearing as if she used parts of the stiff fabric for kindling. He cleared his throat with a raspy sound. "Where's my friend? What did you do with him?"

"*I'm* asking the questions here. This is *my* house. You were on my property. Tell me why. You're from the gang that came here before, the one that took everything!" she screamed madly.

"I . . . I . . . didn't. I don't know what you're talking about, ma'am. Can't you see there's a storm?" Even speaking sent shooting pains through his injured skull. The effort to reason with her was killing him. His head hurt like hell, and his vision kept doubling as he tried to focus on her. She had done a number on his head, and he tasted the resulting blood on his lips.

"We were just driving through," he continued. "The storm caught us, and our truck was stuck. There was no crime against you, ma'am. We thought this house was deserted. We just needed shelter from the storm."

She skirted around him, taking a few steps but kept clear of him in case he tried something. He wasn't sure what she might do.

Deranged, she had obviously been the victim of a previous attack, so she suspected everyone of doing her harm.

"You're here to steal from me again. Didn't you get enough the first time? I won't let you do this to me a second time. I can barely eat."

The honking began to distract her, "Someone else is out there honking that obnoxious horn. How many are there?" She kicked his legs. "Tell me now, or I'll hurt him—the other one botherin' me tonight." She took out a cigarette and a lighter from somewhere in the folds of the worn and tattered rags she wore. She lit it with ease and flair, puffing hard, brightening the tip. She wanted him to know without saying that she meant to torture Mark.

Sam lay silent as he gathered clues from the situation. She didn't seem to have a firearm, but he didn't have his, either. She had to have hit him with something heavy and hard. But she might have as easily shot him dead with his own gun or Mark's, for that matter.

She must have lost them in the struggle outside. Her lack of a firearm didn't make sense, but there she stood with a lit cigarette, threatening to hurt them. Despite that, Sam twisted his head and looked around to catch sight of the boy or their own weapons.

"He's not in here. I'm not stupid," she spit out.

"He's only a kid. Please don't hurt him."

She stopped for a minute, with her lit intention glowing between her fingers. She exhaled the smoke slowly as Sam watched her look up and around the room they were in. She took another drag and stared back down at him, causing the tip to brighten fire-red again. He did not like the look in her eyes. He knew right away what Graham would do. Then he heard the persistent sounds again in the distance, coming in a series of three.

He could see that the sound agitated her. To his horror, the woman snuffed out the cigarette in frustration and warned him, "I'll

be right back to deal with you after I take care of that blasted noise."
She picked up a club by the door and rushed out into the storm.

"No! You leave her alone. She's a kid," Sam yelled and kicked out, trying to follow, but with both of his feet tied, there wasn't anything he could do. She had already slammed the door. His head ached in ravaged pain.

14 Tended

Dalton pounded on the quarantine lab door, trying to send the sound all the way to the lab over the raging snowstorm. The hour was late, and he was pissed. Yet again, after completing his rounds, he'd discovered Clarisse not where she was supposed to be, forcing him to hunt her down.

"What are you doing here?" Clarisse said, surprised, when she answered the door. She quickly ushered him in, closed the door, and brushed the accumulated snow off his shoulders.

Dalton glowered at her. "That's what *I'm* asking *you*." He wasn't prepared to listen to whatever excuse she might try this time.

Clarisse glared back at him. "Addy's spending the night at Rick's with Bethany. I didn't need to come back to camp, and you have no right to take that tone with me." She turned and went back to the lab office.

Dalton blew out a breath of frustration as she walked away from him. "We had an agreement, Clarisse. You shouldn't be out here by yourself."

"I have work to do. I'm close this time. I need every minute I can get."

The toll the work had taken on her showed. There were dark circles under her eyes, and she'd even lost more weight, leaving her almost gaunt. She took off her glasses for a minute to rub at her tired eyes. "I'm fine, Dalton. I'm just as safe here."

"No you're not, Clarisse. Anything could happen to you out here all alone."

"I'm comfortable being alone, Dalton. Steven put up a rope line before he left. I'm sure you saw it on the way in here. I have plenty of provisions and water. If I got snowed in, there's enough for thirty people for a month. There's no reason I can't stay," she argued.

"That's where you're wrong. Because of those provisions and gear stored here, you're in jeopardy. You're a mark. If someone were to stumble on this cache, they'd kill you in a second and take it all." He paused, hoping he'd said enough to convince her. Knowing he was hitting below the belt, he added, "What would happen to Addy if she lost you, too, Clarisse?"

"That's not playing fair, Dalton." Her smile, though crooked, told him she knew he hadn't meant to hurt her. She adjusted her eyeglasses.

Dalton calmed down a bit. She had a rare captivating smile, and he loved to coax it out of her, but when she showed it, the jolt of need within him made him guilty for the effort. "I know, but I'll try anything to get you to listen to me. I'd hate for something to happen to you here by yourself. Please, let me walk you back to camp."

"No. I told you; I'm working on something important. I'm getting closer, I know I'm close." She walked out of the darkened hallway and into the dimly lit lab, and Dalton followed her.

"You can save us all tomorrow. Come on, you need to sleep, Clarisse. You're worn out," he said as he leaned against the door frame, exhausted himself.

She ignored his suggestion. "You know; I've been working on this from two different angles. I've had no success with the new antivirals, but something Addy said to me the other day made me reconsider my ideas, to look at it all again."

"What? You're saying you've been working on another vaccine?" He didn't shout, but raised his voice enough to let Clarisse know his feelings on that issue. No one had been able to come up with a vaccine, and he doubted, at this point, that anyone ever would. Surviving in the world they now found themselves in made more sense to him.

"Don't you think you should give up by now, Clarisse? We both remember the useless antivirals the government stockpiled. There was the barely effective vaccine and one that induced narcolepsy in some people. Remember?" he ranted, shaking his head. "People killed one another to get into long lines for those injections. They exposed themselves and their children to the virus, just to get an ineffective and potentially dangerous shot."

She remained silent while he remembered those awful days. When society had begun to go mad, Dalton had sounded the alert; the one that she had provoked. The approved members came like ghosts, never exposing themselves to others except those in their own family.

Thankfully, the triggers for such an event were clear early on. She was employed by a private research lab near Seattle as a virologist after working first in the U.S. Air Force and then with the Centers for Disease Control and Prevention. When she reviewed the reports coming in, with stats increasing rapidly, she removed her lab coat, grabbed her keys, and quietly walked out the door while her coworkers were scrambling. With all the excitement, no one detected her departure, and that's exactly the way the plan was supposed to work.

After trashing her phone, she pulled out the one only Dalton and Rick knew of. She had quickly called Dalton and relayed the urgent information to him. He sounded the alert and set their plan into action; everything worked as he'd meant it to. Everyone dropped their daily lives, avoided all contact with the public, and made their way to the predetermined entry site.

Clarisse remembered too. She'd already stockpiled all the necessary equipment to continue her research and stored all the equipment safely away in an unassuming van parked in a storage facility that was along her way to the secret destination. She simply pulled up and typed her code into the keypad of the storage facility gate, like so many times before, only this time her fingers shook out of nervous anticipation. They had practiced this many times, but this time their actions were for real.

She drove her little car up to unit 124 and unlocked the roll-up door with her thumbprint scan; she opened the van door the same way and drove the vehicle out of the unit. Following that, she drove her little car into the empty space and lowered the metal door. After she reentered the van and drove to the exit gate, she stopped only to key in the exit code, which she fumbled the first time. While she waited for the gate to lift, a little sign in the shape of a penguin waved a cheerful good-bye. Now, when she thought back to that moment, she wasn't sure why she'd cried, but she had.

Afterward she never looked back and stuck to the predetermined route of back roads. Though the trip took her a little longer, she wanted to avoid any suspicion. Not that anyone would likely take notice of her activities in such chaos. Rick kept her on his radar the whole time in case she ran into any trouble.

Now, even after society had fallen, she continued to work on something that would save them; these few people who had hidden from death. The colossal pressure of such a deed weighed heavily on her every waking moment as well as her darkest of nights.

"Yes, I remember," she said softly now in answer to Dalton's question, "We were very lucky, Dalton, but I can't give up now because you don't have faith in a vaccine. There has to be an answer somewhere."

He stepped close to her. His musky breath blew a few wisps of the dark hair escaping from her tight bun when he spoke. "You can waste your time tomorrow. Get your coat. Let's go." She took a step back and considered him. His expression remained grim.

"I'm not going, Dalton."

"Clarisse, if you don't come with me, I'll have to stay here. With you."

The way he said, "with you," sent tingles up her spine, and her eyes widened behind her dark-framed glasses. She wouldn't meet his gaze, and instead found the flooring below her quite interesting.

"Why are you doing this?" she whispered as her heart began beating faster. She hoped he didn't notice the way her lab coat collar vibrated because of her rapid pulse rate. She turned her back on him before he could see the color rising to her cheeks.

Dalton had to swallow twice before he could answer. "Because it's my job, Clarisse." His voice came out low and raspy. He hadn't meant for it to be this way; he couldn't help his feelings toward her. He was here to make sure she got her ass back to camp. That was what he was supposed to do, dammit. The rest was something that would never be, but he had no control of the first part. He'd never do anything about his attraction for her, but he would keep her safe.

Searching for her parka, he saw it hung by the door. He looked back at her . . . at the back of her long, slender neck, just exposed above her lab coat, with wisps of chestnut hair curling under the usual bun he had more than once imagined taking down.

Speaking now was impossible, so he tugged her by her left arm and started to drag her lightly to the doorway.

"Come with me." He dared utter only those few words finally and even they came out all wrong for a married man.

Clarissa stiffened as his long, strong fingers wrapped around her upper arm. "Dalton, let go of me." She couldn't bear him touching her, was too aware of his heat through her sleeve. She turned. He stopped and stared into her brown eyes. She immediately dropped her gaze and reached up with her right hand to gently peel his fingers from around her arm.

He picked up her parka and held it open for her without another word. She glanced at him briefly and knew by the way he clenched his jaw he wasn't going to let her stay in the quarantine lab. There was no arguing with the man, and no way would she let him stay here with her overnight. Without trying to hide her frustration and irritation, she took off her lab coat, never speaking a word. She turned and slid into her parka as he slowly pulled the collar up and around her neck. The gesture was way too familiar. She zipped up the front and turned to grab her gloves, then found Dalton holding one open for her. She slid her hands in, first one and then the other, while she avoided his intent stare.

She'd taken a step toward the door when he edged in front of her. She was afraid he was finally going to say something about what they both had been denying, but all he did was reach up and pull her fur hat over her head. For a second their gazes met and held as he drew the strings tight to ensure that she was well shielded against the blizzard they were both about to enter.

When Dalton ushered her out the door, the cold took her breath away. He grabbed the lead line and began striding toward the camp. Clarisse followed, but the swirling snow pelted against her glasses, nearly blinding her. As she stumbled, struggling with the depths of a snowdrift, he returned and grabbed her around the waist and behind her knees, hauling her up into his arms. She realized he intended to carry her the distance, and she protested.

"Put me down, Dalton," she said, but her request was lost to the howling wind. She wondered if, in truth, he'd heard her but chosen to hold her despite her protest. He carried her through the blizzard and she knew he couldn't hold her and the rope both at the same time. She felt him stumble at times as the wind buffeted them but knew he'd walked this route many times. He wouldn't get lost. She rested her head on his shoulder, exhausted from her research and the lost sleep, all brought on by what she knew he'd call "her own damned stubbornness."

Just before they came into clear view of the camp, he stopped and placed her down in the snow in front of him. He took her by the shoulders and turned her to face the camp. She walked on with Dalton right behind her. After the guard buzzed them through, Dalton tried to talk to her, to warn her again to stay at camp at night, or he would be forced to take the same actions. She had already anticipated this, and instead of hearing him out, she headed forward hurriedly to her own tent.

Dalton knew Clarisse was angry with him and decided her irritation was for the best. He went in the opposite direction, to the family quarters, where Kim and his boys lay sleeping.

As he passed the greenhouse tent, he saw Tammy busy inside setting up heaters to guard against the freezing overnight temperatures, doing her best to keep their precious seedlings alive. She waved at him as he approached.

He opened and closed the entry door quickly, only to be met with a slight burning odor. "Hey, you're up late. What's that smell? Do you need help?"

"One of the other heaters crapped out on me earlier, so I'm rigging this one up with another extension. I think it's paint burn-off. We can't afford to lose any of these guys," she said while squatting down to plug in the cord. She seemed to have it all under control.

"Do you want me to take the old heater out of here for you?"

"No, that one is unplugged," she answered, her voice nearly lost to the howling wind outside. "This new unit is working fine. I'm camping in here tonight to keep an eye on things."

"Okay, goodnight." He waved and finally walked on to his own quarters, thinking about Tammy as one of those women that men didn't often cross. She could lead a whole platoon if the need arose.

When Dalton entered his own tent, only a nightlight had been left on for him, casting distorted shadows along the walls. He turned it off and listened to the storm outside. At least now he could sleep knowing that all were where they needed to be, safely within camp.

He checked in on his two boys, looking innocent as the ambient light cast a glow over their flannel pajamas. How lucky they all were. If it hadn't been for Clarisse's warning, they might not have been spared.

Why couldn't she understand? She'd already saved them all.

Marcy stared out the windshield as the storm blew around her. She chanted, "Seven, eight, nine, ten," then honked the horn once, twice, and a third time. A desperation overtook her; her pulse accelerated. "Where the hell are they?" she yelled. Alone and terrified, she'd gone through the honking routine just like Sam said to, at least fifteen times now.

She shivered in the decreasing temperature, the vinyl seating crunching awkwardly as she adjusted her position. She considered going against all of Sam's warnings about leaving the confines of the truck. "They're probably already in the house, lighting a fire by now," she reasoned aloud, aware of the tremor of fear in her own voice. *But no. They'd never do that, leave me here alone one second longer than necessary.*

She'd scarcely formed the thought when the glass at her left shoulder caved in, small particles glittering in the glow of headlights reflecting back from the snow. Marcy ducked instinctively, rolled to the right, feeling the fury of the storm as it shrieked through the hole in the driver's-side window.

In the months before — before the end — Marcy would have sat there stunned, immobilized in shock. But not now. Her response was automatic. She drew her weapon without conscious thought, continuing her roll toward the right side door, grabbing for the handle as snow and a rag-covered hand wielding a club invaded the break in the window.

Even as it swept toward her, she flung open the door and rolled out into the fury of the storm. She clawed her way to her feet and took aim. She didn't scream. She didn't warn. She fired. Once, twice, a third time. Just like Graham taught her. She heard a howl over the scream of the wind. Her attacker's arm and club disappeared.

He was either injured or dead. She was certain she'd hit him, but she wasn't through with him yet. She had to be sure.

She kept to the side of the truck and edged her way around the back, not wanting to be outlined against the headlights. Damn! She saw her assailant fleeing across the blinding light and vanishing abruptly into darkness.

Marcy shook from adrenaline as much as cold. Anger flared through her. *How dare someone harm my family!* She had no doubt her attacker had hurt them before coming after her.

She ducked down to stay under the lights and felt along the front bumper for the rope. Letting it slide through her gloved hand, she waded blindly ahead, knowing the monster was out there, still alive and knowing the territory better than she did. She had to find the men. She had to get there before the killer. They might still be alive. If the killer's only weapon was the club, they could just be unconscious, lying somewhere out here in the snow. She had to find them, so she forced herself forward blindly. Every few difficult paces, she stopped to listen for anything besides the howling wind, to search for dark movement against the swirling blizzard. Discerning nothing, she struggled on, then stopped when her boot hit something hard. She searched with both hands. A rifle! She swept through the snow, searching, hoping, but found no unconscious man.

Up again, she lumbered on with the rifle slung over her shoulder.

When the rope end disappeared from her hand, she stood suspended for a second in disbelief. She felt as if she'd been flying high above the storm and, all at once, stood untethered in midair, in the pitch black of night, all alone. Then, some instinct told her she wasn't alone. Intuition made her whirl and jerk sideways as the club careened toward her face.

She lunged at the enemy. Hands smacking against a chest, sending the attacker sprawling backward to the ground. Pissed and frightened, Marcy would fight this person or die trying. She whaled at the attacker with the butt of her pistol, striking out again and again as long, cold fingernails grabbed at her in the darkness, tearing at her sleeves. A skinny, ungloved hand lifted the club. Marcy snatched it free, flung it away. A high, feminine screech rang through the air. "No! No! That's mine!"

Then the woman scrambled up and darted away, and Marcy followed close enough to hear the grunts and cries of her attacker as she stalked her through the night.

"Where are you?" the woman screamed. Marcy crouched down and kept her eyes on the shapeless bundle of rags as the woman searched. For Marcy? For the club? Muttering as she moved in an aimless circle, quickly gathering snow.

Marcy kept her pistol ready in front of her, but soon the woman seemed to get her bearings and scurried off to the right. She followed as closely as possible, keeping the unkempt shape in sight until finally the house appeared dimly ahead of her. The house that first seemed a safe haven from the storm now appeared a malevolent hovel.

The raging woman screamed and mumbled words Marcy couldn't understand as she ascended rickety stairs and crossed the porch. Faint candlelight glowed as the door opened into the lunatic's lair. Marcy ran toward it, crept up the steps, hearing more incoherent ranting from inside. She crouched, weapon drawn, and kicked opened the weathered door of the madhouse.

The woman straddled Sam's waist, about to plunge a large kitchen knife into his chest, and Marcy pulled the trigger.

The shot hit the woman in the back of her head. Blood sprayed—over the wall, all over Sam. Marcy took two long strides and kicked the woman off Sam's chest and shot her again at point blank range, then a third time and then a fourth.

Sam moaned and Marcy turned. When the woman fell, the knife had continued, slicing into Sam's chest. As she stared, it fell over and clattered onto the wooden floor. Sam's eyes were wide open. He stared at her in amazement. "Nice shots," he said. "Now untie me."

"Where's Mark?" she demanded.

"I don't know, Marcy. Untie me."

"Where *is* he?" Her voice went high.

"Marcy! Marcy, use the knife and untie me." Sam rolled to his side, bringing his knees up to his chest.

"Mark!" she yelled.

"Marcy! Untie me, God dammit!" Sam yelled, then gasped as he moved, and she came out of it enough to listen to him. She found the blood-drenched knife next to Sam's curled body and hacked into the tight bindings. Then, she went in search of Mark in the depths of the eerie, darkened rooms filled with litter.

She rushed past broken wooden chairs and couch cushions with their stuffing emptied all over the living room, past rat carcasses and parts of deer flesh, long spoiled, lying by the open fireplace.

She scuffed through litter into what had been a kitchen, then a bathroom, toilet broken, but the stench said the woman had continued to use it anyway. She ducked out of there quickly, then continued into a back bedroom, saw Mark, and screamed.

When Marcy screamed, Sam ripped at the ropes still tangling his feet. Blood poured from his chest. The room spun, but Marcy needed him. He got to his feet, balancing himself on a wall of the hallway, his shirt and coat quickly blooming with bloodstains. Dizziness sent him reeling. His hand came away from the back of his head wet and warm with crimson blood from the injury. Marcy continued yelling Mark's name. The sound of her distress echoed loudly in his cranium. He squinted from the pain.

"Marcy, where are you?" he shouted.

"Back here! Hurry, Sam, I need your help!" Her high-pitched cry dropped down to horrible, hoarse sobbing.

"Marcy, I'm coming! Where are you?" He yelled it, trying to find her as he stumbled alongside a wall that defied its true angle. He braced himself against the illusion, as the rest of the room spun. He closed his eyes and tried to follow the sound of her voice because his eyes couldn't pick a worthy direction. As he trailed her voice, his blood smeared along the dirty wall, trailing crimson waves.

"We're in here!" she called.

When Sam finally found them, with difficulty, he blinked and shook his head to make the two images become one. Marcy crouched, untying Mark as he lay motionless on his stomach, his head in a puddle of blood. Marcy rolled him over, and his injuries were immediately evident. His nose lay at an unnatural angle, one eye was swollen shut, and blood drained out of his ear. Clearly, the crazed woman had clubbed him across the face.

"Mark, can you hear me?" Marcy sobbed, clutching at him, rocking back and forth on her haunches. "Mark!"

Sam staggered to them and dropped to the boy's side. He reached for his neck to check his pulse, afraid of what he might find. Blinking his eyes several times, he tried to ignore the spinning and focused on the task at hand. Finally he was able to determine a faint thumping. "He's alive," Sam whispered hoarsely.

Marcy cried tears of relief. Sam patted her on the back and she leaned against him, pressing her cheek against his blooming blood-soaked shirt.

"She stabbed you," she said, pulling away. Shock glazed her eyes.

Sam had to keep her with him. Though she'd just saved them all, she still had more to do, or they might yet die.

"I know, Marcy, but I'm okay. You need to listen to me now. Can you do that?" He held her by the forearms and shook her until she looked at him.

"Yeah."

"We need to get Mark back to camp. The swelling in his neck could block his airway. Do you think you can drive? It sounds like most of the storm has passed."

She nodded.

"Good girl. Let's get Mark into the main room and get the truck up here."

In no condition to help Marcy move Mark into the living room, Sam could only offer suggestions on how not to injure him further. She did the best she could as Sam followed, holding himself against the wall. She carefully laid Mark down on the floor in front of the entrance, putting a ratty cushion under his head for elevation.

As Sam passed the dead body of the woman, he could see with morbid clarity how she had died. When she'd returned to the house in a rage, she'd been bleeding from a chest wound. Then she'd attacked him with the knife, without thought to her own condition. Even if Marcy hadn't shot her, she'd have died drowning in her own blood. He'd heard her wheezing, fighting for breath.

He worried about Marcy. She shot the woman at least once outside and then again in the house, but the third shot was unnecessary, as was the fourth. Now was not the time to ask her about her actions, but the effect worried him. She was functioning now, but he knew deeper shock would set in soon, and he needed to get her back before she had the opportunity to break down. He needed her to keep herself together long enough to get them home.

He peered at the front window and saw that the storm had calmed down enough for him to see the truck out in the frozen landscape. He tried to speak to Marcy, to tell her what to do, but the effort of walking had left him spent. Slowly, his back to the wall, he sank to the floor and realized he was passing out.

Dimly, he heard Marcy's cry. "Sam!"

He had just enough strength to brush her hands away when she tried to apply pressure to the knife cut in his chest. "Sam, don't . . . don't leave me."

"Girl, go get the truck. I'm fine. Dizzy as hell, but fine," he said as he felt the shadows close in around him.

"Okay," she said, and ran for the door.

He stopped her before she left and said with slow care, "Marcy, it's stuck, remember. Put it back in four-wheel-drive, and follow the dropped wheel. Go straight into the ditch. Listen to me, go straight into the ditch and drive straight up and out to the curve in the road. Don't turn the wheel or you'll get stuck again. Do you understand me?"

"Yes, Sam. I'll be right back."

He nodded with his eyes half closed to keep the room from spinning. God, how he hoped she could do it. He didn't want to be in that house a minute longer, and he really worried about the boy. Glancing in that direction, he could see Mark's injuries were life-threatening. Even now his very breath seemed fleeting.

The warmth in the truck would also beat the drafty conditions in the shack. If they lost the boy, Marcy would be no good, and he needed to get her back to Graham in one piece. The fact that she'd killed the woman outright was impressive but a bit worrisome. He didn't think she really knew she had committed the deed—not really, not yet. No doubt, the fact would hit her later. He needed Graham for that. It was only a matter of time before reality came to her.

16 Decided Chance

Early the next morning, Tala rose before the others and barely made it to the bathroom before the heaving overtook her. The bile wouldn't be held back this time. She hoped no one heard her, but the urgency couldn't be helped. After cleaning up she talked herself into making the morning coffee and beginning breakfast, even though the smell drove her over the edge. Soon Bang's little feet padded on the wooden floor. As always, he rose to meet her in the quiet of dawn.

"Good morning Tala," he said, and poured himself a cup of coffee.

"I know Graham said you could have coffee, but a boy your age really shouldn't be drinking that much caffeine every day. So go easy, okay? You might stop growing," she warned playfully, then attempted to straighten his hair with her hands as she imagined his own mother would have done.

He smiled up at Tala, knowing she had tried to fool him. "If it's good for Graham, it's good for me too," he reasoned as he added nearly as much reconstituted milk as coffee, and then added two heaping spoons of sugar. After observing this, she decided to give up on hassling him about the coffee, and instead, focus on good oral hygiene with so much sugar and no dentists around.

Once again, the coffee aroma threatened to send her to the bathroom, and Bang witnessed her recoil at the smell.

"Are you sick, Tala?" Fear came over his small face, and for good reason: he'd lost his entire family to the pandemic. She swallowed hard and recovered, then knelt down to him and brushed his hair out of his eyes once more.

"I'm fine, Bang. I'm not *that kind* of sick, so don't worry about me, okay?" She handed him a bowl of grits mixed with some dried venison meat for extra protein. He accepted the steaming bowl and made his way to the table.

Tala had worked very hard to gain the boy's trust over the past several months, and she didn't want to jeopardize that bond in the least by keeping a secret. After all he'd been through, he deserved better. So did Graham. She would find a way to tell Graham, and soon.

Keeping the pregnancy a secret would prove to be impossible for much longer, especially with the tight quarters of the cabin eliminating most privacy.

She dreaded Graham's reaction after his response to putting the girls on birth control. She would never agree to an abortion. Clarisse and Graham both believed terminating would be for the best in theory, but Tala would take her chances. She hadn't slept a wink the previous night as she struggled over the decision. To her, abortion was murder; no matter the time of conception. Even with the virus still apparent and the unknown immunity factor, she still felt the child had a chance, a chance at life she was willing to take over a clear and decided death.

Macy was next up, and as usual, she cheerfully entered the kitchen ready for a new day.

"I beat Graham this morning?" she asked, surprised, and beamed a proud smile.

Macy's competitive nature, her determination to beat Graham at everything, always amused Tala. She could almost outshoot him; she could definitely outrun him, and their competitiveness had become a source of entertainment for them all. Once she declared a challenge, it was on. She would practice endlessly and become quite skilled, well beyond her sister's abilities. A strength this keen became essential to their survival.

"We were up a little late last night," Tala said in Graham's defense. "But it's not even light yet. I think we're all up a little early this morning." She let Macy serve herself, and then poured Graham a cup of coffee. Again, she avoided the aroma after a wave of nausea hit her. Sheriff came ambling out of the bunkroom and almost knocked the coffee from her hands. When she finally made it past the doorway, Graham was, in fact, awake and watching over Ennis.

The look on his face took her aback. "Is he okay?"

"Yeah, he's breathing. He was just mumbling a lot in his sleep last night."

She handed him his coffee, and as he accepted the warm cup, she asked, "Does he have a fever?"

"He seems a little too warm, but not like yesterday."

He motioned for them to retreat out of the room to let Ennis sleep longer. He looped his free arm around her waist as they entered the dining area.

"Let's wake him in another hour, and get him to the bathroom," Tala said.

"Yeah, but let me do it. Afterward, I'm going to take the pickup truck into town for a few things. I think we should have those painkillers here for him so he's not in so much turmoil. We need a few other things, too, and I'll check the post office to see if our Carnation boy has arrived yet."

She pulled away, not daring to face him in case he detect her nausea.

The snow had nearly stopped by morning and Graham wanted to get into town and back again before darkness took hold. He wanted to think for a while on his own. Despite Tala trying to hide it from him, Graham had detected she'd been sick to her stomach lately and suspected she might be pregnant, and that brought back recent memories of his wife succumbing to the pandemic and the loss of their unborn child. He didn't feel good about any of this. In fact, he felt like a jackass, but if terminating a pregnancy meant saving Tala from heartache, he'd do his best to convince her to take the drugs. He wanted to save Tala from going through the agony of losing another child at birth, or later, from the virus itself. He knew she'd never agree to the termination, so he would try to prevent the risk. If he spared her the loss of another child, it would be worth the guilt.

Tala peeked out the front window as Graham warmed up the pickup truck. He waved to her and nodded. She was sad from the weight of the secret he suspected, and likewise, pale from morning sickness.

Graham would like nothing more than to keep the child, especially since it belonged to him and Tala. But he suspected deep down that he'd lose her, too, if they dared to try. He had to save her at least. With that last thought, he put the pickup in gear and headed out into town, taking the drive slowly and keeping to the forested tree line where the drifted snow accumulation gave the tires a better grip.

He had never believed much in God, but after losing so many loved ones he had even more reason to negate God's existence. *Why would he allow this to happen to man?* It was a question that would never be answered to his satisfaction. *And don't give me that crap about cleansing the earth. I'm no Noah.*

Despite how bad the storm had been for a brief period, the snow on the drive wasn't bad; there was one spot where it had drifted, and Graham had sweated, despite the cold, while shoveling his way through it. He couldn't wait for Mark to get back home. Graham would never withhold praise where it was due, and Mark was the master of snow clearing.

As he drove Graham thought of how far they had come since the apocalypse began. He knew his father would have been proud of him now. Though he'd struggled against his dad in almost every way, from his politics to his style of dress, he now laughed to himself as he realized he'd become just like the man, with his rifle by his side and nearly the same practical daily attire out of necessity. The irony hit him all at once, and he laughed yet almost cried at the same time. His father, deserving of heaven, was surely chuckling too.

How unimportant the things he'd thought vital this time last year had become. He remembered how he'd tried to convince his dad the marijuana bill being passed in Washington was the right thing to do, and how outraged his father had been. In retrospect, many more important things should have been debated, like the increasing avian flu mutation research for one. What a horrible waste. Even after the shit hit the fan, legalizing marijuana for tax revenue remained the number one issue being debated. Tragically this issue would be the least of their worries. If only they had known what lay right around the corner.

Because Graham's mind wandered, the drive took less time than he thought it would, and he soon found himself well into town. The first order of business was to go to the doctor's house first and grab the meds—both the pain meds for Ennis and the others. When he'd last been there the thought hadn't even crossed his mind that he would need them. Tala took birth control, so they never suspected she could get pregnant, but he knew the pill didn't provide 100 percent coverage—even taking an antibiotic or cough syrup could foul up the system. He should have at least remembered that.

One thing about the breakdown of society was the lack of general rules and laws. One could choose to drive off-road and through sidewalks or front yards whenever necessary. So when Graham found a snowdrift three feet tall blocking the road he simply drove around it, through the front yard of an old weather-beaten white church with a sign in the window that read AA MEETINGS DOWN BELOW. The sign struck him as odd, and he wondered many times a little room below the old church might have been dedicated to those who overindulged. The DOWN BELOW seemed humorous and, to satisfy his own curiosity, he planned to check the location out someday this spring.

Once he reached the doctor's house Graham realized he had forgotten his handheld radio. He had always proclaimed this to be a big no-no, and here he was, the first one to break the rule. "Damn. Well, I'll get this over quick." The door was frozen to the jamb, and releasing it took several encouraging pushes to coax an entry.

A smoky scent seemed to permeate the old home. It wasn't unpleasant, but it took Graham back to his own grandfather's home, where he'd often found the old man toking on big Churchill cigars. The aromatic smoke had permeated every fiber and even clung to Graham's memories. The old home, decorated in what Graham thought of as 1800s antique shop, mesmerized him as a welcomed blast from the past. The deep green plush carpet was accented with fuzzy burgundy baroque wallpaper and floral Tiffany type lamps set atop dark mahogany craftsman-style end tables. Somewhere a clock continued to tick despite the owners' deaths. Graham wished he could conjure up the doctor. His expertise would be useful indeed.

Though they had access to Clarisse on the radio, she wasn't "theirs." After the previous incident, he and Dalton had made an agreement that their first encounter would be the last time they would intervene in each other's camps. Because of Sam being separated from his daughter, he would never allow anyone from his camp to enter theirs or vice versa. With the risk, he didn't want to be responsible for another tragedy, be it death or otherwise.

Graham found himself wiping his feet again, even though it wasn't necessary in these times. Such *a blasted habit!* he thought—one instilled in him by his mother. He listened for anything to indicate he might not be alone, then walked quietly through the kitchen and into the adjoining rooms that served as the doctor's office. These rooms, unlike the rest of the home, were stark white—rooms of serious intention. On their previous visit they had found a lot of helpful supplies here, but had only taken what they thought they might need; they'd left the rest, knowing it would be here if they needed it later.

Well, they had a use for it now. Graham opened the cupboard where he'd found a box containing the pills. The carton consisted of several foil packets of pills. He read the directions and found that the prescription only recommended a dosage for up to eight weeks' gestation. If Tala was at six weeks now, he had little time to convince her to take them. He honestly had no idea how far along she might be. The set contained one larger pill that was to be taken first, and then the others, one by one as needed until the fetus expelled a few days later. Graham took a deep breath. He'd never given abortion much thought before the pandemic, though women's rights had always been a subject of much discussion among his peers and friends. He'd thought of himself as a progressive thinker, and he didn't disagree with a woman's right to choose. But to be faced with such an option now, made him think of the tiniest of details and the subsequent consequences. This aspect of taking care of the specifics couldn't be glossed over.

He shoved the foil pack back into the box and concealed the whole container in his coat pocket. He then scanned the shelves for Ennis's medication, and seeing the bottle lined up under P for phenazopyridine, he took the whole container and closed the cabinet.

He backtracked through the quiet house and out the front door, closing it behind him to preserve the smell within for him to enjoy another day.

Next he pulled up outside the post office. He always checked there in hopes the young man they'd met in Carnation on the way up from Seattle so many months ago would show up at some point. He often thought of the kid, living completely on his own. He and Sam had contemplated going back to check on the boy when spring came, on their way to scout out how things were closer to Seattle. Hopefully they'd be able to convince him to stay with them. The more people they had, the better chance for survival these days.

Always careful in town since the bear incident last fall, Graham checked out his surroundings before stepping out of the truck. Seeing nothing, he took his rifle out of the truck, slung it over his shoulder, and went into the post office to see if there was any word from the Carnation boy.

The foggy gray morning still showed some snow blowing in the wind gusts. He thought of Sam and the kids and hoped they were holding up well through the storm they had had last night.

This trip inside the post office was like many before. The bell on the metallic handle of the door clinked as it always had; the sound still bothered him and provoked little hairs to stand on end. It was a hard habit to break: waiting for someone in the back to come out and ask if he needed help.

After he had stepped onto the tiled floor he scanned the counters for any obvious signs of the teen. He'd done this at least once a week for months now, and he didn't expect to find anything new. But there on the counter, where long-gone patrons had once tossed various pieces of unwanted and discarded junk mail or picked up tax forms every April, lay a piece of paper folded along the middle to stand at attention.

Graham grinned ear to ear. "About time, kid." He picked up the paper and read the few lines:

> I'm the guy from Carnation. I met you last fall. You said to meet you here. I'm staying in a brick house down the road.
> McCann.

"Man of few words." Graham said aloud, then smiled to himself as the phrase echoed in the small, cold post office. At least this good news would bring a smile to the others. They would have another person there to help with things, and Graham could quit worrying about the boy's welfare.

Excited at the prospect of meeting the young man, Graham read the note once again as he exited the door. The bell tinkled as he stepped outside, his gaze still on the note. At that moment, an attack was the last thing on his mind, and he would forever regret not taking the usual precautions.

Three feral dogs sniffed at the truck parked right outside the building, and when they heard the bell ring, they knew a human was close by. As Graham took one step, and then the other, they lowered their chests close to their front paws with their fur raised in alert. When the man looked up, they sprang on him and attacked him with a vengeance.

Graham, caught completely unaware, yelled out desperately. With his rifle slung around his back, he couldn't reach it; one dog already had its fangs sunk deeply into his thigh. Another leaped for Graham's neck from behind, and a third tugged at his calf, ripping it with its long fangs.

He managed to pull away from the second, but the first two had a great hold on his legs and would not let go. Instead, the bastards shook with aggression, tearing flesh free. Again, Graham went for the rifle when the second dog dived for his side, catching him in the chest, knocking him over, and gouging fangs deeply into his upper arm.

A shot rang out. Graham thought for a second he had somehow managed to get a hold of his rifle, then realized he'd never made it. The one dog tearing at his arm lay dead right beside him, but the others attached to his legs would not let go. Graham grabbed at one's head and tried to keep him from doing any more damage when he heard someone yell, "Get out of the way!"

Graham knew that meant he had to let his enemy loose to gleefully resume its mutilation of him, but letting go of his self-preservation held the only hope to free him from the attack. He pulled back and lay as flat as possible to help give his rescuer a clear shot at the beasts. A second shot rang out, and then a third. The gruesome growling ended, and a great weight fell onto his torn-open leg.

McCann had dared to close his eyes for more than a few minutes before his ever vigilant subconscious picked up on something: tires traveling on compact ice. His ears were attuned to the distressed whinny of his horses tied out back behind the one-level brick home he currently occupied. Every hour or so, overnight, wolves continued to try and mark the horses as easy prey.

Coming from Carnation through a snowstorm hadn't been a good idea after all, and McCann soon regretted the trek, but when the flakes began to fall in sheets, turning back made no more sense than going on. He pushed through and had finally made the last stretch the previous morning, but so far, because of wolves and wild dogs, he hadn't slept more than two hours straight.

"Aw shit! Now, someone comes? I'm never going to get any goddamn sleep," he grumbled, even though the prospect of seeing someone—anyone—after many weeks alone brought a kind of giddiness he would not admit to.

McCann lifted himself off the living room couch of the little redbrick house and grabbed his cowboy hat and his rifle from the coffee table in one fell swoop. After inching toward the door, he peeked out the window and spotted someone's truck parked at the post office a block down the road. "I might as well wait for him to find the note," he mumbled.

In the beginning, when the pandemic had first hit, McCann had nursed each member of his family—as in, helping them to die as peacefully as possible. After they were all dead and buried he had no plans to leave his family's ranch. One afternoon while checking on the cattle stock, a movement caught his attention down the dirt driveway. Of all the people in the town of Carnation, he never envisioned his elderly fifth grade teacher, Mrs. Goode, walking to his front door. As frail as her ancient body appeared, having come this far out of downtown must have been a tremendous feat.

Once he approached her, she informed him that they were the only two still alive. She also chastised him for trying to keep up the livestock on his father's ranch.

"Let 'em go, son. They can take care of themselves better than you can. You can't keep doing this all on your own; it'll wear you down. I won't be on this earth much longer, and I'll be grateful for the end when it comes; I don't much like living this quiet. However, you need to find some people to herd as you take care of these cows. McCann, you can't stay here by yourself."

She took up residence in his little sister's vacant room and stayed with him from that point until her death. She stopped taking her heart medication, but McCann didn't know that. He only knew she became weaker every day. It wasn't long before he sat by her bedside one night as her life drifted away in a hush. Later, he found the medication hidden away in her bag and knew what she'd done.

He'd planned to hole up at the ranch as best he could despite what Mrs. Goode had said. However, once winter really took hold, the quiet that snuck in through the doorways and cold windowpanes strangled his hope. He soon realized he wouldn't want to repeat another winter there alone and began to think of the man who had stopped in town months earlier. The blue-eyed girls he'd seen in the Scout's backseat that day visited him often in his dreams, and soon plans to make his way to Cascade formulated in his mind. The next thing he knew, he stood watching the cattle scatter as he held open the metal gate for the last time.

The snarling of feral dogs and the first hollers of pain jerked him back into the present. He spun from the window and took off running, armed and already guessing what had taken place. As he rounded the corner, seeing the man with three dogs on him sent

McCann into action. The first dog went down easily, but the man himself was in the way of other shots. It took some horrified patience and careful angling to get a clear shot of the mauling targets. Immediately the oversight of not warning this man of the wild dog activity he'd already taken notice of in his short time in Carnation weighed on him.

With the dogs dispatched, McCann holstered his gun and reached down, sinking two fists into the deep matt of the dog's gray fur. He grabbed and pulled the weight off the man. With the blood already staining the surrounding snow, his injuries appeared pretty bad. Flesh torn wide open hung out of his upper right thigh. McCann helped Graham sit up and checked the injured left shoulder. It bled, but luckily, the coat padding had saved him from too much damage.

The pain must be gruesome McCann thought as Graham groaned. "I'm real sorry I didn't come sooner."

"Me too. Not your fault. Goddamn assholes," Graham said, staring at the downed menace. McCann tried to help him up, but he yelled out in pain.

"Ribs," Graham said; then he gasped and passed out.

McCann dragged Graham to the pickup, hoping his ribs were cracked or bruised, not actually broken and about to pierce a lung; that would be way beyond his abilities in first aid. He opened the back door and pushed Graham inside. He had lost a lot of blood, and McCann needed to get him back to his temporary residence to stem further bleeding.

He couldn't drive the man to his camp; he didn't know where the hell that might be. Besides that, he suspected more dogs might show up with the smell of fresh blood in the air. McCann hated the damn things. Despite the loneliness, predators were the second-best reason he'd decided to abandon his own home and come here. Well, that was the story he was going with, anyway.

After he got Graham inside the brick house, he instantly went to work to try to stop the bleeding by using kitchen towels and anything he could find to apply pressure to the wounds.

Graham was still out cold, and that was a good thing. McCann had learned first aid on his father's ranch, most of which he'd used on cattle, not people. More often than not, steers tended to open themselves up by rubbing their fool selves along barbed wire or the sharp ends of fence gates. He'd had numerous chances to practice his surgery skills, fine-tuning his techniques with each incident. He'd also helped deliver many calves during the season, and when a heifer had a vaginal prolapse, McCann was the first to replace the tissue and suture the wounds, just like his father taught him.

Before the pandemic, he had far-fetched plans to go off to med school. Now he was just thankful he'd learned as much as he did for everyday survival because, sadly, those dreams were over.

McCann pulled back the compress and saw mangled tissue bleeding badly. Luckily, the injury was on the outside of Graham's right thigh and not near the major arteries on the inside, near his groin. Almost sure the wound would get infected, McCann knew the man was in for a long recovery. He felt for a pulse and then used his pocketknife to rip Graham's jeans open. McCann removed his coat and put another log in the brick fireplace because he had a long day ahead of him. Then he got busy collecting and sterilizing the supplies he would need to treat this guy's injuries if there were any hope of getting him through this.

"Good afternoon, sunshine, what's up?" Dalton asked Rick as he wandered into the media tent after lunch. The morning had been a long one, and he was sure the rest of the day would drag out even longer. He'd barely slept the night before, as he suffered from his own moral conflict.

"Same damned thing; the world ended, but our four corners are secure. Reuben, Steven, and a few others are headed out on their scheduled hunt early tomorrow morning. They're going on the northwest trail since Sam and his group are straight north."

Dalton watched Rick, who obviously had something more on his mind; he sat in his chair with his back to Dalton and was doing that damn tapping thing again, which always led to trouble, as Dalton saw it.

"What else?"

"Macy called in earlier. She said Graham had left camp early this morning. He was going into town for something, but she didn't catch for what or why, and a few of the cameras are iced over despite the fucking auto defrost mechanism. I can't see a damn thing in town."

"You may not track him, Rick. I know what you're thinking. He's probably sick of being cooped up indoors like the rest of us and needed some air. Those trackers probably don't work now anyway. They eventually work their way out to the surface of the skin, and they're out by now."

Rick spun around to face Dalton. "Yeah. Something's off, though. Something's not right."

"That's so prophetic of you, Rick." Dalton stared at his old friend. The stress in his eyes made him appear tired, and Dalton guessed he'd stayed up late with Addy and Bethany giggling into the night. To base anything on less than a fact for Rick was new. Dalton thought perhaps the lowering of testosterone, now that he was past forty, was getting to him. Having Rick PMSing was a frightening thought.

"Why don't you go get a late lunch? I'll man the media for a while."

"All right," Rick said, never one to turn down the prospect of a hot meal. But as he got up to make his way out of the tent he stopped. "Just remembered. Clarisse hiked her way to quarantine bright and early this morning. She said to tell you she had some work to do, and Addy's staying with Bethany for the afternoon. She said she'd be back by dinner."

"Okay, Rick, thanks."

"She'd *better* be back by dinner," Dalton said under his breath.

He checked the existing cameras and surveyed the boundary compound fence. It was clear other than a few snowdrifts. They had no way of knowing if the storm was yet over. It was anyone's guess.

On further inspection, the path to the quarantine building appeared clear as well. He checked the inside cameras and found Clarisse hovering over a microscope again, as always. He wondered if she'd slept at all last night. At least she was inside and safe for now, even if she was still pissed at him.

Tearing himself away from her image, Dalton checked the other cameras in their own camp and noted in the log the time and condition. Next he viewed Graham's camp and found Macy on watch at the drive side, and he could barely make out Bang on the lake side through the partially frosted lens. Tala was in the greenhouse, and he supposed Ennis was still inside the cabin, though without the cameras he had no idea. The absence of Graham's truck in the driveway showed that he hadn't yet returned from town. He missed seeing his kid cousin, Mark, but Dalton was sure he was having the time of his life with Sam and Marcy out on their hunt.

He reviewed all the exterior cameras and found nothing out of the ordinary in the deep of winter after a big storm. He made more notations in the log and turned his attention to the town cameras. One in particular was blacked out completely, and the others were nothing but blobs of grayness.

All of a sudden the radio crackled to life, and the sound was Clarisse's voice coming in, low and sweet. "Rick, can you get Steven? He was on guard duty last night, but I'm hoping he's up by now. I need someone else to take a look at this." By the sound of it Dalton could tell she was pretty excited about something, though he wished she wasn't sharing the news with Steven.

He gazed at her on the screen for a few seconds before he hit the microphone button. "It's me, Clarisse. Rick's taking a lunch break," he said, hearing the tension in his own voice, coming out low and hoarse. He surveyed her body language for any reaction.

"Oh," she said and paused. "Can you please get Steven out here?" By the way she pulled abruptly away from the radio, he thought she still fumed over last night's episode.

"Yeah, I'll send him out right away. Do you need anything from here? Coffee? A muffin?"

"No. I only need Steven. Thank you."

He smiled now, because she was still more than a *little* pissed, and he needed her to be. If she ever turned her steamy gaze on him again, like the night before, he was afraid of what he might do—of what he might discard because he needed her.

He couldn't let her have her own way, either. It was too bad, but she needed to follow the rules like the rest of them. What would they do without her otherwise?

He cleared his throat from all that, and when he said, "All right, I'll send him over," his voice was still gruff. He didn't mean it to be. He had no right or claim to her, and if she needed Steven, he would get the guy for her. But he wouldn't be happy about it.

"Clarisse out," she clipped quickly, as if she couldn't hang up fast enough.

He didn't like that she *needed* Steven, but a relationship between her and Steven would be for the best. He ignored his jealousy for now and went in search of the guy.

Steven was the closest Clarisse had to an assistant these days. In his prior life he had been a paramedic, and before that he served in Afghanistan with the rest of them as a medic.

The first place to look for anyone in the afternoon was in the mess tent and, more specifically, in the coffee line. Dalton liked to get in the dining area first thing in the morning because he hated anyone standing between him and his coffee.

He surveyed the tent and found the man he looked for. With his blond hair sticking up in all directions, Steven looked like he'd just rolled out of bed. He must have just walked out of the shower and lost his comb somewhere along the way to the mess tent. Dalton smiled at the guy, though his instincts told him to strangle him.

"What?" Steven asked, seeing Dalton stare him down.

Dalton knew it was too early for Steven after pulling the midnight guard shift duty.

"Clarisse needs your assistance," Dalton informed him.

"Since when does she need my help?"

"She discovered something, and wants you to come look at her findings," Dalton explained to him.

"Oh. So she needs me, then?" Steven puffed out his chest with mock importance and plastered a big smile on his face.

"Yep, but don't let it go to your head," Dalton barked at him.

"All right! Let me get some coffee. If I can get through this goddamn line!" he yelled, enough for Rick to get the idea to hurry up. He was taking his sweet time mixing his own brew to perfection.

Dalton watched as Rick said with deliberate slowness, "Keep your pants on, man. It's not the end of the world; well, not quite yet, anyway." Then, the other two people waiting in line parted to each side knowing from experience Steven would retaliate. As Dalton expected, Steven walked up behind the unsuspecting Rick and deliberately pushed the other man's elbow just enough that the brew sloshed all over the counter.

Dalton gave up and walked back to the media tent as Rick's explicative retort wafted behind him. These proceedings would be the beginning of a tit-for-tat game that would both entertain and drive others crazy for days until they both called it a draw. To Dalton, Steven's antics meant that, without a doubt, Clarisse would not settle in the long term for anyone so childish. That acknowledgment both thrilled and terrified him.

Steven finally got his coffee fixed and changed his now sodden and coffee-stained T-shirt; Rick had dispensed the rest of his remaining brew in one impressive splash aimed directly at his chest. Steven had called a temporary truce, then headed back to his tent to change and don his outerwear before he made his way over to Clarisse in the quarantine building. As he opened the lab door, she turned, looking impatient. It was obvious she had been waiting for him.

A really broad grin wasn't something he'd ever have expected to cross Clarisse's face, so when one did, it creeped him out a little. So much so that he shot a quick glance behind himself in case Rick had somehow appeared there with some kind of sadistic reprisal.

"What is going on? I like you better bitchy and arrogant. It's too damn early for this, even though it's nearly evening," he complained like a little boy as she led him by the elbow over to the microscope. "At least it's too early for me."

"Look," she commanded, pointing to the microscope.

He sat and took a peek through the scope. After a few seconds, he gave up. "What am I looking at here?"

"Antibodies."

"Clarisse, I treat the wounded. This isn't exactly my thing. Please explain."

"Okay, so, as you remember, before the pandemic we had no vaccine for the avian flu. The government stocked antivirals, but they did little to affect this mutated version of the avian flu, and actually, it prolonged suffering but did not prevent death.

"Then they tried the vaccine, which included the adjuvant they needed to stabilize the vaccine, but that caused narcolepsy. As if we didn't have enough to worry about already." She was pacing in front him now. "That vaccine never worked to begin with. It was for a different variation altogether."

She stopped pacing. "Really, Steven this is so sick and sad. If only our government had funded the research we needed to come up with this variation, not nearly so many would have died. But no, they had to give millions to fund farming in China or video game research in California."

Steven interrupted her, "Hey, I for one miss video games, and you're ranting. Get to the point. I need more coffee."

"I think I have it. You're looking at the antibodies I took from subject twelve."

He scrunched his eyebrows together.

"You mean Harry? You gave Harry H5N1 and a vaccine that actually produced antibodies?"

"Hey, I *told* you not to name the ferrets. And, actually, no, not quite. I gave Harry and three of his ferret buddies a vaccine containing *HA* (hemagglutinin) with aluminum phosphate, plus a new adjuvant that I've been working with to help stabilize the vaccine to allow it to absorb better. I followed up three weeks later with a second dose, exactly the same, then waited four weeks and gave them the challenge virus.

"This is the first time I've had all test subjects show no sign of the virus. There was no increase in temperature, no runny noses, no weight loss, and no loss of activity, but they do show strong antibodies."

For a while Steven acted bored, but as she babbled on he soon realized what she was saying—something he hadn't heard before: *strong antibodies*. She'd tried over and over for months, and now, she'd finally developed a viable vaccine.

He ignored her babbling while he digested the information. He lifted one eyebrow and said, "Wait a minute. Are you saying you created the *vaccine*? *For real?* You did it?"

She nodded, and to his surprise, tears started flooding down her cheeks. Her shoulders heaved with suppressed sobs.

Steven got up off the lab stool with arms opened wide and yelled, "You did it? You *did* it!"

He lifted her up and spun her around a few times, then set her back down carefully. He fixed her collar while she adjusted her glasses. "Oh, my God! Why doesn't everyone know about this?" he asked as the realization set in.

"Because I wanted to be sure my data was correct. I wanted to finish checking the results last night, but Dalton wouldn't let me stay, so I came out early this morning."

"That bastard! Is the vaccine ready for the first round?"

"No, I'm using the cell-cultured method, so the process should take about four weeks; then we can begin giving the first injections."

"So you're saying that once we are inoculated and show antibodies to this one, we can interact with the carriers?"

"Yes. Full immunity will take about two weeks, but yes," she nodded, glassy-eyed. "It means Addy can be with her dad again." It took all of Clarisse's strength to keep her voice from cracking as she revealed the triumph. Steven reached out to hold her again, more softly this time; even the Quarantine Queen needed a hug now and again. He held her there for a moment until she recovered and pulled away from him again.

"One thing no one knows yet, though, is if this virus will naturally mutate next season. We have to assume, based on recent history, the likelihood that the virus will continue to transform. We're still not safe from H5N1, and neither are the carriers, for that matter. Next year we could be dealing with a much different mutated form of the avian flu—call it a subtype variation. The only thing now that might save us is this drastic decrease in population allowing a greater buffer between societies."

"Will this vaccine give us any immunity to another mutated subtype form?"

"It's possible, but not something we can count on."

"Can we tell everyone?"

"Um, I've been thinking about that. I don't see why not, but instead of having everyone on edge again for four weeks, why not just keep the secret to ourselves until we have only one more week to go?"

"I see your point, Clarisse, but you have to tell Dalton. And I can't not tell Rick, he'll do something evil to me for sure. If he finds out I knew and didn't tell him . . ." Steven shuddered at the thought.

"I tried to tell Dalton, but he doesn't want to hear about a cure anymore."

When he heard her say that, Steven diverted his attention away from what he thought Rick might do to him and gave her his attention, nodding in understanding. They'd been through so much, and after a while, like Dalton, many people built a shield to protect themselves from going through the cycle of hope, crushing disappointment, and desperation over and over again.

"Well, I'll let Rick know, with the disclaimer that we don't announce until the last week. And you *must* tell Dalton; he needs to know." As Steven headed for the door, he added, "Great job, Clarisse, you saved us all again."

Marcy closed the guys inside the wretched house. Dawn came in a mist of blue with everything in sight frozen. The evergreen trees loomed like dark imposters. Though the snow had left the ground piled high in drifts; she could barely make out the lead line. After carefully descending the slick and rickety porch steps, she ran out the long driveway to the Scout, careful not to slip on exposed ice; the last thing she wanted to do was to injure herself and be of no help to the men.

Though the whiteout had dissipated, snow still swirled with sharp gusts of wind, stinging her exposed, tear-streaked cheeks. She began to run faster along the rope line left on the ground until she spotted another rifle laying half buried under crusted snow.

After picking up the gun, she eyed the spotlight poking through the snow farther ahead. Either the two guys had managed to throw the gun and light when they were attacked, or the woman had seen no need for them or had missed them altogether. The visibility then had been nil.

Marcy tried to push the terrible memories out of her vision, but they returned in flashes. A shot in the dark. A mad woman astride Sam. A butcher knife raised high. Her own finger pressing the trigger. The blast of sound when her weapon fired. The blood that splattered against Sam. *I killed her. I killed her.* Forever, the mad woman would remain in her mind, branded as *the one I killed.*

Graham's "no regret" rules were there for a reason, but the statute didn't stop Marcy's stomach from dry heaving or her mind from remembering. She tried to focus on what she needed to do now but flashed back to Campos, remembered horror, the newer vision of blood on the wall. Blood of *the one I killed.*

The nausea would not subside, though what had just happened seemed like a dream, a nightmare. One should be able to tell when tragedy strikes because the drag in time, right before the event, seemed scripted now, and somehow slowed, with colors more saturated and conversations foretold. As if she might somehow recognize the pattern now, she would predict when a tragic event might happen again and avoid another tragedy. She saw herself again as she leaned over the seat and kissed Mark. Even then she'd known Sam would have to go find him, knew she shouldn't have let them go, should have somehow stopped them. But she hadn't. And now she would forever be *the one who killed another.*

She retched again and again, bent to retrieve the spotlight, and fell. She wanted nothing more than to curl up somewhere and sleep, to forget all of it, but something told her to get up.

Graham. The voice was Graham's. He'd kept her alive once, and she knew she needed to keep moving or else Mark and Sam would die from their injuries and then their deaths would be on her conscience too. Her head spun, and her hands were frozen through her gloves to the ground as she braced herself still with a stream of fluid still hanging from her bottom lip and nose. She closed her eyes and pulled her hand away from the ice. She wiped her mouth and sat farther back. Then she took several deep breaths of the icy cold air and thought of Mark inside, needing her, and pushed herself up off the ground without looking down and made her way farther to the truck.

The drive ahead would be on the icy roads. She needed to get herself together — and fast.

Marcy quickly untied the line and flung it into the snow bank, then opened the passenger side door and climbed in. *I must have closed it out of habit. Good thing, or the battery would be dead for sure.* Shards of glass littered the driver's seat. Marcy took off her knit cap and used it to brush the sharp pieces off the seat and out the driver's side door.

With the keys in the ignition she tried to turn the engine over but all she got was a small attempt at life.

Marcy rocked back into the driver's seat and said to herself as Graham would have lectured her, "It's just cold. Don't flood the engine." She looked ahead of her at the derelict old white house in the distance. *I have to get the damn truck moving — now.* She gave the key a second try, again the rumbling dragged on, and she said, "Come on!" Finally the engine finally roared to life. She almost cried. "Oh God, thank you."

"Okay, now I've got to drive the truck *into* the ditch?" She remembered what Sam had told her, but now she doubted that logic. The truck rolled into the ditch in the pitch dark of night, and Sam wasn't here to look the situation over in the light of this new morning.

With one wheel over the side of the ditch, Marcy slid out of the driver's door with the engine running. She had to get an idea of the direction she needed to go. She instantly recognized the sunken footprints of her assailant and how she had fallen into the snow and then climbed out on the other side of the incline. Marcy chased those memories away and studied the placement of all four wheels and how she might maneuver the Scout. If she didn't do this and managed to turn the wrong way, the delay in getting help from home might mean the death of them all.

"God! Why don't we have cell phones or tow trucks?" she screamed out loud, mainly to interrupt the cold quiet around her to remind herself that she was alive. "Okay, Sam said to drive straight into the ditch and keep the truck straight to the driveway." But the more she looked at the depth of the ditch with the deep tracks from the woman's escape and how much snow accumulation there was, there was no way that made any sense to her.

"There's no friggin' way that's going to work. Why can't I just back the truck out and then go forward?" If Sam were to see what she saw, he'd agree with her.

Right. She was here and he wasn't. The job was hers to do, so she'd do it—her way. She checked out the back tires and where Sam had previously dug into the snow and ice in his attempt to reverse last night. He'd dug shallow divots in the ground.

She began looking around for anything she could get her hands on that would help provide grit and traction. Spotting a cluster of trees across the street, she tramped through the snow and pulled off several pieces of bark casings and gathered armloads of sticks and debris to put under the back wheels.

"Okay, let's give this a try," she said, the sound of her own voice in the silence giving her courage. Although Graham had taught both girls more about the art of driving since their first adventurous attempt, she still wasn't totally comfortable behind the wheel. She moved the stick into R like the first time, when she'd learned by trial and error, because then she'd had wild man-eating dogs on her tail.

She applied a little gas and could feel the tires spin before they caught on the brush she'd laid down behind them. She hadn't realized she was holding her breath until she felt the front end come to rights and lurch up and backward. "Oh, thank God, thank God!" she cried.

"Okay, okay," she said quickly to herself as she let the tires roll backward another five feet and clear of the forward obstacle, then moved the stick to D.

Marcy didn't precisely follow the long driveway. She was careful and drove where the path made sense, avoiding drifts and favoring the few open graveled areas where she could gain more traction. Even with four-wheel drive and snow tires, driving conditions were treacherous.

She pulled up as close to the front door of the house as possible and jumped out of the truck, leaving the engine running. When she opened the door, she heard an awful noise that sounded like someone drowning.

Sam held Mark and the boy had a death grip on his forearms, his face nearly blue, his eyes wild, as he struggled for breath. She'd seen this before, but this was Mark, not Campos, and she jumped into action. She understood his panic as Sam tried desperately to hold him still with one hand and to cut a hole in his windpipe with the other.

"Marcy! Find a straw, a pen, anything small and hollow. Quick, he's going to suffocate."

Marcy left the front door open and frantically ran around the small, filthy house but soon gave up as she remembered there were a few straws and pens in the glove box of the truck. She rushed through the opened doorway to the truck, grabbed what she needed, and flew back.

When she returned, Mark's eyes were rolling backward and she feared the worst. She handed Sam the straw, stripped of its paper wrapper. He grabbed the tube and pinched one end and stuffed the end through a hole he'd already cut in the boy's throat.

"Breathe, Mark—God dammit, *breathe!*" Sam yelled.

He did, sucking in as deep a breath as the small hole in his trachea permitted, but it clearly wasn't enough, and the wild-eyed panic returned. Sam had to grip him by the shoulders to get his attention. "Slow down, don't panic. Take one long slow breath," he said, trying to calm the boy down as Marcy watched, terrified she would lose him.

They could not have been closer to watching him die. She had never seen Sam scream or panic. She knew he'd really feared for Mark's life. Soon Mark got the idea and began trying to control the urge to gasp for air. Marcy knelt down to him and held his hand. He looked up at her and wiped one of her tears away after he regained control of himself.

"You're going to be okay," she promised him. *Please make it so!* she begged silently for both of them.

With the knife he'd used to make the incision, Sam shortened the straw now sticking out of Mark's neck. "Marcy, get the tape and find something clean we can wrap around his neck," Sam said, out of breath himself.

She ran back out to the truck and grabbed one of Mark's clean t-shirts and a roll of duct tape they'd packed for the hunt.

As she came back in Mark watched Sam, who had slumped back against the remains of an old ratty couch. Clearly, his injuries were taking a toll as well.

Marcy ripped a few pieces off the roll and placed the tape around the tube to hold the device still. "Do you think you can walk?" she asked Mark after his breathing had steadied.

He raised his right hand and gave her a thumbs up—just to make her smile, she suspected. He wanted to get out of there as much as she did. She helped him stand while he held the straw in place with one hand. He leaned forward once he was up, and for a minute, she thought he was passing out again from the lack of oxygen, but he strengthened again and she led him out to the truck. She put him in the backseat, and he used his feet to push himself farther across, then lay down. When his breathing steadied again she knew she could risk leaving him.

She returned for Sam, who seemed barely conscious as he stared at the form on the floor and the spread of blood in a growing puddle.

"Sam, come on, let's go."

He sat silently, as if sifting through the events. She eyed him, worried about what he might say or what judgment he might make.

"Why'd you shoot her again, Marcy?" he finally asked, his voice hoarse.

"Let's talk about it later, Sam. We need to go now."

"I'm not judging you, Marcy, I just want to know. She was clearly dead the first time."

She, too, stared at the body. "Graham's rule; make sure or it'll cost you later." After a moment, she was able to meet his gaze. "I had to be certain, Sam. You were hurt. I didn't know if Mark was alive or dead. So I did what Graham taught me. I'm not proud of it, but it needed doing and I was the only one who could."

Sam looked at her for a long moment, then nodded. "Let's go, girl."

She helped him up, and his weight leaned on her, then away from her, then back again. "World's going in circles," he said.

"Just close your eyes, Sam, I'll get you there."

She led him out to the truck, stopping and starting, taking as much of his weight as she could as he staggered. When she got him there, she buckled him into the front passenger's seat, grabbed a tarp from the back and folded the plastic enough to fit over the driver's window. She taped it in place. She couldn't see out of that side, but she had to keep heat in the cab while she drove home.

With that taken care of she scanned the area for the best way out, then climbed up behind the wheel. She grabbed the shift knob to put the truck in reverse, and Sam placed his hand on hers.

"You did good, Marcy. Good job."

"Thank you, Sam. Let's go home." She looked back at Mark, whom she loved now as much as Macy—even more. She smiled at him as he gave her the thumbs up again, and she backed the truck around, eyeing the opened front door of the house, hoping to never see the image again.

She headed out on a long trip over icy roads back to Graham's camp, toward home.

McCann held a toothpick in the side of his mouth. It wiggled from time to time as he chewed on it, focusing on the delicate job of stitching up the torn tissues of Graham's leg wound. That's when he realized he didn't know the man's name. He recognized him as the one who had stopped him in the street months ago and invited him up to Cascade.

He recalled again the blue-eyed girls he'd seen in the truck at the time, and a young boy, so he knew the guy would be missed. Certainly someone would come searching for him soon.

Nearly done with the last stitch, McCann left in a piece of a flexible straw to help drain out any fluids that accumulated in the wound. There would be more swelling, and almost certainly the wound would become infected. Inserting a way for the discharge to release would help the healing process by his way of thinking. *Plan ahead*, his father had always taught him.

The man already ran a fever and mumbled off and on. McCann had poured whiskey down his throat whenever an opportunity, between the mumblings, would present itself. McCann hoped the stitching pain he'd inflicted wouldn't be remembered once the man awoke. He was used to working on cattle, after all, not men, and cows didn't tend to hold grudges after surgery. Men held grudges and acted on them with revenge.

With the last suture tied off, McCann snipped the ends and then wiped the sweat from his own forehead. He kept everything as clean as possible. After he had cleaned himself up, he sponged off Graham's leg and shoulder again, hoping to minimize the risk of any infection.

He covered the leg wound with several large gauze bandages, staggering them to fit the large area, and taped them down lightly so they could easily be redressed. The puncture wounds on the man's arm needed only three small stitches. The other ones he left to heal on their own. He had cleaned the deep wounds out as well as possible.

McCann listened to his patient's chest for any sounds of lung problems. He thought his ribs were at least bruised, if not cracked. His breathing sounded good, but large contusions already appeared. In McCann's estimation, the man's chest would be black and blue by morning.

He remembered when his father had been thrown from his horse not too long before his family started dying off. They'd wrapped his chest with compression bandages before he agreed to go in to see a doctor, only to find out later that wrapping suspected broken ribs was the worst thing you could do for a chest injury. Instead of helping him, the tight bands around his chest had curtailed his breathing too much, and he developed pneumonia. He went downhill from there. When the virus hit, with already damaged lungs, his father died first. So, instead of wrapping the man's chest, McCann applied clean, icy snow wrapped in a towel, off and on, in an effort to keep the swelling down.

He stood back, figuring he had done everything he could do for the time being. Healing and fighting the infection were up to the man now.

The little house became dark and dreary as evening approached. This wasn't how McCann had envisioned his meeting with the other survivors. He tossed his worn toothpick into the old fireplace and added another log. He knew he had an additional night of fighting off wolves and wild dogs ahead of him, trying to keep them away from the horses he had tied up in the back. To eventually be able to sleep through the night would be great; this constant vigilance was wearing his energy reserves too thin.

McCann had just turned twenty and had lost his entire family to what he referred to as "the plague." He had hoped to join a good group of people and now looked forward to settling down and starting over.

After watching the man's chest rise and fall, McCann backed away. He needed some fresh air after hours of leaning over a stranger and pushing a needle and thread through his skin over and over.

He headed for the front door of the stuffy little house and peered at the truck parked in the driveway. *Maybe there's a radio or a map in there or something that will show me where he came from.*

Out of habit McCann checked his sidearm, which he kept in a holster about his waist and began to walk toward the vehicle. His pistol was one handed down from his great-great-grandfather, who'd made his living as a deputy sheriff down in south Texas in a county named Refugio. There were nicer guns to be had, but he'd learned to shoot with this one, and now the weapon felt a part of him, like his own left hand. He also had a few rifles, but the old Colt .45 served him well. The fine-looking gun had nickel plating and ivory grips, with a five-and-a-half-inch barrel.

The pistol had a twin somewhere in this world; legend had it that the gun was originally one of an identical pair. Sheriff Herd, around the time of Pancho Villa, had given them as gifts to Will Franger and McCann's ancestor, Elmer. There were wild tales from that time, and to carry the treasure with him on this new adventure seemed fitting.

After checking around him, McCann had already absentmindedly plucked another toothpick from the supply in his pocket and chewed on it while he studied the inside of the man's truck for any sign or clue as to where he'd had come from. The tracks left in the snow led down the street, but he didn't think following them now would be a good idea. The need to find his camp and people would have to wait a day or two until he came to, long enough to talk to him at least. In the meantime, McCann would have to fight the boredom and the ever-persistent wolf packs after his horses.

Dalton held Addy by the hand as they stood in line for dinner. After spending the night and most of the next day with Rick's daughter Bethany, she was ready for some downtime. Bethany, like her father, had a knack for constant conversation.

Addy scanned the crowd continually; she was looking for Clarisse, Dalton thought. The surrogate mom had promised to catch up with Addy at dinner, and he knew the little girl wanted nothing more than to share the rest of the night quietly in their own quarters. As soon as Addy had come into the tent looking for Clarisse, he'd guessed she needed rescuing from her talkative friend. Her face was drawn, and she hugged herself while nodding at Bethany's constant jabber.

When he asked her if she would eat dinner with him, since she had neglected him lately, she'd immediately agreed and said good-bye to her exuberant friend.

"Are you looking forward to sleeping in your own tent tonight?"

"Yeah, but where is Clarisse?"

"She'll be here, honey. Don't worry."

Just as Dalton began to scan the mess tent again, Clarisse appeared in the doorway. "There she is," he assured Addy, patting her on the back.

Dalton studied Clarisse as she beamed at the crowd of people lined up for dinner. Her bright smile was unusual. Something was up. The first thing that came to mind was her and Steven embracing in the lab this morning, which he'd been forced to witness on his screen. It had made him instantly jealous, even if he had no right to be. Still, her involvement with Steven didn't make sense. They were completely different types. She and Steven had always just acted like colleagues. Dalton had never suspected more of a relationship would develop between them.

Steven wasn't married, but he had often dated before the world went to hell; Dalton and Rick had kidded him about all of his missed chances. Now, after the apocalypse, it was unlikely he would ever find a wife. He'd become Rick's kids' Uncle Steven, and lived his life as a bachelor, though when he'd first made his way to the prepper camp, he'd brought along his off-and-on girlfriend, Lydia, an equipment specialist. Unfortunately, what had always been a problem for them before the apocalypse still existed and even became amplified here in camp.

Not surprisingly, Dalton had heard through the grapevine first, then later from Rick, that Steven's girlfriend had found "true love" a few tents over from Steven's. She'd gone there—accidentally, on purpose—one night to make him jealous. And that was that, because Steven wasn't jealous at all. In fact, he was happy for her and now she was stuck with her decision. Steven had never held much hope for the relationship to begin with and was happy to stop pretending love existed between the two of them.

Dalton cleared his throat and told himself that if Clarisse and Steven decided to give a relationship a go, he would be happy for them. Other than Tammy, they were the only singles left at the camp. Even though they were light-years apart in terms of compatibility, their getting together made sense. He just couldn't make himself feel happy about the relationship.

Dalton kept his gaze on Clarisse as she scanned the room's occupants, and when she finally caught sight of Addy, her earlier happy grin turned into a full-fledged, beautiful smile. The grandeur of her expression stunned him. *She really does love this child as her own—and God, she's beautiful.*

"Hi, Addy, I've missed you all day," Clarisse said, gathering the girl into her arms to hug her tightly. "Yum," she said, her face in Addy's hair, "you smell like crayons and peanut butter, two of my favorite things." She came close to Dalton, as well, to claim Addy from his grasp, and he drew in a deep breath of Clarisse's own scent.

He wondered if she'd avoid speaking to him now because of the previous night, but she glanced right up into his eyes and said in a whisper over Addy's head, "Dalton, we need to talk after dinner. I've got some big news to discuss."

He didn't want to hear her big news; she was going to confide in him her newfound love for Steven or some such nonsense. He would listen to her, though, even if the idea killed him.

"Okay, I'll stop by your tent after dinner."

"That would be perfect," she said, then turned her full attention back to Addy, who clung to her side with the insecurity of a lonely child.

Clarisse observed the group chatting away with their friends and families. She hoped, more than anything, she would be able to keep them all healthy so they could continue to move forward in this new life they now shared. Later, at the table, Addy went with the other children to retrieve a rare cookie treat.

Clarisse watched as Kim handed Addy a huge peanut butter cookie, an action that appeared staged. Kim smiled down at Addy and smothered the girl with a hug. Addy made the best of the situation, plastering on a smile just to appease her, but was clearly uncomfortable with the woman.

Clarisse wasn't sure if Kim did this in public to do away with any suspicion she didn't care for the girl or if in fact she genuinely did care for Addy and this was her way of showing affection. Her efforts didn't matter either way. What was clear was the child only tolerated the embrace. *Sometimes*, thought Clarisse, *children instinctively use shyness as self-preservation, and for good reason.*

After Addy trotted back with her prize, Clarisse asked, "Are you ready to head back to our quarters?"

"Yes! Can we go now?" Addy begged.

"You bet," Clarisse answered, knowing the girl had had too much stimulus for one day, and they began to clean up their trays and trash to make a hasty exit.

Dalton watched them get ready to leave and tried to make eye contact with Clarisse when his six-year-old son, Hunter, ran up to Addy to give her his own cookie. He had detected Hunter eyeing the girl often, and even though she was almost a year older than him, the age difference didn't stop the boy from being sweet on her. His son's first heartbreak was about to happen right before his eyes because, surely, Addy was done with people for the night and wouldn't give the boy the time of day. But to Dalton's surprise, she turned and smiled at him shyly, accepting the offering. Then Hunter turned abruptly and fled straight for the opposite exit. Dalton smiled to himself, knowing what his son was going through.

Confused, Addy asked Clarisse a question Dalton couldn't hear over the chatter. He could guess, though: *Why did Hunter give me his cookie?* Clarisse shrugged, but her little smile and a twinkle behind her glasses told Dalton she was as aware of Hunter's crush on Addy as he was. What an ideal mother she was turning out to be for the girl.

~ ~ ~

Later in the evening, Dalton stopped by Clarisse's quarters as promised. "Knock, knock," he said outside her door flap, opening the flimsy entry. Clarisse looked surprised, maybe even a bit startled.

"Oh," she said, a touch breathless. "You're here already."

"Am I too early?"

"No, no. Addy's already down for the night, happy to be back to her familiar routine."

Dalton felt more than a touch breathless at the sight of Clarisse. She'd obviously showered off the day's grime. Her hair was still wet from washing but combed in long ringlets. She stood before him in only her battle dress uniform pants and a white tank top. He loved the fact that current conditions finally made wearing makeup senseless but suspected Clarisse had never made use of the stuff anyway, even when cosmetics were in fashion. She certainly never needed anything to enhance her own natural beauty.

Clarisse's skin smelled like soap and, as if he were on a difficult military mission, Dalton's brain yelled, *Abort!* He didn't turn from her, though. He couldn't; he wanted to keep on looking at her. He forced out the words, "I'm sorry. I can see I'm too early. I can come back in a few minutes."

Clarisse blushed and turned away from him. "I'll just, um, find my shirt." Her BDU top hung over the end of her cot, and he reached out to retrieve it for her. She grabbed it from him and slid a slender arm through one sleeve, then the other. He watched her button the shirt up, her attention focused fully on the chore.

She spoke softly, shoving her feet into her boots. "We can walk around and talk outside, since Addy's asleep." She sat on the side of her cot, bending to tie her bootlaces.

Dalton only nodded, continuing to gaze at her until a blush rose from her chest to her neck and cheeks. *Damn!* He stepped back half a pace so she could reach for her army green coat.

"Let me help you," he said, but his voice came out all wrong again. He reached for her coat and held it out for her like he had done the night before. When she turned around to face him, he again pulled her hood up. With the length of her hair hanging down one side in front, he reached in, brushing the back of his hand alongside her neck, and gently folded the length back inside the hood. "Don't want you to catch a cold going outside with wet hair in these freezing temperatures."

She slowly pulled away from the touch he couldn't bring himself to break, and headed for the tent flap. He followed her out into the cold.

"Well," she said after looking around and noticing several residents of the camp lingering after dinner, shooting the breeze in the middle of the compound. "I need to talk to you about something that's happened," she whispered. She didn't want others to hear their conversation. They strolled away, the snow-covered gravel crunching under their boots.

"Dalton, I've—"

He cut her off with a slicing motion of his hand. He didn't want to hear her say it. Somehow he knew that if the words came out in her voice, he'd hear them over and over. "Look," he said. "I know you and Steven see each other, and I'm . . . happy for you. Why you guys getting together is any of my business, I don't know, but I thought I'd let you off the hook and tell you I already know."

He was two paces ahead of her before he realized she had stopped in her tracks.

"Dalton?"

He turned back to her. She looked at him like he'd lost his mind.

"What you are talking about? I'm not *seeing* anyone. Steven? Ugh! I mean he's a nice guy, but he's not for me."

Dalton berated himself for feeling relieved. Staring at her, stunned, he felt as if his lungs were empty of air. *What the hell is wrong with me?* "I, um, thought you were trying to tell me . . ."

"Why would I tell you anything like that," she murmured, "even if it was true?" She looked completely bewildered now.

"Okay, obviously I've come to the wrong conclusion about this whole discussion. So, why don't you tell me what this is all about?" His embarrassment shattered his attempt at discretion, and he almost yelled, bringing curious glances their way.

"That's what I was trying to do, Dalton," Clarisse answered, quietly cool now, her voice sounding as if it came from between clenched teeth.

He took a deep breath. "Please, go ahead and tell me. I've got other things to check on tonight before I head back to my tent." He was furious with his inability to control his own emotions around her.

"Fine," she said, facing him with her hands on her hips. "Here goes. I've created a viable vaccine for the virus that will produce good, strong antibodies. The inoculations will be ready in two weeks. Steven and I thought keeping the news a secret from the general populace until shortly before administering it would be best. The vaccination will be a series of two shots, two weeks apart."

He stopped in his tracks this time and looked at her doubtfully. "It works this time?"

"Yes."

"You're certain?"

"Yes, I'm certain, Dalton. I've created strong antibodies. This is the first time I've replicated the procedure. The results are not an anomaly."

"Anything else?" He should be more excited, but he had become jaded by so many failed attempts at a cure. He'd resented Clarisse spending so much time and energy on the impossible mission, and now he even resented being proven wrong. He was acting like a lunatic.

"Yes." Her tone, though she kept it low, was taut. "This vaccine will work for the current strain. However, next year, or even later, we may be dealing with yet another variation, which will make this one ineffective, so it's not over yet, Dalton." She took a deep breath. "However, with the drastic decrease in population, our chance of exposure to a different strain is less likely."

He stared at her, and this time he managed a smile; she deserved that from him. In return, she rewarded him with a brilliant return grin. He patted her on the shoulder, and they both headed back to camp from their short walk.

"Who else knows?" he asked, trying to keep their conversation going.

"Only Steven, and probably Rick. Steven was going to tell him."

"So, the whole camp, you mean." *If Rick knew, then so would the rest of the camp in short order.*

"Oh, well." Clarisse tossed her hands up. "When we announce the vaccine, we need to make sure we emphasize the fact the virus will mutate in the future, and this vaccine will not work on that one. Not even the current carriers will likely be immune to the next strain. There's no way of measuring what will happen in the future. Since our community is now so small, the virus won't spread nearly as fast, and we may never see another sign of the darn thing. Which makes it important for us to continue to quarantine ourselves from any new people we come across until we're positive they aren't carrying anything new."

They had practically walked all the way back to her tent when he said, "What would we do without you, Clarisse?"

She beamed at him, making him glad he'd finally let her know he was grateful for her accomplishment, one in which she could rightfully take pride.

Dalton had just said goodnight to Clarisse and headed toward his own quarters when Rick called out from the media tent across the open area. "Hey, Dalton, we have a situation."

Dalton strode to the media tent. "What's up?"

"I just talked to Tala," Rick said. "She's concerned because Graham hasn't returned from town yet, and Ennis has taken a turn for the worse."

Dalton stood there, weighing his few options. He and Graham had agreed they would not intervene again, risking a fallout like what had happened last time. Perplexed with the situation, he said, "Did you try the tracker?" He knew full well Rick had by now.

Rick paused before admitting he had, "Yeah, you were right, damn thing's not working."

"When do Sam and his crew get back?"

"Day after tomorrow, maybe."

"Why did Graham go into town?"

"Tala said he went to collect a few things. The trip was supposed to be quick."

"And Ennis is really sick?"

"Yeah, he has a high fever, and he's mumbling a lot. He keeps telling Macy to come help us. He's delirious."

"Okay, let's get Clarisse in here. She can help with Ennis. As for Graham, maybe he decided to stay in town for the night. There's nothing we can do about finding him. We both agreed we wouldn't intervene again. If he's not back by morning, I suggest either Macy or Tala go looking for him."

"Yeah, I thought you'd say that."

"Our hands are tied, Rick. Any fanciful ideas this time?"

"No. I keep checking the damn cameras, but there's nothing to see. The temperature dropped again, and they're still fogged over or frozen over, even though they're equipped with temperature controls. Damn things, wish I could call in a warranty on those fuckers." Rick slumped his head down between his folded arms in frustration and exhaustion. "I didn't get much sleep with the girls up all night giggling."

Dalton reminded him again. "We don't intervene physically. It has to be this way—for now, anyway."

Rick grunted his response. Dalton wanted to say more, but he wasn't sure if Steven had told Rick yet about the upcoming vaccine. In another few weeks this would likely not be a problem, and Dalton would already be in town by now with a group to track Graham down. The fact that Graham was out there, probably injured, or worse, and needed his help, drove Dalton nuts. Worst of all, Rick had no techie tricks to offer him—a rare occurrence.

"Yes, I know, Dalton. I can't think of anything to do anyway. I'll let you know if something comes to mind."

"Okay, at least for now, Clarisse can offer help concerning Ennis. I'll go get her and be right back."

Once Dalton returned with Clarisse, her first question of Rick was, "What can I do?"

"Okay, here's the deal. Tala called in a few minutes ago. Graham left on a quick trip to town but hasn't returned yet. The worst part is the old man has started running an awful temperature, and Tala's scared out of her mind. She's the only adult there, with just Macy and the boy taking care of Ennis. Is there something else we can tell her to do to bring his fever down?"

"I just spoke to her the other day. There must be something we're missing. He's been suffering from a UTI. Graham probably went into town for the medication they needed," Clarisse speculated. "Did something else happen with Ennis?"

"No, not that I know of. Sam, Twin One, and Mark are still out hunting. Graham left this morning and still hasn't returned. It's dark now, and the town cameras are on the fritz with these low temps. I can't see a damn thing. Tala has only the old Escort, but it has no gas. Hell, I think they use the car for parts these days anyway."

"What about the trackers?" she asked, looking up to Dalton.

Dalton deferred to Rick, knowing he had already tried using them

Rick shook his head. "I tried, but they only work while the device is still in the skin. It's been months now, and they're no longer active."

Dalton felt they were wasting time going over the same conversation. "We've already discussed this. Let's see what we can do for Tala at this point with regard to Ennis. Can you talk to her about how to bring down his temperature? She said he's delirious, and he keeps yelling out in his sleep. They can't get him to take anything by mouth."

"I'll do what I can. There are a few tricks to getting the fever reducers down him. Let's call in." She settled herself into Rick's chair, and he pulled up another one beside her in the small media room.

Rick placed the familiar call. Usually the time before someone picked up was only two rings; this time the call took five rings before someone answered. Twin Two picked up the call.

"Hi, Rick, we're busy here with Ennis. He's really . . . upset," Macy said with the sound of stress in her own voice, clearly frightened by the situation.

"That's okay, Macy, that's why we're calling. I've got Clarisse here with me. Can Tala come to the radio, hon?" Rick asked her.

"Sure, just a minute." While they listened to her they also heard Ennis moaning in the background and Tala attempting to comfort him.

"Poor girl," Dalton said under his breath as he stood near the doorway with his arms crossed over his chest, feeling at a loss as how to help them.

"I'm here," Tala said.

"Tala, it's Clarisse. What's his temperature?"

"It's a hundred and four! I don't know what to do. I'm putting cold compresses on his chest and forehead. I tried to get him to take the ibuprofen, but he keeps spitting the pills out. He's shaking and screaming, and Graham's gone!" She sounded on the verge of tears. Tala was worn out from the stress of it all, and Clarisse wished nothing more than to be able to help her friend.

"Tala. Has Ennis gone to the bathroom today?"

"Yes. I'm sorry. Um, he did a few times, in fact, which isn't usual. He can't verbalize much, but he's acting like he's in a lot of pain."

"Okay, he's spiking a fever due to the UTI. Maybe he's resistant to the antibiotics. The elderly don't usually show signs of high fevers unless the infection is pretty bad. So I want you to get two of the painkillers and crush them along with one of the antibiotics. Crush them all together and mix them into a few tablespoons of something sweet. Chocolate pudding or applesauce work well to disguise the medicine flavor."

"We have a jar of applesauce."

"Okay, crush the meds into a powder and mix them into a small amount. Enough to mask the taste, and to get the medication all into him at once. So, maybe three tablespoons of applesauce in a small cup. You can even add sugar to the mix to make the taste even more appetizing if you need to."

Tala started to speak, but Ennis yelled out in the background as Macy and Bang tried to soothe him. "Try to keep him there, Macy," Tala said as Ennis attempted to get off the bed. "Sorry, Clarisse, he's out of control. I'll do my best to get the meds down him. Any idea where Graham might be?" she begged the answer.

"No, Tala, I'm so sorry. If we get any news, we'll tell you right away." Clarisse looked up helplessly at Dalton. "They've even tried the trackers, but those things no longer work. The town cameras are frozen over, so we can't see into town. I'm sorry to say, we don't know where he is," she said. Right now, though, it did little good to worry about Graham. They needed to keep Tala on the task at hand.

"Tala. Tala, listen, I'm sure he'll turn up somewhere soon. Focus on getting Ennis medicated, and call me back in one hour. I'll be here waiting, for your call, okay?" Clarisse said, not wanting to turn off the link to her friend in trouble.

"Okay. Thank you, Clarisse."

"Don't worry about it. I wish there was more to offer."

"I'll call back in an hour. Tala out."

After the conversation had ended, Clarisse took a minute to think, then looked up at Dalton and Rick. "We've got to find him," she groaned, agonized by the turmoil she knew Tala was going through.

"No. We will not risk exposure again, Clarisse. Not again," Dalton said. He hated the look she returned to him.

"He's never gone off like this. Something is wrong," Rick said.

Clarisse huffed, then shook her head silently. "You're right, I feel so helpless. I'll go check on Addy and be right back. I've got to be here for her."

After she left, Dalton and Rick stood silently. Rick finally said, "We don't know if anything's happened to Graham or not. His truck probably broke down, and he decided to stay overnight in town."

Dalton mulled the theory over for a minute. "No, he would walk back to camp. No matter how long the trip took him, he'd do it."

"You're right, Graham is like you. He would walk back to camp in a blizzard, during an apocalypse, with wolves on his tail." Rick rubbed at his tired face. "Shit, something bad has happened to him, man."

"Yeah, my thoughts exactly. Damn, it sucks to be powerless."

"He wouldn't want you to risk a rescue anyway," Rick said, "so we wait it out. That's all we can do." He leaned forward, again laying his head on the table.

Dalton couldn't stand the sound of defeat in Rick's voice. He was exhausted. "Have you been having that nightmare again? You look like hell and about ready to collapse."

"Yes. Who else gets plagued by these strange goddamn nightmares? One minute, I'm standing in a large white room watching in horror as a man runs like hell screaming while a gigantic fucking unhooked safety pin chases him down, sticks him through the end of the pin, and then the fucker starts running toward me. The screaming wakes me up every time."

Dalton cut loose with a surprised laugh as he pictured a gigantic safety pin chasing after Rick screaming his head off.

"Go ahead and laugh, man. I know the whole thing sounds funny, but it's a fucking nightmare, I'm telling you."

"Whose screaming wakes you up? Yours, or the other unfortunate fellow's?"

"Both, I guess," Rick shook his head. "I've had this same twisted nightmare since the third grade, and I never find out if the damn thing gets me or not because I wake up so fast with my heart pounding out of my chest. I thought it would finally go away or be replaced by others once I went into the military, but no such luck. Not even nightmares over the apocalypse can match this one."

"Hey, if you let me get a few hours' sleep first, I'll come and relieve you the rest of the shift and check on things." Dalton started to leave, then remembered something. "Oh, and don't let Clarisse out of your sight, man. Make sure she goes back to her quarters after the next call. I don't want her to come up with some grand scheme and risk herself."

"No problem. If she tries anything, I'll sit on her and hogtie her. All right, boss. Get some sleep," Rick said, and waved goodnight.

McCann wiped the sweat off his patient's face again and again. The fever was predictable, but he hadn't expected it to be so severe. He checked the bandage. The major leg wound had swelled. Keeping everything as sterile as possible in the process, he cleaned and redressed everything.

Outside, his horses whinnied in sudden fear, so McCann jumped up and grabbed his Colt, running for the back door to chase away the wolves, yet again, tonight.

When he swung open the door, their eyes glowed in the dark. "Get out of here, you fucking assholes!" he yelled. Not only did these nightly vigils exhaust him physically, those damned carnivores were going to exhaust his ammo.

The scent of moldy hay, damp manure, and fresh snow stung his nose. He would have to leave the injured man on his own while he cleaned up the area. It wouldn't help either of them to neglect the horses. Before getting busy with that, he checked on the patient once more. The nameless man slept fitfully. He shook his head from side to side and muttered what McCann thought was the name Tala. *Must be the missus.* He wiped away the man's sweat once more.

Afterward, he rolled up his sleeves and mucked out his makeshift barn, the covered back patio off the old brick house. The only hay he'd found was across the street, and moldy fare, so he opted to give the horses some of the oats he had found in the house. Refined oats were not their usual diet, but these were not usual times. "One must make do with what one has," his frugal mother used to say.

The sick man called out from inside the house, so he finished up quickly and laid out as much straw as possible on the ground. Then he used lawn furniture and miscellaneous yard paraphernalia to build a blockade around the open patio. He found a lantern in the kitchen, lit the wick, and hung the light up along the doorway in hopes the flickering flame would hold the wolves at bay.

Inside he found the man conscious for the first time, though delirious and shuddering in massive pain.

"Where am I?" Graham asked.

"You're here, in Cascade. You were attacked by wild dogs. Don't you remember?"

The guy grimaced as he tried to adjust his position so he was more comfortable. "Got to get up. Got to get back to Tala. She needs me."

"No. You can't move yet."

"You need to help them. Please."

"I don't know where *they* are. It's too late tonight. I'll try in the morning. What's your name?"

"Graham. You're . . . the Carnation boy." The pained surprise on his face contrasted with the sweat pooling down his forehead. "You made it! I needed you to chop the wood."

McCann smiled at him; being needed was what he desired most.

"My name's McCann, and yeah, I made it. Just in time, by the looks of it," he said as he checked out Graham's leg wound again.

"How bad is it?"

"Bad enough. You should probably try to sleep more. Your fever is pretty high, and we need to find you some antibiotics."

"We have to go to the camp." Graham tried to maneuver higher but yelled out in pain as he tried to move his leg. "They're alone. I'm sure she's worried." Graham slurred his words, and he fell unconscious once again from the pain and fever. McCann helped him lie back down again.

"Nice to meet you, Graham," was all he could think to say as the man slid back to his fitful sleep.

He walked away and went through it all again: he checked the horses, called the wolves "fanged bastards," redressed Graham's wounds, and wiped him down again. Finally he sat by Graham in a sturdy kitchen chair and, with his boots still on, crossed his legs on the end table in front of him. He let his cowboy hat slide down to his forehead, and fell asleep with his toothpick lolling to the side, and hoping he would wake up if Graham needed him again.

In Ennis's dream, Tala kept telling him, "It's okay, Ennis, just one more; don't worry, it will get better," as she added log after log, placing them horizontally across his chest as he sunk farther and farther into the rushing water of the creek. At first he believed her, but now he was running out of breath and would soon drown with the heavy weight upon his chest. Still, she continued to add more logs, running through the water in the dark to retrieve yet another to place upon him.

"Bang, can you get another wet towel?" Tala asked. She began to wedge the spoon between Ennis's lips to sneak in more applesauce while Macy held onto Ennis's hand, trying to soothe him.

"Please, Ennis, you'll feel so much better if you can get this down," Tala pleaded.

With his fever so high, Ennis was delirious. He pushed at them, worn out from the hazy, unseen battle. "No! No more," he cried out in anguish.

Tala dropped the spoon back into the cup and looked at Macy in tears of defeat. "I . . . I don't know what else to do. I can't get the meds into him without choking him." With Ennis like this, and Graham lost to them for now, she lost her battle to keep a brave face around her young charges and sobbed.

Macy tucked Ennis's hands to his sides as he thrashed about in his bed. She went over to comfort Tala and guided her into the dining room.

"Tala, take a break. Let me try something," Macy urged.

Macy went back into the kitchen with the applesauce bowl and poured the contents into a small cup and added a little cool water to make the concoction thick but drinkable. She listened outside of the bunkroom for a minute with the cup in hand. Ennis had continually writhed and kicked the sheets since his fever spiked.

Bang brought the wet towel Tala had asked for to Macy, who gazed at Ennis from the bunkroom doorway, wondering what she could do for him. The sopping cloth dripped onto the wood floor, and she absentmindedly accepted the waterlogged mass while she formulated a plan.

Suddenly, everything seemed to be falling apart. Ennis might die if they didn't get the medications into him. Even though Tala hadn't mentioned it, Macy suspected Graham was hurt somewhere or possibly dead. And, as Macy stood in the doorway, Tala softly cried in the other room. To top off Macy's worries, her sister and the others were not back yet from their trip, though she didn't expect them to return for a day or two.

With the cup in one hand and a dripping towel in the other, she stood until the *drip, drip* caught her attention and wondered briefly how the wet cloth came to be there in the first place. She glanced at Bang standing by her side with an expression of fear on his little face.

"Um, thanks, Bang. I don't think I'm going to need these actually. Can you put the towel in the sink?"

He nodded and accepted the bundle, holding it to his chest and soaking his own shirt in the process.

She walked back into the bunkroom to meet the battle to save Ennis's life despite himself.

"Let's try something different, mister," she whispered to herself and pulled a chair up close to his side.

She rubbed his forearm and called his name lightly. "Ennis. Ennis, it's me, Macy. I have your water. I didn't forget tonight. It's story time."

She waited another minute more, repeating the phrases until he had quieted down further.

He glanced at her with wild, anguished eyes for only a moment. She had the glass held high for his viewing. Once she was sure he had seen it, she set what she hoped would be the cure on his bedside table where he always kept his water at night, and picked up a book they continued to read together every evening.

"It's time for bed, Ennis. I've got the story ready." She patted his arm with her free hand while she began to read, holding her voice in a melodic rhythm in hopes of drawing him home.

Macy barely perceived Bang retreating from the doorway after watching them for several minutes. She sensed Bang's helplessness, but she needed to focus on Ennis's troubles right now. Graham had taught her to take one thing at a time, to finish one job before moving on to the next. She had learned that it worked with chores around the cabin and with people.

After Macy had read the third page, Ennis relaxed significantly and his eyes remained at a constant slit and were focused in her direction.

She turned the page and continued. Two additional pages later, he turned his head and acknowledged the glass on the side table. This action was routine for them, the water and the reading. She would always retrieve his water glass and sit beside him to read each night before he went to sleep. The complaints he made if she didn't bring the water before she sat down bordered on tantrums.

Another page and then another. Macy began to worry he would never ask the question. If she preempted the query, the opportunity would be lost, and they would be back where they were before. She chanced a glance up at him between paragraphs, hoping his eyes would still be open as she patted his forearm with a steady cadence.

His milky stare opened in half-moons, and he must have detected in her own eyes the question she wanted him to ask. Instead of uttering the words, his rough, fever-heated hand gently clenched her elbow. He eyed the cup and pointed his chin toward it.

As if in the presence of a skittish deer, Macy shut the volume on her finger and reached out with her free hand, emulating nonchalant grace. She lifted the cup and held it for him as he sipped at the concoction he needed. As he swallowed, she gently stroked his throat with two fingers to encourage the elixir to stay down.

The triumph almost sent her to tears, but she instead placed a timid kiss upon his forehead. His eyes pleaded for more water, and she ran for the tap to oblige him.

As she filled the glass, Bang stood from a chair beside Tala, the question in his eyes reflected in hers as they both held their breaths for an answer. She only uttered, "Yes," under her breath as she passed by them, still on her mission.

Out of the corner of her eye she saw that Tala smiled, her face streaming with tears of gratitude. Bang was fidgety with joy, but managed to contain himself. Although she'd already accomplished what she'd hoped for, Macy was still on the task of fixing Ennis. She returned with the glass and helped him take regulated sips until he motioned for no more. He lay back down, and she left the room quietly to join the others.

With that done, she should have thought to rest, to relax, but she did not.

Now I have to find Graham.

"He drank it?" Tala asked, hopeful.

"Yes," she whispered back, still in awe that the procedure had worked. "Thank God!" she said, and sobered at her next thought. "Now we'll just have to convince him it's story time again in another four hours."

"Oh, I better get the radio out of there," Macy said. "Clarisse will be calling us in a few minutes." She tiptoed back into the bunkroom to retrieve the device.

"Tala, where's Graham?" Bang asked again.

"I don't know, sweetheart," Tala said and brushed the boy's hair out of his eyes. "He must have stayed in town overnight. I'm sure he'll come back to us in the morning. Don't worry." To Macy, who overheard the conversation on her return with the radio, it sounded as if Tala was trying to convince herself along with the boy.

"Ennis is sleeping well now. Bang, let's go take care of the chickens, and we should all try to sleep while we can," Macy said. She noticed how pale Tala had become and suspected what wasn't being said. She had heard Tala throwing up, and the signs of pregnancy were apparent to her. She thought if Graham didn't recognize the signs, he was the most stupid smart man she had ever known. She was also certain Graham would return if he was able to, and the fact that he still hadn't come back worried her. She planned to go looking for him early the next morning, but she had to get Tala and Bang to sleep before she could sneak out, knowing Tala would never agree to let her walk into town.

As Bang and Macy began to bundle up for their outdoor chores, the radio buzzed and Tala answered. Macy waved good-bye while Tala took the call.

"How's he doing? Were you able to get him to take the meds?" Clarisse asked.

"Well, I wasn't able to, but Macy was. She's a sly one, that girl. He's asleep now and much less agitated, thanks to her."

Clarisse laughed. "Oh, thank goodness. Now, try to do it again in another four hours. If he's sleeping, though, just wait another hour or two. Try to get him to drink more water as well. Whatever works for him, repeat the process."

"We will. Thank you, Clarisse. On the cameras there, do you see any new changes in town?" She knew she shouldn't ask, but couldn't help herself. When Clarisse didn't answer the question right away, she wanted to put her face in her hands and cry again. She wished she had never told Graham of her concern for the girls. He shouldn't have gone into town anyway, not right after a snowstorm. If it hadn't been for their conversation, he would still be right here, helping with Ennis.

Clarisse had hoped Tala wouldn't ask and looked wearily to Rick for answers. He took over the radio from there. "Tala, I keep checking, but no, I don't see anything new. Sorry. Most of the town cameras are still frozen over. All of us here are trying to figure out if there's something we can do," Rick said.

"I know, Rick. Don't feel bad. You guys have done so much for us already. I'm sure the truck just broke down or something. Hopefully, he'll show up tomorrow, and I will have worried needlessly," Tala said, trying to sound reasonable.

"I'm sure he'll be fine," Rick said, but Clarisse could tell by his face he hated having to lie. So did she, and doing so only prolonged the pain. He handed the radio back to her. Poor Rick. He did not have the stomach for this.

"Well, hopefully Sam and his group will return tomorrow, and then they can go looking for him. Maybe he went out too far and got stuck, and he's just waiting for Sam to figure it out when he gets back in a day or two. I'm sure Graham's fine." Clarisse tried to reason out a scenario with Tala. It was plausible, not probable, and Clarisse knew many different and more dire scenarios might also be playing out.

"Yeah, maybe that's it," Tala said. "He wouldn't want me to worry about him."

"We will call the minute we detect anything. Try to get some sleep, Tala. You sound so tired."

"I will. Take care. Tala out."

With the lack of sleep and the recent trauma she had gone through, Marcy felt exhausted. She had pulled over once to check on Mark's breathing. He'd fallen into a light sleep, and the flesh around his neck wound swelled, but he still breathed slowly and steadily through the straw. A few times he panicked, but Sam was able to calm him down enough so that he remembered to take short and shallow breaths.

Sam also fell into a fitful slumber. Marcy inclined the passenger seat back for him as far as it would go, and he rested as comfortably as his injuries would allow, but he moaned and often jerked.

As she drove, the wind flapped the tarp where the window used to be. The cold was so intense on her side of the truck that she had to run the heat at full blast while trying to drive as fast on the icy and snowy roads as she dared. Before he fell asleep, Sam had moved his hand up and down a few times to tell her to slow down whenever he feared the truck might lose control. The last thing they needed was another accident, and she agreed.

She wanted to ask Sam how much farther they had to go to get home, but he slept well now and she didn't want to disturb him. The drive out had taken more than a few hours with a few stops, so she reasoned they had several more hours to go before they got close to town. The road ran straight south now, unlike the winding curves from before, and she would recognize the familiar scenery of Cascade when they arrived.

Marcy stopped to refill the gas tank with the fuel they kept in the back and to check the chained tires, because she had seen Sam do the same thing at every stop and she didn't want to miss anything. Everything looked well as far as she could discern. By the time she climbed back into the cab her hands were frozen; her breath was a shining vapor in the cold and clear evening air. She checked the pulse of both men, then started the engine, heading again toward home.

The stars shone brightly, which brought Marcy back to recent memories of sitting up in the deer stands on watch over her newly formed family. She still felt confused by this new situation. One minute she was lucky to be alive and grateful to Graham for having saved her; the next she resented the parental authority he now held over her, the power to control her destiny.

Almost in a daze with her own thoughts, she fought to stay awake on her drive home and remembered over and over what she'd done earlier. The muzzle flare and the blood splatter flashed in her mind. *The woman I killed. The golden-green eyes, staring.*

She hadn't eaten anything and ran on adrenaline alone, just to get back to Graham; he would help her get through this. But first she needed to keep herself together and get home. His voice rang in her head, "Keep moving forward, Marcy. You're almost there, girl. Don't regret. Finish strong . . ."

Clarisse surveyed the display screens for any detectable movements while Rick read through the tech booklets on how to defrost the town cameras. These particular cameras came with a remote defrost chip, but at these historic low temperatures, the damn things didn't work well. He kept yawning; his lack of sleep was catching up with him.

Clarisse listened to him cuss and whine while she continued to monitor the cameras outside of Graham's camp, following Macy and Bang back into their cabin, where she hoped they would lock themselves up for the night. She thought about Tala, and suspected something more in their earlier conversations, but kept silent. The extra emotion Clarisse sensed from her friend might have just come from her lack of sleep and worry over Ennis, even though Clarisse thought Tala as stoic as they come.

She would have to wait to share the big news about the vaccinations until they completed the injections and the antibodies were revealed through lab testing. Two weeks seemed an eternity for inoculation day, but then their vulnerability would be over.

"Rick, I'm too wired, and Dalton will be here in another hour or two. Why don't you go get some sleep? I'll keep watch until he arrives. I want to be by the line in case Tala calls in again anyway."

"Are you sure? I can wait," Ricks said with a yawn and a minor contemplation of Dalton's warning, but he trusted Clarisse well enough to know she would not abandon the post to do anything risky.

"Seriously, I'm fine, but you're exhausted, and I have a good view of my tent door from here in case Addy comes looking for me. It's already midnight," she said, checking the time. "I'll buzz Dalton by three if he isn't already here."

Taking her up on her offer, he slapped the manual onto the table. "Sounds good to me. Maybe I'll come up with something if I can get a few hours of decent sleep."

He patted her shoulder on his way to the door. "Thank you, and if anything happens, just call me."

Clarisse was happy to be able to do this for him. Rick had always sacrificed sleep for the camp, and he needed a few hours of uninterrupted downtime to be at his best annoying self. She checked the time again, double-checked the logs, and viewed each camera as Rick had taught her to do in the past; then she updated the mundane information.

In between the boring little jobs she read Rick's manual for the cameras, dusted the electronic equipment, and began a list for supplies she would need in the quarantine lab and another list of her favorite childhood books she had hoped to beg, borrow, or steal for Addy to read.

That's when she first got a whiff. Something was burning nearby. She checked the cameras again for anything unusual, then the wiring and equipment she'd dusted prior to list-making. Perhaps she had loosened something?

She stood up from under the desk table and thought the odor must be coming from the equipment, but as she came to a standing position, the smoky odor became even stronger. The smell of burning plastic hit her with alarm. Then the first visible sign of smoke drifting through the ambient light of the camera aimed through the dark part of the family resident tents.

"Oh God!" she yelled and wrenched open the door to find the source of the fire. Smoke billowed in the northeast end of camp. "My God!" She gasped. "The family quarters! The greenhouse!" She ran that direction, shouting, then flames erupted within the greenhouse, spewing toxic smoke from smoldering plastic into the air. She first thought of Addy, of course, but she slept in Clarisse's own quarters, safe on the west side of the camp, where she and many of the other singles lived in smaller tents.

At this point training set in, and Clarisse ran back into the media tent and sounded the alarm to signal a fire emergency. Soon the camp was in a state of strategic mayhem. Clarisse ran for the water hose they kept for emergencies and began to drag the end toward the greenhouse, now engulfed in massive flames.

People spilled from their tents, armed and ready. Soon they realized the present danger and immediately went into fire contingency mode, manning their various posts. Strong voices yelled commands in the distance, but people ran around in alarm all the same.

Reuben was the first man on the scene to assist her with the hose, relieving her enough to set up a triage for the injured, out of harm's way.

She searched the crowd for Steven, the medic, when she saw Rick out of the corner of her eye, running with something in his arms, shouting, "Clarisse! Help me!"

She sped toward him as he held his daughter, Bethany, who lay limp in his arms. Clarisse checked her pulse; the rhythm was there, but weak. All the while, Rick coughed, crying, "Save her! Save her, Clarisse!" His words were an order, not a plea.

He was desperate, almost insane. "Give her to me, Rick," she demanded, forcibly taking Bethany from his arms. She laid the girl down on the cold ground in her fleece-footed pajamas and began CPR.

Rick put his hands on his knees and coughed again, trying to clear his own lungs. He swayed backward and took one last glance at his daughter as Clarisse worked on her, then ran back into the smoke for his wife.

Bethany began to cough, and Clarisse picked her up and ran beyond the media tent to the guarded entrance, where she would bring the other injured, away from the chaos. "Keep her sitting up and coughing," she told the guard. She hoped there would be no more, but she could tell by how few were helping to put out the fire that the injured would likely be many.

Clarisse peered into the chaos before her and saw people scattering about, trying to put out the flames; by now they had grown massive, aided by the plastic fuel of the greenhouse walls. She searched the crowd for Steven again, needing his help. After glancing at her own quarters, ensuring they were still safe from the smoke and flames, safe for Addy, she turned back. A hoarse voice shouting her name spun her around. Steven came toward her with Rick, the pair of them carrying someone.

"Over here!" she yelled above the noise. They lay the body down and Clarisse stared, stunned, at Dalton's unconscious form.

She suppressed all emotion and, with Steven's help, went into work mode.

Bethany shouted, "Daddy!" and continued to cough smoke out of her laboring lungs as she ran to him.

"You stay right here by Clarisse," Rick shouted. "I'm going to get your mom. She's fine; she's sitting with the boys. I'll be right back with her." He disappeared quickly once more into the smoke after taking another horrified glance at Dalton.

"Clarisse!" Steven shouted. "I've got to go back now. Kim's still in there!"

"Go!" she yelled. She quickly assessed Dalton's condition while somewhere deep inside she screamed in mad denial. Dalton could not be hurt!

But Clarisse's professional self took over. Dalton was covered in soot and reeked of burned plastic, the fumes from it stinging her eyes. She tore open his shirt and laid her ear down onto his chest to listen. She heard his heartbeat, heard the struggle going on in his lungs. She wished she had the oxygen equipment from the quarantine building, but when his breathing faltered, she pulled his chin down and opened her mouth over his, pinching his nose as she breathed for him.

In moments he rolled away, coughing and retching. He pushed up on his elbows, contracting in coughing spasms while trying to open his eyes. She saw they were bloodshot and tearing excessively. Each time he tried to speak, the relentless coughing fits took over again.

Someone delivered yet another patient, and Clarisse turned her attention away from Dalton as he grabbed her arm, imploring her to wait until he asked what he needed to know.

He needed answers, but until he could speak, she needed to treat the others coming to her faster than she could assess them. She pulled gently away from his pleading grasp. So many were lying around her on the frozen ground needing help. Clarisse had no idea who had brought them or when they had arrived; she just went on doing what she could, encouraging people who could to sit up to cough out the poisons they'd inhaled.

She was dizzy with exertion but looked around for the next worst patient when Dalton finally found his voice and croaked out, "My sons? Kim?"

"I don't know, Dalton," she said.

She turned away again for the next one who needed saving, peripherally aware of Dalton rolling over and struggling to his feet, driven by pure will.

Rick rushed over with his wife Olivia, who had sustained minor burns on her arms while trying to reach the occupants of Dalton's tent. Each of them carried one of Dalton's sons. Both boys were conscious, but traumatized, and covered in soot. Bethany cried again and held her arms out imploringly when her mother approached. Rick sat the boys down with them, and Olivia stayed to comfort the children, cooing soft reassurances.

Rick searched for Steven through the smoke, knowing he was trying to bring in Kim, who'd looked too far gone when he helped to pull her from the smoke-filled tent. Clarisse performed CPR on another victim nearby, ignoring everything around her while trying to bring life back to just this one.

Steven finally made it through the heavy smoke and into clearer air. He knew he couldn't wait to get Kim to the triage area. Instead, he laid her down hastily while the smoke rolled up and away. For the third time, he performed CPR on her. The first two times she hadn't responded, but this time, without so much smoke around them, he hoped he could get her breathing.

He rhythmically compressed her chest and forced his own air into her lungs, continuing the routine over and over. "Help me," he said when he saw Rick. "Take over compressions. I'll breathe her."

Rick dropped down and complied, counting out loud. Steven puffed air into the lungs he now feared would never draw it in again of their own volition. Patients with the worst of traumas sometimes have a look about them, and you know, despite your efforts, that they are beyond your reach; Steven recognized this in Kim. It was as if death marked her, and Steven's efforts would be in vain.

He looked up, saw Dalton standing by, weaving and coughing, and redoubled his efforts. On and on it went, he and Rick working over Kim. They traded places, and Steven took over the compressions until his arms and shoulders ached, then he stopped, leaning back on his haunches.

"Switch?" Rick panted, but Steven only lowered his chin to his own chest. He shook his head slowly, sadly. "No."

Dalton pleaded. He cried and yelled in agony and begged them to keep trying.

In no time Clarisse was there and crouched beside Steven. She rested her fingers on Kim's throat, feeling for a pulse, but Steven already knew there was none. As her eyes confirmed it, he stood and took Dalton by the arm, wanting to lead him away, take him to his sons, but Dalton refused.

He reached for his wife, shoving Rick aside, and checked her pulse himself, coming away empty. Steven tried to hold him back. He tried to ease the coming reality from the man. In denial, Dalton shook his head. "No! You stopped too soon! Try again," he pleaded, his voice ragged and cracked through his raw throat as the reality sunk in. He reached for Kim again to continue the work of saving her himself. He could barely move, but he made the effort.

Steven let him try, even though it was clear Kim was beyond retrieval from death's grasp, and he knew Dalton was doing himself further harm with the effort. Finally Rick grabbed him by the shirt and pulled him squarely in front to face him. "Dalton. She's gone, man. She's gone."

"No!" Dalton cried, causing another spasm of painful coughing. He dropped to his knees, and Steven held him while he choked out his grief. When he was able, Dalton asked in anguish, "Boys?" The word was more a plea for mercy from this horror, but in that small question he also accepted the finality of his wife's death.

"They're fine, they're with Olivia," Rick assured him. He helped Steven get Dalton to his feet and slung one arm over his own shoulder to lead him to his now motherless sons.

Steven picked up Kim's body and carried her over to one side where he laid her beside two others Clarisse had been unable to save.

"We need to take count," Steven said softly to Clarisse, who looked ghastly, exhausted, and as covered in soot as any who'd had to rush from the burning tents. She nodded, and covered Kim with a sheet.

Reuben suddenly showed up at Steven's side. "Fire's out, finally. We had to use a lot of our water supply, and the damage is extensive."

There were broad burns on Reuben's arm. "Over here!" Steven called to Clarisse, who was still staring down at Kim's body.

"Oh, heavens!" she said, "Reuben, let's get your arm bandaged." Gently she tried to pull him away.

"No, I can't," Reuben answered. "There's a body in the greenhouse still. It's hard to tell who it was."

Steven could see that the man was dazed, probably in too much shock to even be aware of his own injuries. "It doesn't matter now, Reuben. Let us take you to the guard station. I'll do a head count, a role call; we'll find out soon enough."

While they brought Reuben into the guard station, they heard the whimpering and saw the shock as tragedy finally seeped between the cracks in the plaster of what they'd all seen as their safe haven. Dalton desperately hugged his boys, holding them so tightly the older one looked out wild-eyed from behind his father's shoulder.

Nearly everyone they passed was either crying or staring vacant-eyed at the smoking rubble, stunned by this terrible turn of events. As Clarisse tended to Reuben, Steven knew he and Rick would have to take over for Dalton right now. People were huddled in the dark and cold, unable to go back to their quarters, unable to function.

"Clarisse, can we get everyone into the quarantine lab?" Steven ordered more than asked.

She looked around as if doing a mental head count. "Yes, there's more medical supplies and cots in there. Some of these people need to be on oxygen, and soon," she said as she taped the end of the bandage on Reuben's burn.

Rick heard the plan too, and said loudly, startling everyone out of their misery, "Okay, folks. Listen up, we need to move to the quarantine building. Pick up what you can and follow us." Rick began leading the procession with a flashlight through the snow.

Clarisse and Steven helped those who were struggling, and Dalton coughed constantly in an effort to clear his lungs, clinging to his two boys, unwilling to let anyone take them from him.

As Clarisse left the gate, helping Bethany, she remembered Addy. Without a backward glance, she ran to the untouched side of the camp to retrieve the girl. After a moment, she reappeared, looking even worse than before. "She's gone!" she screamed. "Addy! Addy! Where are you?"

Steven caught her as she began to run aimlessly, still calling the child's name.

The glow of a fire in the distance held Marcy's vision. She had finally entered the outskirts of Cascade and the closer she drove, the more worried she became.

She debated a few minutes about waking Sam. She wasn't sure if he would wake up, considering how tired he was, but thought he would want to be told about the potential danger in the distance.

"Sam," she said and tried to nudge him a little to rouse him from sleep with her free arm. "Sam," she said louder, and heard him stir in the passenger side seat of the Scout's dark cab.

"What?"

"Can you see this?" She pointed, "There's a fire up ahead."

He blinked and glanced around, then sat up a little higher in his seat. He squinted his eyes a time or two and tried to get his bearings. An expression of dread washed over his face. "That's the prepper camp up there!"

"Oh. Oh, my God. Your little girl's there."

"Pick it up, Marcy," he growled.

She sped up as fast as possible on the icy roads.

Sam had spent a lot of time in the forests around Cascade and mentally calculated how long the hike would take him if he went first to Graham's cabin.

"Stop right here," he commanded. "It's closer to the prepper place." The truck skidded to a halt. "You go straight to Graham's camp. They probably aren't aware of the fire yet. I have to make sure Addy's all right. Then I'll come back." Sam stepped out, pulling his gloves on and turning up his collar against the cold.

"No!" Marcy called after him as he took his first few unsteady steps "You can't do that. You can barely walk!"

Sam didn't dispute her claim, but he trekked out into the woods with his rifle slung over his shoulder, raising one hand in salute behind him.

"Sam!" she yelled in exasperation. He heard her, but kept on into the woods. After a moment, he heard the truck's tires bite into the crusty road again. She'd bring Graham, he knew, but he'd get to Addy faster this way.

Sam ran as best he could through the forest, blinded by darkness, slowed by weakness and pain. He stopped every few minutes to lean against a tree and listen to the distant shouts coming from the preppers' camp. Something terrible had happened there. Was his daughter safe?

He continued on, though the world spun every few minutes and he had to slow down and lean against something sturdy before he dared continue. He trusted his hearing more than sight, but even that was impaired from the pounding in his head thanks to that crazy woman's club. His chest wound bled through his coat. He pressed a hand against it and lunged on; his one thought, *Save Addy, save Addy, save Addy*, thrumming along with the pounding pain.

He finally came to the edge of the prepper enclosure. Residents ran in all directions, shouting orders. Some sat in groups, huddled as if in shock, holding children. He did not see Addy among them.

He stayed far from an exposure point, but as he circled the camp searching for his daughter, he told himself it would be enough just to catch sight of her, a glimpse, some insurance she was all right. He lurched forward, wanting to help as he watched Steven come out of the family tents bearing the weight of a body. An adult. Way too large to be Addy.

Though he wanted to help, he couldn't risk exposing anyone. Keeping his distance was hard, but he had to remain a spectator to the disaster and search in stealth as he circled the camp. His vision blurred, and the vertigo made him reel. He knew he could easily make a mistake, get too close, but the need to be certain Addy was all right drove him on, searching, always searching, as he staggered between trees.

~ ~ ~

Marcy drove on to Graham's camp as fast as she could go. Smoke hung between the trees, obstructing her vision, but she squinted and managed to stay on the familiar road, hardly slowing until she was nearly at the cabin. On any other occasion Graham would have threatened to tan her hide, but in this case she thought he would understand. The moment she stopped, right alongside the front porch, she jumped out of the truck and leapt for the door. Giving up right away on the locked entry, she pounded her fists and yelled, "Graham! Graham!"

Macy was the first to open the door "Marce! What? What's wrong? Oh, my God. Where's all the smoke coming from?" she asked, waving her hand in front of her face as a cloud of it swept out of the trees.

"There's a fire at the preppers' camp! Sam and Mark are injured, but Sam made me stop to let him out on our way back. He's going to search for Addy. But he's hurt pretty bad." She shook her head. "I can't explain it all now. Get Graham, quick!"

Macy shook her head, and Marcy thought her sister was just being obstinate.

"Macy!" She shook her twin's shoulders. "I'm serious. Get him!"

"He's not here! Graham's not here, Marcy. We don't know where he is."

Tala and Bang appeared beside her, and Sheriff rushed between them and out the door, his nose seeking answers from the wind.

"Where's all that smoke coming from? Is there a forest fire?" Tala asked, eyes wide with alarm as deeper bands of smoke curled toward them and the burning odor becoming stronger.

"I . . . I don't know," Marcy said to both questions. "I've got to get Mark inside. He's badly hurt."

Sheriff began to bark and whine at the danger he sensed, startling them all. He rarely barked unless there was a good reason.

"My God, can this get any worse?" Tala asked of no one. "I think we might have to evacuate the cabin." She pulled on Marcy's arm. "Is the fire headed this way?"

Marcy couldn't care less about the fire. She wanted to get Mark inside, then get Graham to go find Sam. "No! I think it's just drifting smoke. I don't know for sure. Mark's in the truck, hurt bad, and Sam is out there, looking for Addy. He's injured too. I need to get Mark inside! Help me! Where did Graham go?" She didn't understand why they weren't taking this more seriously.

Macy shoved past her. "Come on, then. Let's get Mark out."

"No. Leave him there," Tala said, trying to hold both girls back. "We might have to drive out if the fire comes this way."

"It won't," Marcy argued, shaking loose. She flung open the truck's back right door and reached in for Mark. He moaned, and air tainted by smoke sucked in through the straw in his throat.

Macy yelled at Tala. "He's really, really hurt. Come help us carry him!"

Tala shoved her feet into boots and grabbed her coat. Marcy heard her gasp as she took in the extent of Mark's injuries. "What happened to you?" Tala's voice shook. Marcy knew Mark was a scary sight, neck covered with duct tape and dried blood from his nose smearing his face.

Mark managed to push himself up onto his elbows, and Marcy sidled in on the floor, then climbed up behind him, helping him sit. "Don't cough, Mark," she begged. "If you breathe in smoke, you might cough it out of your trachea." Tala passed her a soft, knitted scarf. With care, she draped it loosely over Mark's throat. Macy helped him swing his legs down.

With Marcy pushing and Macy pulling they got Mark out of the truck and on his feet.

"Can you walk?" Marcy asked.

Mark began to move, and the sisters helped him make the journey to the porch.

"Does Sam look like this too?" Tala asked, leading the way to the bunkroom.

"No, I think she got him more to the back of the head," Marcy offered.

Tala turned the covers back. "Who?"

"A madwoman we met. I . . . I killed her."

Tala nodded and helped ease Mark down. "Macy, you take the truck down the road a mile or two. If the fire's spreading, get back here quick. Only go a mile or two and no more. If you think the fire might be heading this way, come back right away, and we'll all get out of here."

Macy slipped out the front door with a radio in her hand. The smoky air tried to hold back the dawn. Macy whistled low for Sheriff, and he appeared at the tree line. She patted his head and pointed at the cabin. "Guard the cabin, boy."

As she slipped behind the steering wheel, Sheriff panted on the porch. Macy saw him sitting on the alert as she backed the truck, turned, and headed down the driveway.

McCann slept only a few minutes near Graham's side.

When the howling started in his dream, he was a fifth grade boy again, standing at the school's curb, waiting in line for the school bus with the other kids. They all turned their heads, first hearing the dogs' howling, followed by the squeal of the county sheriff's car whizzing by. Soon a fire truck raced after the police car, and the neighborhood dogs gave chase.

He clearly heard Mrs. Goode's voice. "Wake up," she said, her whispered warning close to his ear. Startled by the dead woman speaking, McCann jerked wide awake.

He plopped his boots to the floor and sat straight up. "What the fuck?" He rubbed his ear and realized immediately he hadn't dreamed the whole thing, though he swore he even felt Mrs. Goode's warmed breath blowing in his ear.

He stood, recognizing the sound of an alarm clanging somewhere in the distance. Wolves howling never surprised him, but that alarm did. "What the hell's going on?" he asked himself quietly, annoyed that just when he had been able to finally fall asleep something interrupted his peace. He looked at Graham's sleeping form as he passed on his way to the front door, pistol out before him.

McCann checked outside. Here, where no one lived anymore, there shouldn't be anyone capable of making such a racket in the middle of the night. In the dark he saw only a faint glow to the northwest. That's where the ringing seemed to come from, way off in the distance.

Could that be coming from Graham's camp? Shit! What if they're looking for him? McCann worried. He never imagined Cascade's population as big enough to sustain a community with alarms. The intrusive sound seemed completely foreign now after his months in solitude.

Only one way to find out what the hell was going on. He strode back inside and crouched beside Graham. He tried to rouse him out of his sleep to give him a little water and more meds, and to get some information.

"Graham," he said, as he shook him by his uninjured shoulder. "Graham, wake up, man," he said again, but his efforts were of no use. The guy slept deeply, and he wasn't coming to. McCann was jealous. Then suddenly, the distant alarm went silent.

"God dammit!" he said in frustration. He gave up on waking Graham. McCann started to suspect a grand conspiracy to keep him awake had taken place, and the ploy was some form of new torture.

He went back outside. With the alarm now subdued, so was the glow of a fire. "Okay, so there's nothing I can do about their emergency right now. Whoever they are, they apparently have it under control." He closed the door, shutting out the night, hoping to get a little more sleep before dawn. He assumed his previous position and nodded off once again.

"Addy!" Clarisse yelled as she ran through the ravaged prepper camp. "Addy!"

Reuben had turned back after hearing her voice in alarm. She ran up to him and grabbed him by the shoulders. "You said there's a body in the greenhouse. How big?"

Not used to seeing Clarisse scared out of her mind, he said gently, "Calm down, Clar—"

"Is it a child's? Could it be Addy's?" Silently she begged him to tell her it was not.

"I don't know, Clarisse. Let's get everyone to quarantine. She's probably in there."

She released her grasp on him and backed away, faking a stoicism she didn't feel. "You're probably right." She nodded. "I have a few things to grab. I'll be along in a minute."

He let her go while she ran back to her tent to see if Addy had left any clues. Only her coat and boots were gone. "Oh, my God, Addy, where are you?" she yelled. She had to find out for herself if the burned body in the greenhouse was Addy's.

Clarisse pulled a green army blanket from her bed and grabbed her flashlight. With everyone having deserted the camp, she headed for the burned out greenhouse. She approached it with trepidation. *Please, God, don't let it be her.* Steam rose where the fire had won the battle over ice. Water pooled and mixed with the earth underneath.

Clarisse held her arm over her nose as she stepped over some of the smoking debris. The noxious fumes still rose. She was about to enter the burned-out frame when movement caught her attention through the dark end of the long building. Someone bent over the charred remains. She shone her flashlight on him, and when he turned toward her, he shielded his vision from the light and staggered backward.

"Turn the light off, Clarisse."

She recognized his voice. "Sam?" she gasped and sucked in her breath at the same time. She remembered the danger he posed to her and jumped back several feet farther, shaking with raw fear though she was probably at a safe distance.

"What are you doing here?" she whispered loudly and scanned the area, terrified someone else would detect his presence. She flicked her light on him once again, and he swayed as he took a quick step to the side.

"Is she safe, Clarisse? Is she?" he asked, pleading, his voice broken.

"You, you can't be here, Sam! What were you thinking?"

"Where's my daughter?" he howled in grief.

Clarisse shook her head. "I . . . I don't know," she stuttered. She pointed at the charred body, "I just came to find out if"—she whimpered—"if that was her." How it hurt to utter the words!

"It's not. It's Tammy."

Clarisse doubled over and cried. "Are you sure?"

"Yeah," he said gravely. "I'm sure. I looked."

"Okay, okay," she panted, standing erect and pointing the flashlight at him again. The dried blood on his coat had become wet again, and he swayed and staggered from another dizzy spell.

"You're hurt, Sam. What happened? Weren't you on a hunting trip?" she asked, confused, trying to make sense of his presence here.

"On our way back, we saw the fire. There was some, um, trouble on the trip," he said, his voice weak and halting.

Fear shot through her. Had the entire prepper colony been exposed to the virus? "Are the others wandering around here too?" As if dealing with the fire hadn't been trauma enough.

"No. They're at Graham's camp. It's just me. I need to know if Addy is safe. Where is she, Clarisse?"

She avoided the question. "Did you come close to anyone here?"

"No. I kept my distance. I'm not trying to hurt anyone. I heard you ask about the body in here. So, after everyone left, I came to check. I have to find her. I have to know she's all right." Clarisse heard the desperation in his tone and saw it in his strained face, though they stood the length of the greenhouse apart.

"You can't be in here, Sam. I'll find Addy. Please, go back to Graham's camp, and get medical attention," she tried to reason with him. "I'll send word as soon as I find her."

Before she completed her thought, he had already turned and scaled the perimeter fencing to the other side. He obviously would not take her advice right now and would continue his search for his daughter. She had to find Addy first, or Sam might accidentally expose the child to the virus—an outcome they'd all regret.

She also needed to keep his presence in the camp a secret. By their own rules, he would be shot dead on the spot if found within the perimeter. The penalty was a law they had to enforce for their own safety, but Clarisse only had time to worry about Addy right now; she had to find the child.

There was only one place Addy might go to if she had walked out of the tent into the mayhem earlier. The thought scared her. Addy, frightened, would head for the river in the dark, waiting for her father to come and save her.

She took off toward the quarantine building. The others would not understand what she needed to do, but the dawn's light was beginning to break and she had to get there before Sam thought of the probability first and accidentally expose her to the virus.

Upon entering the crowded quarantine building, Clarisse saw most of the preppers hacking and coughing, even as the stronger ones aided those who were injured.

Rick had cleared a conference room and rushed around setting up cots from a storage closet. Steven tended to Reuben's youngest daughter, who had burns to her feet. Clarisse heard her say, "I had to run through the fire when I got out of our tent." The child coughed and wept as Steven worked over her.

Steven's head jerked up from his task as Clarisse hurried past to her office. She pretended not to have noticed him, though guilt stung her as she made her way between those huddled in the hallway with varying expressions, from horror to dull acceptance. Stepping around and between bodies, she hurried on.

"What's going on, Clarisse?" Steven's voice called after her. "Dalton's down. We have three dead, and you're MIA?"

"*Addy's* MIA," she snapped back at him. "I'm going out to look for her right now. I'll take a radio."

She began to rummage through her supplies, snatching up the things she needed. With a glance over her shoulder to make sure she wasn't observed, she opened the refrigerator and pulled out a syringe with the new serum. She quickly capped it and carefully tucked it into her backpack with her other supplies.

"We need you here, Clarisse," Steven said as she stepped out. "I can't do this all by myself. Look at these people." He waved toward the injured with a wad of gauze in his gloved hand.

That pissed her off, partly because she knew it was true and partly because she was damn near her breaking point. "Addy needs me more. Keep everyone out of my lab." She strode away despite the pleas of the injured and Steven's angry demands she stay. She didn't dare stop; she could not forsake Addy.

Outside the dawn peeked over the horizon, casting into stark light their marred oasis, surrounded by the forbidding forest. The few people Clarisse ran into outside were trekking their way back and forth between the burned camp and the quarantine building. The refugees toted random supplies in a daze. Each was on a mission, barely making eye contact, glazed with the unbelievable events of the night. Not surprisingly, they didn't even ask Clarisse what her intentions were when she unfolded and donned a sterile suit over her outerwear and trekked south from camp.

A new day began to form, whether they were ready for it or not. The voices of those earlier in distress and confusion replayed in Clarisse's ears. In that state, she could only imagine that Addy must have woke, emerged from the tent, and run into the bedlam around her not knowing what to do. In her terror she'd have run for the only person she knew would never let her down—her father.

Clarisse quickened her pace to the rendezvous spot where she had taken Addy so many times before to visit with Sam. Now, as the daylight grew, he probably watched her every move from a safe distance, or he was searching for Addy on his own. That could mean death for the girl if he didn't keep a safe distance.

Clarisse's heart ached. She, too, truly loved Sam's daughter, but did she love her enough to take the action she feared she might have to? And if she did it, and Addy knew, would she ever forgive Clarisse? She checked the cylinder of the revolver before palming it closed, the familiar click resounding before she placed the gun in her harness. She knew Sam was desperate, and desperate people often made terrible mistakes, no matter their love and good intentions.

At five in the morning, the February sun had barely began its ascent toward dawn. It cast a lavender hue against the atmosphere, slowly creating a dark silhouette of the mountains to the east. Unfortunately this dawn met Macy mixed with smoke and a trepidation for what she might find.

With only the rumble of the truck engine, the morning held a silent foreboding. She leaned farther out the broken window to peer through the hazy woods. The glow of the distant fire ceased along with the sound of the alarm right as she turned out onto the main road into town. Seeing no immediate danger, she assumed whatever had caused the fire was now under control, meaning her camp was no longer in any danger and that she was free to search for Graham.

"Tala, come in. Over."

"Go ahead, Macy."

"The alarm's off, and no flames are present. I think they've got it under control now."

"Whew! Okay, come on back."

"Roger, Macy out," she said, not exactly lying but not conforming either.

She continued on, easing down the main road of Cascade, scanning for Graham's truck. With residual smoke billowing out of the woods, the haze settled like a persistent fog along the icy streets, causing her to occasionally rub at her irritated eyes.

She had to find Graham first, to learn what had kept him away. She hoped to find Sam as well, but it made sense to check the streets of Cascade before she went tromping through the woods. She figured she had at least an hour before Tala began to panic.

She scanned the side streets until she caught a glimpse of something brown in front of her. She hastily slammed on the brakes, causing her truck to slide five feet forward as deer crossed the road.

One of the wide-eyed deer stopped right in the middle of the street and gazed at her, only moving again when the last one in the herd caught up. Macy continued her drive, peering through the forest to catch a glimpse of them, but they were already gone, having escaped into the woodland depths like ghosts.

As she turned the corner to get to the post office, she spotted three snow-covered mounds by its front door. They had been there for a while, since the drifts to the right of them were at least two feet deep. "Oh, Graham, *no!*" she moaned aloud. "Please, please don't be there!"

She pulled up, turned off the ignition, and examined her surroundings while taking off her seatbelt, ever prepared for danger. She pulled out her pistol and grabbed her flashlight before cautiously approaching the mounds. She sucked in a breath so cold it made her teeth ache when she saw the brown oxidized blood on the snow. She quickly brought her hand to her mouth. "Oh God, no," she whispered, shaking from more than the cold.

Macy swallowed the rising bile, and with the tip of her boot she began to brush away a little snow from the first camouflaged dune. She uncovered the fur of a dog's side, and with hope she quickly checked the other mounds to be sure they were dogs too.

After confirming that Graham wasn't among the carnage, she stepped back and tried to piece the scene together. She peered down at the dead dogs, frozen stiff in their snowy graves, with a lot of what she suspected to be Graham's blood too. There had been a struggle with the dogs and Graham had gotten away. At least she had hope. *He must be somewhere nearby. He's got injuries, or he'd have driven home yesterday.* Then, through the drifting smoke, she spotted his truck a few houses down the street.

Gun at the ready, she crept—one methodical, quiet step after another—to inspect the passenger side of the pickup for any clues.

Maybe he made it inside that house?

She jumped back and took safety behind the truck as loud, frustrated yelling came from somewhere behind the house. "Get the hell out of here, you fucking assholes!"

At first Macy thought the unfamiliar voice bellowed insults at her, but as she peeked around the truck, she saw no one. She circled around to the back of the building, hoping to get a glimpse of whoever yelled and, perhaps, what he was shouting at. As she rounded the back, she saw a young man waving his arms, shouting to defend his horses from three approaching wolves. She didn't want anything to do with an unfamiliar person, but the stranger had Graham's truck and probably also had an idea of what had happened to him.

The wolves were down low, crouching for an attack. The guy stood waving a lantern in one hand and throwing what seemed to be old potatoes from the other. He was clearly armed with a gun in a holster around his waist, and the fact that he was using potatoes as ammo didn't make sense to Macy.

She crouched there, trying to piece together what might have happened to Graham, all the while staring at the potato-throwing man as he continued to berate his attackers. Obviously he had been attacked by the dogs who now lay dead in front of the post office and was likely the one who killed them, because there was no one else around. Maybe this guy had the answers, but maybe he'd also killed Graham. She didn't have any idea, but would not take chances with a stranger.

She needed the guy alive to question him and he wasn't doing a good job of staying that way just now. Graham always said, "Stay away from the crazies." Macy wasn't sure if this guy was crazy or what, but he certainly wasn't acting sane at the moment. She had no doubt she was about to witness his own mauling.

One of the wolves cut low and to the left, coming in for a side attack at the man. Macy stayed where she crouched, aimed carefully and fired. As the wolf dropped to the ground, the other two took off without looking back. The stranger swiftly pulled his pistol, whirled, and locked eyes with her.

She knew him! In that instant, Macy could only remain frozen in place, stunned, held captive by the intensity of the contact. An inexplicable sense of panic rushed over her, and she broke away, running for her truck.

McCann recognized those blue eyes. He had seen them before in the back of Graham's truck last fall. He wasted no time running after the girl; he jumped over the side gate and ran around the front in hopes of intercepting her in the road.

Just as he crossed to the neighboring house, another shot rang out behind him.

"Hey! Stop shooting at me, dammit," he yelled. He wasn't sure where she hid. He stopped in his tracks, with his hands up, pointing his pistol high into the air. "I'm not going to hurt you," he yelled out, hoping she would come out of hiding.

"Where's Graham?" Macy demanded. He heard a tremor in her voice, one she probably hated. A girl who could take out a lunging wolf with one shot was no coward, and a damn good shot, too. But scared and armed was not a good combination. He didn't feel like getting shot today.

"He's fine. He was attacked by some wild dogs."

"You're not telling me where he is," Macy said, even more frightened, and chanced another shot at a safe distance from him as a warning, "I will shoot you next."

McCann flinched. "Knock it off, God dammit! I've had enough of this shit." He could now see a pickup truck parked at the post office, and he suspected that she was going to make a run for it. Just then Macy's radio crackled to life, giving her position away. "Macy, are you okay?" came a female voice.

The sound of the radio tipped him off to her exact location. He ran to the edge of the post office and got down low and holstered his pistol. She bolted from a neighboring yard toward the truck and McCann took off running after her.

Though she sprinted fast with him on her heels, McCann knew he would catch her if she stopped to open the truck's door, but to his surprise, she right raced past the truck. He could barely keep up. He was exhausted from fighting off the wolves earlier and taking care of Graham all night, not to mention the alarm waking him after he'd caught only a few minutes' sleep. "Stop running!" he yelled in frustration, but she wasn't stopping. He had to get this chase over with and, using what little energy reserves he still had in him, kicked his pace into a last surge of high gear. He aimed for her legs, diving down onto her. She slammed into the hard icy road, hands first, and as she sprawled, her gun skidded off a few feet in front of her.

Macy tried to wiggle out of his grasp to reach for her weapon, but even as tired as he was he managed to hold her. She began kicking and punching the hell out of him, but he flipped her over and grabbed her around the left thigh, hauling her body beneath his. She continued to struggle with every ounce of strength she had.

"Get off me!" Macy yelled.

McCann tucked his head down and let her continue the assault while he laid his entire weight onto her. When he'd had enough of the abuse, he took both of her arms and shoved them down against the cold, hard ice. "Not until you calm down!" he said.

With her breath coming in rasping gasps, Macy glared at him and tried to buck him off, but he held tight.

She raised her head in an attempt to bite him.

"Don't you dare!" he warned her. "I'm too tired for this shit."

"What have you done to Graham?" she spat, venom flaring in her eyes as she fought and tried to catch her breath.

McCann remembered those blue eyes as curious, interested, and warm, and he wished she wasn't so pissed off right now. She was a little bit of a thing, yet she fought like a demented giant. "I told you, he's fine. If you'd listened to me the first time, you'd be with him by now." He couldn't help but grin.

She didn't seem to think it was funny. "I don't trust you."

"I can see that," he conceded, and waited until he felt her body relax beneath him. "I'll take you to him, but you have to promise me you won't shoot me, bite me, or run from me again."

"I will promise no such thing," she said, glaring at him again.

"Hey, I've got all day, missy, though I'm tired as hell because I've been up all night. You, on the other hand, will freeze your ass off lying here on the ground with me sleeping on top of you. It's your choice."

Macy glared some more, those gorgeous blue eyes stormy and a bit confused, as she clearly pondered her options. To show her he meant what he said, McCann snuggled his head into her neck and let her feel his dead weight again.

"All right! Get off!"

"Promise?"

She nodded, muttering a resentful "I promise."

He smiled again and got up quickly, grabbing Macy's gun before she could. When she reached out to take the weapon from him, he shook his head and raised his eyebrows at her while holding the weapon up and away from her.

"I don't think so. You shot at me. I'll just hang onto this for now."

"If I'd wanted to hit you, I would have," she said. He turned her toward the house, pushing her ahead of him because he believed her. After seeing how she had dropped the wolf not three feet from him, he had no doubt she aimed straight.

"Just walk up ahead of me where I can keep an eye on you."

The radio strapped to her belt crackled again with Tala's now frantic voice. "Macy. Are you okay? Over."

She stopped and turned to him, her eyes beseeching. No man in his right mind could refuse her. "I have to answer her. She's scared."

"Go ahead, you're not my prisoner, Macy. I just have a problem with people shooting at me."

She rolled her eyes at him, knowing how he'd just learned her name. "I'm fine, Tala. I think I might have found Graham. Are you okay? Over."

"You did? Is he all right?"

She hadn't thought to say "Over," but Macy put that down to relief. "I haven't seen him just yet, but I'll let you know as soon as I do. I have to go now. I'll call back soon. Macy out."

She began to walk again, but stopped in her tracks and turned to look at McCann. "Is Graham hurt badly? Please tell me before I go in the house."

"Yes, I'm afraid he is, but he's alive. It's been a long night. He's probably awake by now. I would have driven him to your camp last night, but I didn't know where you lived. I figured someone would come looking for him eventually."

He could tell by the way her lower lip trembled just slightly that she was scared of what kind of shape she would find Graham in. The sun was fully up now, and McCann watched the back of her head as the light picked up the highlights in her golden hair. "Don't you remember me, Macy?"

She looked up at him with a hesitant smile in her eyes and nodded. "You're the Carnation boy?"

"Oh, no," he didn't like the sound of that. "I came from Carnation, but my name's McCann," he said, wanting to get that straight right away.

She caught on to his annoyance, "Oh, we call you the Carnation boy. You might as well get used to the name."

"McCann," he repeated, wanting to hear her say it.

"Can Graham travel?" she asked more seriously.

"I think so, I patched him up as well as possible."

They continued to walk in silence until they came to the door of the brick house. Before Macy could reach for the handle, McCann reached around and opened the door for her. Her wide gaze shot toward him as if she thought this was strange. He guessed it was. The way things were now, people had probably stopped expecting good manners.

Macy took a step through the door and halted so abruptly that McCann ran into her back. The air smelled putrid inside the house. Macy swayed, and McCann slipped an arm around her waist as she emitted a low moan of distress.

Graham lay on a couch covered loosely with a sheet. Recovering, Macy slipped loose and rushed to his side. As she lifted the sheet, McCann saw more blood had seeped through the bandages on Graham's open thigh.

"Graham?" Macy was probably trying to keep the alarm out of her voice, but again McCann could detect a frightened tremor.

"He's probably still asleep."

"Graham!" She ran to him and knelt down beside him. "Graham, wake up. It's me, Macy." She looked pleadingly at McCann. "He's the strongest man I've ever known. To see him like this is awful."

"I know," McCann said gently, using a cloth from the back of the couch to wipe sweat from Graham's forehead.

"What happened, exactly?" Her voice cracked and tears spilled from her eyes. "He risked so much to save me and my sister, to save all of us."

McCann spoke quietly. "I heard a truck pull up down the road early yesterday morning and then yelling. I knew the wild dogs were attacking someone; I've been dealing with them and wolves here since I arrived. I ran over there and shot one of them, but the other two would not let go of him. I killed them, but not before they hurt him. A lot."

Macy's low moan of distress cut into McCann.

"Macy, I promise you I tried the best I could. He lost a lot of blood. He's been running a fever, and he mumbles a lot. I was up with him off and on through the night. I have experience with stitching up cows on my father's ranch; I did the best I could with his wounds." He was afraid she might blame him for Graham's condition.

"I'm sure you did, McCann." She sniffed and blew out a breath. "It's just hard to find him like this. Did you know he's been waiting for you?"

McCann shook his head.

"He takes care of all of us—my sister Marcy, and the little boy Bang, but also three others we've encountered since getting here." She smiled. "Looks like it's time for us to return the favor, and it's all thanks to you."

McCann didn't want her gratitude, so he changed the subject. "So, we have two trucks to bring back to your camp now. We'll put Graham in one, and I'll hitch my horses up to the other. We'll have to drive slow, but I'll just follow you back." Then he set to work as fast as he could to gather his gear and his horses.

Meanwhile, Macy checked on Graham. His temperature was still elevated, and he looked pale and fragile. She examined his wounds and noted how neatly McCann had stitched him up. There was a long gash coming from two directions down his thigh, with a lot of swelling, and Macy detected an odor. They needed to get him back to camp fast so that Clarisse might tell them what more they could do for him.

As Macy redressed his wound, Graham began to stir, and his eyes fluttered open for a bit. "Hi, Graham," she said, so happy to see him come around, if even for a minute.

When he recognized her, he said, "Macy, girl. The dogs got me." He tried to swallow.

"It's okay," she said as her tears dropped down to his chest, "McCann killed them."

"Yeah, he came just at the right time," Graham said, then his eyes began to flutter shut before Macy could say anything more.

She wiped her tears, and then went to the bathroom. She could hear McCann retrieving first the Scout, then the pickup, from in front of the post office. He left both engines running and came in through the front door.

"I think we're all set. You know there's a frozen deer strapped to the roof of your truck, right?"

"Yeah. My sister and two others just returned from a hunting trip, and I took the truck to look for Graham as soon as they got back."

"I'll help you get it down when we get there. I hope Graham's still asleep, because moving him is going to be painful for him," McCann speculated.

"He came to, just for a second. At least he knows I'm here," Macy said. "I'll help you carry him to the truck."

McCann swept a gaze over her. "No. No, you won't."

"Maybe I'm not very big," she argued, "but I'm strong. I can help."

"Look, he weighs about as much as I do. He's probably going to yell out in pain. Are you going to be able to handle that? If not, you need to go get into the truck now."

"I can handle it, Carnation boy." She glared at McCann. "You don't even know me."

"I'm just trying to help, Macy."

"Then pick him up, and I'll help you get him into the truck."

As McCann began to heft Graham into his arms, Macy saw the strain it put on even his muscular frame. He didn't object when she took part of Graham's weight, laying his legs across her arms. "Don't think he weighed this much when I first hauled him into the house," he muttered, grunting as he lifted Graham higher and swung into a turn. Macy followed. Graham's legs, wrapped in the sheet, hung heavy and limp against her.

Graham moaned when McCann accidently brushed an arm past his incision in an attempt to not drop him. Macy covered him the best she could against the cold. Walking sideways, she opened the door for McCann and escorted him to the Scout. She braced the truck door open with her back and helped to slide Graham into the backseat. "Okay, go ahead. I'll follow behind with the pickup, but drive slowly. With the horses tethered to the back, we can't go too fast."

"Oh my God, I nearly forgot. You are a carrier? Right?" she asked with sudden fear.

"Yes, Macy. I'm the only one left from my town. I never came down with the virus."

She nodded with bittersweet recognition.

McCann went to the pickup truck and waited there for Macy to pull around him. She turned around several times to check on Graham, who had settled back down and didn't seem to be conscious of his surroundings. She pushed an errant sheet back over his chest with her right hand and continued on slowly to keep from jostling him around too much.

Macy put the Scout in gear, and McCann followed close behind as they made their way slowly toward camp.

The brake lights brightened ahead of him, causing McCann to stop. He got out and went to the back of the pickup to check on his two horses tied to the tailgate. Calming them in unfamiliar surroundings, he patted each one and rubbed their necks a bit. Afterward, he walked around to the front and found Macy standing by the side of the road looking worried and confused.

"What's up? Graham okay?"

"He's still asleep." She pointed with the radio toward the side street. "This is the spot where Marcy said she let Sam out last night."

"Who?"

"Marcy is my twin sister, and Sam is another guy living at our camp. I need to call in again and find out if Sam went back to camp. If not, I'll go looking for him after we deliver Graham."

"Tala? Over," she said, waiting for a reply.

After no answer had come in more than a minute, Macy resubmitted the call, thinking they were probably busy with Mark's injuries when Tala finally answered.

"Macy! How is he? Over." Tala's voice crackled on the radio waves.

"We're on our way back. Graham was attacked by a couple of dogs, but he's going to survive." She flashed her eyes and smiled mischievously at McCann. "The Carnation Boy arrived just in time and saved him, but Graham's got a long recovery ahead of him. Carnation Boy is coming back with us. Um . . . Is Sam still missing? Over."

"Oh, it's such a relief"—Tala's voice choked up for a moment—"to hear that Graham's with you. Um, no; Sam still hasn't come in yet. Please hurry, and bring Graham home. And Carnation Boy too, of course. Macy, I have more bad news, though. Bang. He and Sheriff went off to track either Sam or Graham. The other radio's missing, and he took Sheriff along with him. I . . . never caught him slipping out while taking care of Ennis and Mark. Over."

McCann watched as Macy's face drained of all color. "Oh no!" Her blue eyes flew up to McCann's, filled with alarm. "Tala, he's aware of the rule to stay away from the prepper camp, so don't worry. You tried to call him? Over."

"Yes. He didn't answer. Oh, Macy, Bang always copies your every move. I'm sure he figures if you went off to find Graham, it was his duty to go track Sam." Her voice broke again as a sob escaped.

"This time he's gone too far. As soon as we find him, I'm going to kill him, if he's not already dead." She fell silent for a minute, then clicked the radio again. "Tala, I'm sure he'll be back soon. Sheriff is with him. We'll be right there, Tala, and then I'll find him. I promise. Macy out." She turned to McCann, and he could see her fear. "We should go," she said.

"Wait a minute," McCann said. "Prepper camp? Does this have anything to do with the fire last night?"

The prepper camp is located north of ours. They're still susceptible to the virus, so we keep away from them. There was a fire there last night. I've tried to radio them, but they don't answer. One of our guys, Sam, has a daughter who lives with them. He's injured, but he still went to look for her to make sure she was safe. Bang, who is the five-year-old boy you must have seen with us back in Carnation, is now searching for Sam, I think. It's a lot to explain; all you need to know now is that the preppers are friendly, but we don't cross into their territory—ever, for any reason—without prior permission."

"And who's Sheriff?"

"He's our dog. Don't you remember the dog we had that growled at you?"

"Oh, yeah. He's tame?"

"Yes, he's part of our family now. He was a police dog," she said as she slid back into the driver's seat, and then her radio crackled to life again unexpectedly.

"Bang here. Macy? Over."

McCann stopped in his tracks as he heard a little boy's hushed voice pipe over the radio waves and stopped to listen as Macy barked, "Where are you, Bang?"

"Someone's walking around in one of those suits, Macy. I had to get away to call you. I found Sam. He's hurt real bad. I need you to help me get him home. I can't move him by myself. Over."

She began to tremble in fear as she asked him, "Where are you exactly, Bang? Over."

"I'm near the bend in the river. On the other side. Over."

She took in a sharp breath. "I told you never to go over there!" Tears of fury or frustration spilled down her cheeks now as she held one hand over her opened mouth.

"I had to. Sam's lying in the brush. So, I went around and found him. Then, one of the preppers walked over here. Hurry, I'm afraid they're going to find me."

McCann asked quickly, "How far is it?"

"About twenty minutes on foot," Macy answered. "If they find Bang and Sam, they'll shoot them. Those are the rules we agreed to."

"Let's take the horses," McCann offered.

"We can't. They'll make too much noise. I have to go alone. I don't want them to shoot you or your horses."

McCann grabbed her arm and stopped her short before she headed into the woods, alone and unprepared. As he spoke, he replaced her pistol into her harness. "Listen to me. Graham needs to get back to camp. I can take my horse and follow the river from here to get them both back on the right side. I'll be quiet. I'll get them both and then bring them all back to camp. You need to get Graham home." He gave her a little shake. "Macy, trust me enough to get this done. Go on. *Move.* Graham's getting colder and weaker each minute we stand here talking."

McCann could see the war Macy had to fight with herself, but eventually she nodded. "Okay," she said, "I'll get Graham home, then come back here for you. Let me talk to Bang." Quickly, she outlined the plan to the boy, telling him not to be afraid of the man on the horse, to come with him when he got there. "You'll have to take my radio so you can talk to him," she said to McCann after logging off.

McCann mounted his horse, slung his rifle over his shoulder, and was about to move out when she grabbed his knee. "Just remember, going over there, into their territory, means they can shoot you. It's our agreement with them. If you come across anyone other than an injured man or a little boy, please hide from them."

"Macy, I'm not going to let anyone kill a five-year-old kid because he crossed over into their territory. If they want to shoot at me, they're fair game as far as I'm concerned. If I have a confrontation with them, I'll try to reason with them first, but I'm not making any promises that I won't shoot someone aiming at me or a kid. I should be back within an hour. It'll be all right, Macy, I promise." With that, he tipped his hat at her and headed the chestnut mare into the ravine leading down through the forest beyond.

Macy gazed after him for a moment. *Who is this guy?* Then she hopped back into the Scout and began to drive away. "He thinks he's a cowboy," she whispered to herself, shaking her head.

"Maybe he is," Graham murmured low from the backseat through the pain and fever combined.

Macy turned really quick and saw that he was conscious, but barely, with his eyes mere slits.

"Graham! I didn't know you were awake."

"Well, I am. You need to tell me what's going on with Bang," he said as he tried to reposition himself. He grunted and groaned through the excruciatingly painful effort.

"Nothing. He's fine." Macy tried to sound casual though she had never been able to lie to Graham. "He went looking for Sam. He'll be home soon. Nothing you need to worry about right now." He groaned with agony she knew he couldn't suppress as she drove on.

"Macy, thanks for trying, but you never could lie to me worth a damn."

She guided the truck carefully, trying to avoid any dips in the icy road. Some obstacles couldn't be avoided, so she tried to warn him when they were coming up. When she pulled up in front of the cabin, Tala looked like she had stood outside on the porch waiting since their last conversation. Her face held creases of worry, and her skin was pale.

Wiping away tears, Tala ran to open the truck door, and Graham smiled upside down at her in the backseat.

"Sorry, I forgot my radio this time," he said sheepishly.

The sweat pouring off his forehead was the first giveaway that his condition wasn't good. Tala tried not to cry, but she couldn't help it, seeing him in so much pain. She reached down and kissed him. "You're forgiven, but next time, you might not be so lucky," she said.

"I wasn't so lucky *this* time," he whispered, trying to swallow though his mouth felt thick. He began to shiver with the fever and the cold.

"I'll get Marcy to help you inside, Graham," Macy said, and with Tala's assistance, tried not to cause him any more pain than necessary. They got him onto a canvas stretcher and carried him into the cabin. Soon, he lay on his bunk next to Ennis's.

Tala still cried and Graham said over and over, "It's okay, Tala. I'm going to be fine. It's my own fault."

He was clearly not fine. Tala found that his temperature was over 102 degrees, and his leg injury was flaming red. With all the movement, the wound bled again, and she patted at the sutured area with gauze, wondering who had stitched him up so well. Marcy retrieved fresh dressings, as well as antibiotics, and passed Macy as she left the bunkroom, seeing that Graham was now in good hands.

Macy glanced at Mark on the living room sofa to see how he fared, and though he still couldn't talk, he waved at her. His face displayed black and blue marks, but he seemed to be in good spirits.

She'd begun to back out the front door when Mark beckoned her over to him. She shook her head, but he looked stubborn and patted the table next to him to make her stop. She put her finger up to her mouth, asking him to be quiet. He glared at her and shook his fist forcefully, but she backed out the door all the way and ran for the truck. She didn't want to explain about Bang's whereabouts or hear any other questions she wasn't ready to answer. Especially about going over to the preppers' side.

This was turning out to be another long day for McCann. He hoped he would locate this kid named Bang and the man named Sam fast. Then he planned to get back to their cabin and find a quiet spot somewhere so he could get some decent sleep.

The day became dreary and overcast. The hue of the snow only a shade or two lighter than the horizon, contrasted to the dark, monotone of the trees. Unlike the other seasons, when the shades of different tree species stood out, in the dead of the winter they only revealed one predominant color, a damp charcoal black. The ride to the river involved trekking through trees, dodging low-hanging branches, and watching for holes that could trip the horse.

McCann heard the river before he saw it. At this point, with much of it frozen, it was little more than a trickle from the north as it meandered its way through the rock maze. It sounded like lazy chimes rather than the rushing resonance of meltwater that would come in the spring. As he neared it he searched for the easiest path to cross without being seen by these prepper people hell-bent on killing friends who put one toe over the line. It was one thing to track a person; it was a completely different thing to track a person when you knew unfriendlies were out and about to get you.

McCann stopped and waited, looking both ways before crossing the stream. Seeing no foe—animal or otherwise—he guided the mare slowly through the waters to the other side. She barely made a sound.

McCann reasoned that if he stuck to the tree line and headed west, he had to come to the bend in the river and find the boy. The search took no more than ten minutes, and there the boy hid behind a small pine, kneeling beside a man who lay much too still on the frozen earth.

He had a bad feeling about that, but before anything had time to fully register, the dog roared toward him, barking ferociously. So much for stealth.

"Call him off," McCann said as the kid just gaped at him and his horse in dazed silence. "Hey, kid. Call off the dog," McCann said again.

Finally Bang jumped to his feet and called Sheriff, got hold of his collar, and made him sit, murmuring calm into ears that still pricked alertly.

McCann dismounted and stood still, letting the dog get a good look at him, but Sheriff stood his ground with a low growl. McCann reached into his saddle bag and ripped off a hunk of beef jerky. Crouching low, he tossed bits of the treat to Sheriff. In order for this to work he needed to befriend the dog quickly.

"I'm McCann," he said to Bang. "From the radio, remember? Macy told you I was coming." He continued to toss little pieces of jerky ever closer to where he kneeled; Sheriff inhaled one piece after the other without even tasting them.

"Yeah, she said you would come on a horse," Bang said. "We don't have horses around here." His eyes fixed admiringly on the mare. McCann liked the kid already.

"So, how's he doing?" McCann asked Bang, pointing to Sam.

Bang raised his shoulder and dropped it. "His heart beats, but he's not awake, and he's cold."

By this time Sheriff took jerky out of McCann's hand, and he reached carefully to let the dog sniff him. "Why don't you come over here and show him we're friends."

Bang came to McCann, who stretched out his hand for him to shake. "Pleasure to meet you, Bang." Sheriff showed no more aggression, and again McCann reached over carefully with slow ease to let the dog smell him, then reached under his muzzle for a scratch.

McCann slowly rose to his feet and led the mare to where Sam lay. The guy had a pulse, but it was weak. The injuries to his head and face were ghastly. "What the hell happened to you, man?" he asked rhetorically and then straightened Sam's arms at his side and prepared to lift him up and over the horse's saddle.

"We need to hurry. There are preppers around here," Bang warned again.

"When's the last time you saw one?"

"Um, a while ago."

McCann nodded. This was a lot to ask of a five-year-old; could a kid that age even tell time? "Okay, let's hurry up, but if they show up, you take the dog and run across the river and don't look back. I'll handle the preppers."

McCann hoisted Sam's body up and over the saddle so that he hung evenly from side to side. The head injuries were pretty bad, and McCann had an inkling the guy might not make the trip if they didn't get out of there soon. He probably suffered from hypothermia after spending the night out in the freezing temperatures. McCann wrapped a blanket around his body in a feeble attempt to warm him.

"All right, Mae," he said to the horse. "Let's get this guy back to camp." He'd just patted her rump to get her moving when an angry yell rang out, and an armed man came out of the tree line, stopping a good distance away.

"What the hell are you doing here?" the man demanded. "Put your hands up where I can see them."

McCann thought about complying, but he was tired, and Macy had already warned him of the dangers here. With the horse between them and the guy with the gun, McCann had a small window to act before things got out of control. "*Run*, kid," he said quietly to Bang, and, at the same time, pulled out his long rifle and pointed the weapon up the hill.

McCann watched the guy, daring him to so much as aim at the kid and the dog running away. He'd have had no remorse over blowing a hole through the prepper's plastic suit. Unfortunately for Sam, he remained unconscious and precariously balanced between the pointed firearms.

"Hold on! I only came to get this guy. He's badly wounded. We're headed right back to our side now. So put your goddamn gun down, man." McCann tried to reason with him like he'd told Macy he would, but he'd also let him know, in no uncertain terms, that he would defend himself if he had to.

"We have rules here. You've broken them," Reuben said.

McCann interrupted him. "Hey, man, I'm new here. I came to pick up this guy. I've been warned. I'll be on my way now," he said and nudged the horse to take a few steps when White Suit shot a warning round into the air causing McCann to stop midstride.

"You don't get off that easy!" the guy shouted. "Someone set fire to our camp last night, and you people have a guy on our side. Not only that, we're missing a little girl. I think you know a lot more than you're letting on!"

McCann was about to shout back that he wasn't responsible for little girls, and they should keep better track of them themselves, when another person in a plastic suit showed up.

"Reuben! What are you doing?" This one was a woman. She huffed and puffed, obviously out of breath after running up through the woods toward the other prepper. "I didn't find her. Only her footprints in the mud between boulders. Why did you shoot?"

"I think this guy might have information for us. I caught him down there with Bang, but the boy took off. I'll take care of this, Clarisse. You keep looking for Addy."

The woman named Clarisse stared at Sam draped over the horse. "Did you shoot him?"

"No! I fired a warning shot. He already had the wounded guy over the horse," Reuben explained.

"Sam! Reuben, I think that's Sam! Is it?" she demanded, taking one step more down the hill toward the river. The man she'd called Reuben hauled her back.

"Yes, ma'am," McCann said. He was confused by this turn of events but, if the woman could get the rude guy off his back, then that would be fine with him.

"He's got some pretty serious-looking head injuries, and he's probably hypothermic. I need to get him back to camp, but this moron keeps getting in the way!" McCann pointed his rifle at Reuben.

"Who are you?" Clarisse asked.

"Name's McCann. Graham asked me to come up to his camp when I was ready. I got in a few days ago." He shivered because the cold wind had begun to pick up and now made its way through his jacket. "Look, I really need to get this guy back to Graham's camp."

"Graham was missing. Have you seen him?" Clarisse's voice rose over the wind.

"Yeah, he was attacked by some wild dogs. He's back at camp now. He'll be fine after he recovers. I would have brought him back sooner, but I didn't know exactly where the camp was."

Clarisse kept looking back and forth between Reuben and McCann, and McCann inferred they were trying to decide his fate. Perhaps they were trying to make sure his story washed with the current events, or perhaps they were wagering on who would get to kill him first.

To try to speed things along, McCann offered more of an explanation. He yelled, "Then Macy came looking for Graham, and on our way back to camp, someone named Tala radioed to say the kid, Bang, had sneaked off looking for this guy." He pointed to Sam's body. Still there was no reply from the two preppers, who were engaged in their own discussion. "Hey, I don't have time for this, and neither does he. He's getting colder by the second." He began to take a few steps, muttering to himself about the fact that he was tired and didn't have time for this crap, when Reuben broke free of the argument he was having with Clarisse.

"Wait a goddamn minute," Reuben demanded angrily, while Clarisse continued to try and reason with him, attempting to push his rifle barrel down toward the ground.

"No, you look, asshole. I'm trying to save this guy's life. I didn't come all this way to have a girl shoot at me and some fucking Teletubby threatening me. I'll tell you what, I'll be at Graham's if and when you guys make a decision to shoot me or hold a trial, but be prepared for a fight.

"In the meantime, I suggest you stop screwing around and find that little girl. It's cold out here." He led Mae into the river, even though this wasn't the best place to cross. He wanted them to understand he was doing exactly as he said he would. Before long, they had cleared the river, and McCann welcomed the dark forest.

Trekking through the snow in a sterile suit, armed and carrying a backpack with supplies she hoped she would not need, became harder for Clarisse with each step. Every few minutes she called out for Addy in hopes she would say "Here I am!" and be found safe and sound. The day had started to cloud over, and more cold weather was bound to be on the way, yet still no sign of the girl presented itself.

Clarisse had tracked Addy's small boot prints to the river spot, but with no further luck. Peering around the forest edges for any clue that Addy had found refuge near the river, she turned up no trace. Beginning to despair, Clarisse muttered in frustration, "She didn't vanish!" In an attempt to reason logically with herself, she whispered out loud, "She's got to be somewhere nearby." As she was about to admit Rick's desire to inject tracking devices into all of them might have been less foolish than she'd originally thought, her nerves were further shattered by a sudden gunshot. That blast, coming from the east, drove all further thoughts from her mind beyond the imperative: *run.*

Clarisse crushed down fear that the gunshot might have ended Addy's life, running so hard the landscape became a blur in her peripheral vision. No. More likely, Sam's life had just ended. Someone must have found him. Reuben was searching for Addy as well, by now, and if he'd found Sam here, she had little doubt he'd shoot to kill. Sam's presence—any carrier's presence—was a threat to them all. Reuben would not listen to claims of good intention from a man determined to save his daughter. Reuben would see only a threat to the safety of the prepper domain.

When she rounded the bend above the river, Clarisse saw a man draped over a horse. Was he dead? Another man, one she'd never seen before, stood with the horse between himself and Reuben. She thought she was hallucinating. *A horse?* She hadn't expected this, but on the bank well above them, out of likely infection range, Reuben, outfitted in a suit just like hers, pointed his gun at the man. "Don't shoot them, Reuben," she begged. She feared she had little time to convince him. He shook his head at her as if she didn't understand the situation.

"Don't interfere, Clarisse," he advised.

"You're making a mistake, Reuben," she countered as she quickly made her way to him. She recognized the color of Sam's hair, the shape of his head. "I think that's Sam!" she shouted. "Is it?"

The stranger said it was, and spoke of Sam's serious injuries.

Clarisse closed the distance between herself and Reuben. "I need to help him. He's injured."

"No! You're not going anywhere near them, Clarisse. There is no way Dalton would allow you close to them, and I won't either."

She glared at him. As if the threat of Dalton would stop her.

"Look, Reuben, Sam knew his daughter went missing last night. He had injuries already when he started searching for her. I need to make sure he's all right."

"No, Clarisse, I mean it. You take one step toward them, and I'll shoot. We can't lose you to the virus."

"Then let them go." She said it calmly; she knew she had won, could see it in Reuben's eyes. She slowly pushed the business end of his rifle down while Reuben continued to send verbal threats over to the invader.

Whoever this stranger was, he led the horse away across the river, waving good-bye while she continued to try and distract Reuben. He faded into the forest without another glance back.

"What the hell is going on here?" Dalton asked. He had spoken briefly to Rick and Steven after his little boys had fallen asleep, worn out from the nightmare of losing their mother. When he learned of Addy's disappearance during the chaos of the fire, and that Clarisse and Reuben were out now searching for the girl, he pulled his sorry, grief-stricken ass together and went to where he thought the child might be—the bend in the river where she often went to talk to her daddy. He jumped, then froze momentarily as the gunshot rang out.

When he found Reuben and Clarisse arguing, he got right to the point: what was the shooting about? He had already concluded they hadn't found the girl yet.

"Dalton, I stumbled onto this guy with a horse who was over here picking up Sam," Reuben explained. "Sam was injured and unconscious on our side. The young boy, Bang, and his dog were here too. The shot you heard was a warning."

"Was the guy Mark?"

"No," answered Clarisse. "I think the guy might be the boy from Carnation that Graham talked about before. The one he's been checking the post office for. He came to retrieve Sam." She glared at Reuben. "That's all he was doing, and he wasn't close enough to harm any of us."

"We don't know how the fire started last night," Reuben shot back. "Arson at the hands of the carriers might explain it, for all we know."

Dalton held a hand up to silently stifle the accusation. When Reuben simmered down, Dalton said, "No, I'm pretty sure the fire started because of the faulty heaters in the greenhouse. Tammy"—Dalton's voice cracked at the mention of her name—"had trouble with them. I'm an idiot for not insisting on checking them out. She thought the smell was from paint burn-off. What the hell was I thinking?"

Clarisse tried to soothe him. "The fire was no more your fault, Dalton, than it was arson by the carriers. It was an accident," she insisted, flinging another glare at Reuben, who suddenly looked ashamed.

"Yeah, Dalton. Come on, man, you can't do that to yourself," Reuben said, "and I shouldn't have been mouthing off about the carriers. I know one of them's family to you."

Dalton pressed his fingers to his eyes, then looked up. "Our first priority is to find Addy now. Anyone tried to radio the carriers? We need to find out what is going on with them. They know better than to come over here, so they must have had a damn good reason for crossing into our territory. Reuben, don't shoot at them again. Not even warning shots. We've had enough accidents lately, and we can't afford to make enemies of them now. We've lost all of our spring starts and seeds. We might need their help soon."

Reuben didn't argue. With a chastised nod, he acquiesced to Dalton's logic and leadership.

Leadership. Yes. Dalton saw that fact acknowledged in Reuben's face. No matter what, he had to continue leading these people.

"Clarisse, you need to get back to camp," he ordered. "They need you in the infirmary. I'll keep looking for Addy."

"No," she protested with a rapid shake of her head. "Dalton, once I find her, I'll go back to camp, but not a moment sooner. Not until she's safe. She's been out here since midnight." Clarisse pleaded further with her eyes.

He'd expected this reaction, and truly, he didn't blame her. She had become the girl's mother and held the honor like no other.

"All right. Reuben, you go back to camp. Whoever's not injured needs to get supplies together and retrieve the station's four supply trucks. Get the extra tents. Set another crew to sort through the debris, and ask Rick to place a call into Graham's camp for their status and let them know we're still missing Addy. Make sure they understand that if they find her they are not to approach her," Dalton said.

Reuben nodded and began to turn away. Then Dalton added, "Oh, and Reuben. Make sure Rick reiterates that they *cannot* cross the river again. *Any* of them. All they have to do is call us, and we can work our side. We don't want any mishaps."

"You got it, boss." Reuben hesitated a moment before turning away. "Uh, Clarisse? Thanks for intervening. I really didn't want to shoot the young man, but with the fire and the threat of the virus, I was afraid I might have to. I wouldn't want to have to live with that."

Dalton returned his attention to Clarisse. "Where would Addy go, other than the river rendezvous spot?" Right now, this was the only conversation he could have with her.

Clarisse shook her head. "I tracked her to the river, and then, nothing but footprints. She just vanished. She left during the commotion last night. She was scared, I wasn't available, and she ran. She took her coat and wore her boots. I know she came this way, but her tracks ended there by the river. Most of the river is ice, so I don't think she fell in. Oh, God, do you think she crossed and went to the carriers in search of Sam?"

Dalton had already thought of that. "It's sure possible. That's why I want the carriers warned not to go near her if they see her."

He took up his radio. "Rick, Reuben's on his way back. Hey, we're pretty sure Addy has crossed the river to Graham's camp. Call in there immediately. Tell them again to stay away from her if she shows up and to let us know ASAP. Also, someone needs to recheck the cameras in their direction. She might be hiding somewhere over there," Dalton said.

"Got it. I'll call in now," Rick said and added, "Hey, boss, we need Clarisse here. We're trying to move people around, and some of them are still pretty injured. We think Reuben's youngest is still going to need surgery to remove dead tissue that Steven couldn't treat."

Dalton surveyed Clarisse's conflicted expression as she listened to Rick. He knew she would do the right thing. "We'll be back in a few minutes," he said, staring at her and letting the reality sink in. "Dalton out."

"There's nothing more we can do for Addy right now," Dalton said to Clarisse. She'll show up, and we'll take care of things then. Look, I have to get these people moving in the right direction. I need to be able to depend on you, Clarisse. I can't deal with everything all by myself right now."

After a long moment, she looked up at him and let him take her by the arm and guide her back to camp.

"Crap, where's that kid?" McCann said to himself as he led the horse gently up the incline to where Macy waited for him. He didn't think she'd be too happy with him once she found out he had lost Bang and Sheriff after finding them once.

Sure enough, the first thing she said as he came to the rise was, "Where's Bang?"

"Uh, we had a little trouble with your neighbors. I told him to run for the other side of the river, and I thought he'd come back here, but maybe he went back to your camp?"

She didn't have time to question him further after she detected Sam lying unconscious over the mare. "Oh my God! Is he okay?" she asked.

"The only thing I can tell you is he's breathing. Here, help me get him down and into the truck," he said as he grabbed Sam by the back of his waistband. Macy helped to steady him as McCann hefted Sam's weight over his shoulder just briefly enough to walk the four steps to the open back door of the Scout and arranged him on the backseat. Macy tucked a blanket around Sam's stone-cold body.

"Jesus, Sam," she said, seeing his condition.

Once he was settled, Macy grabbed the radio from McCann and called into Bang. "Where are you?" she demanded. McCann listened to her conversation as he readied Mae for their trip to Graham's camp.

"I'm walking back to camp through the forest. I'm halfway home anyway. I thought it would be faster this way. Did that guy get Sam back?"

"Yeah, he did. Are you okay?" she asked more quietly.

"Yes, I'm fine. I just don't want to turn around now, I'm halfway there. I'll see you back at camp. Bang out."

Christ, McCann thought. For a kid of only five, that little guy sounds pretty mature. What a shitty world, where a kindergartener has to grow up so fast.

"He sounded a little irritated," Macy said, but the statement was more of a question to McCann asking what actually went on in the business of retrieving Sam.

"Like I said, we had some trouble with your neighbors." He removed the saddle from the horse and put it in the back of the pickup truck.

"You didn't shoot anyone, did you?"

McCann looked sidelong at her, the toothpick between his teeth moving as he talked. "No, Macy, I didn't, but I should have. I don't know what kind of arrangement you guys have with them, but it's not okay to point rifles and make threats for nothing more than crossing the river to help one of your own. I don't care who you are or what you're carrying. Luckily for him, another Teletubby showed up and talked some sense into him."

She stifled a snicker at the Teletubby comment. With Sam injured in the backseat, they didn't have time to laugh.

"I wish you'd spit out that toothpick," Macy said, sounding crabby. "My dad used to do that. Seeing you do it bothers me." She sniffed and hauled herself up behind the wheel. "Okay, follow me into camp. Let's get Sam home."

By the time Clarisse and Dalton returned to the quarantine building, Reuben had formed a team to retrieve the section 4 supply truck. The stash, hidden in a secure location for contingencies like this, was an ace in the hole. Dalton nodded to Reuben as he passed by, knowing the man had things under control.

When they entered the building, several people still milled around, dazed, while others rested in the cot room, previously the conference room. The lights were off, and the darkness encouraged whispering. Outside, military surplus trucks started up and idled while an occasional yelled direction disturbed the quiet; inside, grieving still reigned for the ones lost in the tragedy. They had come to feel secure in their situation, only to have that precious gift stolen overnight.

"Hey, buddy." Dalton knelt down, level with his youngest son Kade, who walked hand in hand with Bethany as she led him down the hall to the bathroom. The boy's bewilderment, his look of uncertainty, was heartbreaking.

Not fully understanding his loss, but knowing life was now drastically different, the boy looked up at his father. "Mommy's dead," Kade said. His words came as a statement of fact, as if maybe Dalton hadn't been informed.

The raw simplicity of his son's declaration shocked him. Dalton held Kade's hands and brushed his thumbs over the soft skin of his son's grip while trying to find the right words to express what would become a lasting memory for his son. "Yes. Mommy died last night. We will miss her very much." The tears came forth for both of them as Dalton quietly uttered the words. He drew the child into his arms, only dimly aware that Clarisse was ushering Bethany away to give them privacy. He held Kade tightly, and the boy allowed himself to be hugged as, with ragged sorrow, his father wept into his small neck.

Clarisse wanted to help, but she was powerless against Dalton's immense loss. She wished, somehow, she could bring back Kim to ease the broken hearts of this devastated family. Though she had disliked Kim, had found her cold and been angered by her treatment of Addy, she'd never have wished for something like this. Even as, last night, she'd thought to spread a sheet over the dead woman's body, she'd felt she did it out of some kind of guilt.

It's ironic, Clarisse thought. *You never really know, in life, who will be the one to do this kindness for you when you die.* She never would have guessed she'd be the one to do this for Kim. It was a morbid honor, being the last one to see Kim, with all her flaws and all her beauty, and then to view her with compassion, to shield her deadness with a cloak from the eyes of the living before decay set in. Even though she'd felt Kim was as selfish as might be socially acceptable, and she'd resented her for imposing that selfishness on a child, she still wished there was a way to bring her back—for Dalton, for his boys, for the camp itself.

Kim's enthusiasm for life would be missed by many. And for those reasons, Clarisse regretted losing her to death.

As soon as Steven saw that Clarisse had arrived, he bombarded her with details of injuries that needed her expertise, then stopped for a moment to ask about Addy's whereabouts. When she told him she hadn't found her yet, he said, "I'm really sorry she hasn't turned up. Thank you for coming back. While you're working, I'll let you know if any news comes in."

"Thanks," Clarisse said. Reuben's youngest daughter's foot injuries were the worst, so she started with her. The nine-year-old girl, Lawoaka, held herself stoically as Clarisse numbed several points around her injury and began the process of removing first a bit of tissue that would never heal properly because there was no circulation to it. She avoided the large blister rising in the center of Lawoaka's arch and applied silver sulfadiazine to the affected area. After loosely bandaging the wound, she spoke to the girl's mother. "I know the burn looks bad right now, but it should heal up well. Other than the one spot, the remaining area is just a second-degree burn. We need to watch the area for infection, and she needs to keep her foot elevated. Absolutely no walking on it." Steven had already fitted Lawoaka with a pair of crutches, and the girl was in good spirits despite her injury.

"It could have been so much worse," Lavinda, Reuben's wife, said. "We were so lucky."

Lucky? Clarisse wondered how much luck they still harbored. Apparently luck had a shelf life, and to her mind it had expired.

Clarisse heard Rick's voice coming from down the hall. He relayed the information to Dalton about the carriers, and she wondered what he had learned about Addy. When Rick muttered to Dalton, words not intended for Clarisse to hear, "The girl's as good as dead," Clarisse nearly fainted.

Sheriff slowed by Bang's side, his attention suddenly focused forward, one forepaw lifted midway. The forest darkened up ahead, but this was familiar, even welcome. When the dog went to attention, his rigid pose alerted Bang to pending danger. He wrapped a fist in Sheriff's thick ruff and stood as still as the dog.

Sheriff's low, deep-throated growl seemed too immense for his lean body. Scared, Bang began to back away, but a muffled cry brought him back to a standstill. That didn't sound like an animal; it sounded like a person. The small, frightened whimper came again, and Bang realized there was no beast in the trees, but maybe the little girl Sam had gone looking for on the other side. Nothing else made sense. Girls didn't just turn up in a winter forest. "Hey, girl!" Bang yelled. Sheriff sank back on his haunches.

For the life of him Bang couldn't remember her name. "Hey, *girl!*" he called more loudly, since no one had responded. Sheriff sat panting next to him, with an occasional glance at Bang as if questioning the reason for the delay.

Addy's head appeared, peeking around a large cypress trunk farther up the deer path, but she ducked back out of sight just as quickly, and Bang began to wonder if he had seen her at all. "Hey, are you Sam's daughter?" he yelled.

She peeked out again. "Where is he? Where is my dad?" Her voice wasn't very loud, and Bang could tell she was crying. "Do you know Sam?" she asked.

"Yeah," Bang said cautiously, because he remembered something important. Sam had come to stay with them because he was a carrier now. The rest of the details didn't interest a five-year-old. He didn't keep track of adult conversations very much, but he heeded what Graham had taught him. One of the biggest rules said to stay away from the preppers because they were still susceptible to the virus. "Are you a carrier?" he asked the girl.

It seemed to him she took too long to answer, as if she was trying to decide to tell the truth or not. Finally, she said, "I don't know. Do you know where my dad is?"

Bang was suspicious; she had taken too long to answer the question. Graham had taught him better. "Yeah," he said again. "He got hurt. A man on a horse came and took him to our camp."

"A horse? My daddy's hurt? How? I want to see him."

"Well, I'll show you where he is, but you have to stay far away from me. I don't want to give you the virus if you don't have it already. So come on. Walk that way," he told her and pointed the way for her to go well ahead of him through the trees.

Sheriff stayed right at Bang's side as they kept their distance from the girl, who continued to look back every few minutes to make sure she was going in the right direction. Bang wasn't used to talking to young girls, so he shyly pointed or nodded his head when she looked at him.

Bang watched her stagger a bit as she walked, and she shivered whenever the wind snaked its way through the trees, lifting her long, matted hair. He was sure she would fall over soon. "Hey, girl. Maybe you should stay here, and I'll go get someone," he cautioned her. "You don't walk very well."

"No, I'm going where he is. And my name is *Addy*," she yelled back at him.

She appeared to be upset, and pouting. Bang just shook his head; he would never understand girls. Mark had told him they were often unreasonable, and so far he had found that statement to be true. Marcy, in particular, drove Bang crazy, and he didn't understand why Mark "*like-* liked" her.

Finally they came to the area where their trail would skirt the edge of the frozen lake and then lead right, and up to the path to camp. She looked back at him, and Bang yelled, "Go right!" He pointed, but as she began to traverse the ice-covered boulders leading up around the lake edge, she stumbled and fell over the side, completely out of Bang's sight.

He and Sheriff ran over to her, and, as they climbed up a small cliff, Sheriff began to bark, looking downward. She had fallen through the ice and in the lake and was sinking into the shallow, freezing waters.

Bang peered over the edge, trying to be careful to keep his distance, and she only lay there in the water. She wasn't even trying to get out. This made no sense to him, and he briefly contemplated the importance of keeping his distance, balanced with her drowning, until Sheriff scrambled down the rock face. Bang teetered at the top.

He gazed toward camp, uncertain of what to do. If he got nearer to her, she might catch the virus, but if he did not take action, she would drown or freeze right there before him.

Sheriff looked up at him, prancing on his paws. He barked at Bang for his inaction, as if to say, "Do something, man!"

Bang waded out into the frigid waters, through the broken ice, and pulled Addy's face up out of the shallow water. He gripped her pink jacket and dragged her over to the shore. She was freezing cold and turning blue. Panicked, he pulled her up over to the forest edge, where she would be safe from the now open water where her fall had broken the ice. Sheriff licked at her face and jumped around in a panic. Bang stared down at her. There was no way he could carry her the rest of the way to camp. She was taller than him by at least three inches. He listened for her breathing like he had listened to Sam's chest earlier that morning, but instead of the heartbeat he expected, only a void remained where her jacket soaked his ear.

The only thing he could do was run the short distance to the camp and get help. The girl might die one way or the other, but there was a chance she would live if he could get help fast. Sheriff seemed to have the same idea as he ran ahead, barking madly.

Macy pulled the truck to a halt and watched as McCann came in behind her, with the horses ambling at the back of the pickup. Mark, on his feet but pretty unsteady, came out onto the porch. Macy greeted him and opened the back door of the Scout as McCann stepped out and waved a greeting at him.

Sam had regained consciousness, complaining of a pounding headache on the bumpy drive home; Macy had kept reassuring him they would be there soon. He shook heavily with the cold, and she suspected hypothermia, though she was no expert in these matters. He had kept asking about Addy's whereabouts, and she didn't have an answer for him. She warred with herself. Should she confess they hadn't found her yet or pretend everything was okay so he would calm down?

Once Macy opened the back door, he tried to sit up, and she had to press him down. "Sam, wait. Let me get some help. You can't even walk—"

She was interrupted by Sheriff bolting toward her, barking frantically. McCann looked alarmed, ready to leap into the Scout and away from the dog. "He's not after you!" Macy shouted as McCann pulled his pistol. Macy scanned the horizon; something was obviously wrong if it had set Sheriff off like this.

Bang, panting, emerged from the woods right after the dog. "She fell in!" he shouted. "Help, she fell through! We have to help her. *Hurry!*" he screamed angrily, as Macy only stared at him, trying to figure out what he was yelling about, but Bang's frantic cries and the dog's racing first to her, then back toward the trail, got her moving.

"Hurry, she fell through!" Bang kept repeating, his breath rasping out in sobbing coughs. "I know I shouldn't have gone near, but she fell through the ice. She was gonna drown, Macy!"

As Macy caught up, she yelled to him, "Bang, wait!" But she knew it was already too late. The exposure rule had been thoroughly violated at this point. If the child was Addy—and who else could it be?—and she hadn't died of hypothermia or from drowning, she might die of the virus. She watched as Bang bent down beside the small body lying on the icy earth. Addy's face already had a blue cast, and her pink coat was soaked with lake water and draped in lake scum.

"Is that Addy?" Macy gasped. "She can't be exposed to us." By the looks of her, the child was dead; she bled from a cut on her forehead, and her lips were deep blue.

"Yes, hurry. She fell through." Bang gestured with his little hand as he leaned over her body and cried as if he were responsible for her death and admitting a wrongful deed. Macy stood shaking her head in horror for the girl, Sam and, ultimately, Bang.

McCann caught up to Macy, skidded to a halt, and dropped down beside her, Bang, and the too-still child. "Is it always like this here?" he asked incredulously.

Macy stared mutely at the little girl on the ground, then gaped at McCann when he pushed her aside and bent over Addy.

"It's a little too late to worry about exposure now," he muttered. He checked Addy's neck for a pulse, which Macy realized should have been her first move.

Without hesitation McCann began CPR. Macy took off her own coat and draped it around Addy. McCann checked again for a pulse. "Got one," he said, as if to himself. "Weak, but it's there." He pushed on Addy's thin chest with only the fingers of his hands, and puffed every few moments into her mouth and nose.

When Addy coughed and turned her head away, he said, "That a girl," then scooped her up, adding his jacket to Macy's, and rushing up the trail. "Hurry, let's get her inside. She might have a chance!" he yelled.

Macy ran ahead to let the others know and to clear a space for the girl. They would need to get her warmed up as soon as possible. As she ran, her heart broke for Sam. His daughter had certainly been exposed now, and, if they managed to save her, her life might not be a long one. She could die of the virus in the next few days even if they managed to save her from the drowning. Macy consoled herself in the thought that at least Sam would get to say good-bye to her.

As Macy neared the clearing, Sam was being helped out of the truck by Mark and Marcy, the two men hobbling together. Sam saw Macy's shocked face as she stopped and stared at him; she didn't have time to warn him. McCann came into the clearing with Sam's daughter in his arms, draped in death's blue cast; he rushed her into the house, disregarding any obstacles. McCann never acknowledged Sam's alert presence; he focused only on the girl.

"No!" Sam yelled in terrible anguish. "No!" he screamed again, and the sound of it ripped through Macy. Tala held the door open as McCann barreled through with his burden, the expression on her face saying she couldn't believe that one more tragedy could enter their home today.

"Oh, my God! Addy," she said, as Macy pushed in beside McCann.

"Shut that door. Lock it. Keep Sam out for now." He looked at Macy. "Where?"

"Living room. Warmest." She shoved him in that direction.

"I said lock the door!" McCann yelled as he hurriedly laid Addy down on the couch. "Blankets!" he yelled to Macy, just before he began CPR on the girl once again.

Tala complied and pushed in both latches as Sam stumbled up the front steps. She turned to back to Addy and began removing the girl's sodden boots and socks and rubbing her blue feet, hoping she was more than the corpse she appeared to be. Addy's whole frame jerked with the effort of the adults to save her life. While Macy tossed and tucked more blankets around her, McCann gave her CPR, and Tala worked on removing her clothing. The whole time Tala yelled, "Come on, baby! *Breathe!*"

Macy picked up the chant. *"Breathe, Addy! Breathe!"*

Sam broke away from Mark and pounded on the cabin door, screaming for his child. Mark himself only stood by pure will, gazing in shock at the scene while, along with Marcy, he recklessly strained to hold Sam back. Marcy wept, "Sam, Sam, please don't! You're hurting yourself. They have her. They'll save her! You can't help!" But the enraged father continued to battle all restraint.

Bang clung to Mark's legs, also crying. "I—I had to pull her out. She fell in. I didn't know what to do. I'm sorry, Sam, I'm sorry."

McCann bent to repeat the breathing in the little girl's mouth when a watery choking sounded from Addy's throat. She struggled, and McCann turned her over to her side, where she expelled water. Most glorious of all, her eyes blinked open wide as she looked at McCann almost questioningly.

She coughed out more water and cried, "Dad-dee!"

Outside, Sam heard his daughter's voice. The door flew open, and he stumbled through, his broken heart swelling, healing, as he dropped to his knees beside Addy. He reached for her, held her, crushed her to him as she coughed and cried. It was the sweetest sound he'd ever heard, the greatest gift, having her skinny arms wrapping around his neck, however feebly she clung. He knew he shouldn't give in to the selfish desire to have her back with him, even if only for a little while, but he couldn't help himself.

"Daddy! Daddy!" Addy cried again and again between spasmodic coughs. A strange man helped Tala keep blankets around her, and Sam shoved the man's hands back.

"Get away, from her!" Sam wrapped her tighter in his arms, half turning as he spoke.

McCann stepped back. "If it's exposure you're worried about, it's too late for that, Sam."

Dimly, Sam wondered who this man was, and how he knew his name, but none of that outweighed the need to simply hold his little girl, feel the icy cold of her skin as he pressed kisses to her face. She was so cold! Why had they taken her clothes off?

The man snapped out orders. "Close that door. Get this room as warm as possible. Heat water and fill containers to put under the covers beside them."

Sam grew aware of being pulled by the arms to sit on the couch with Addy on his lap. "Take your jacket off," McCann commanded. He didn't know why, but the man seemed to be in charge, and Sam complied, though doing so hurt his chest wound. "Now your shirt. Hold your daughter against your skin. Come on, man. We're fighting hypothermia, here."

Macy tucked more blankets around them both, and then Tala was there with something that felt hot against his skin as she tucked a towel-wrapped object in beside Addy, then another on the other side. Within the pile of blankets around them, he felt his daughter begin to shiver.

"Ah . . . good," McCann said. "Now, something warm for her to drink. We'll heat her from the inside, too."

~ ~ ~

Graham hung in the doorway, watching the scene unfold in the living room as others saved Addy from the effects of cold and drowning. As Tala ran to the kitchen, she saw him and stopped, staring at him. "What are you doing up?"

"Need to use . . . radio. Call . . . Dalton," he slurred. It had felt like miles from his bed to the radio desk, but he'd made it. He'd had to.

"You and Sam," Tala said, with both admiration and admonition in her voice. "You guys, you pull fumes from adrenaline."

Graham leaned on the side of the desk. "Rick, come in. This is Graham. Do you copy? Over."

"This is Rick." The voice cracked out of the receiver. "Did you say *Graham*? Over."

"Yeah." He didn't know how much longer he could stay on his feet. "We found Addy. Alive."

There was a pause. "Is she hurt?"

"She fell through the lake ice." Graham tried to keep his voice steady, but the effort of being upright and imparting the bad news made his voice wobble. "She's alive, but she's been exposed, Rick. It doesn't look good. Over."

"Oh, Jesus!" Rick said. "I'll tell Clarisse right away. Maybe she can do something to help."

"We're really sorry, man. There was no time to wait for one of you to come here, and Bang . . . well, he had to get her out of the water."

"No, no, I understand. Stay tuned. I'm sure Clarisse will want to talk to you. Rick out."

Clarisse watched the doorway as the voices got louder, heading her direction. Dread built within her, a feeling she often found herself vulnerable to after becoming a surrogate mother. Somehow she sensed what she was about to learn would cut a hole clean through her heart. Becoming vulnerable was a price she would gladly pay again to have loved this child as her own.

She hardened her resolve as Dalton entered the room with Rick right behind him. Dalton's expression told her everything she dreaded and more.

"Clarisse. Rick got the call from Graham. They found Addy."

"Is she—?" The words would not come.

"She's alive. She fell through the ice. She's been exposed, Clarisse. They had to expose her, they didn't have a choice."

"I need to go to her," she said quickly. She began to grab necessary items out of refrigeration and put them into her backpack.

Rick glanced at Dalton as if pleading with him to step in, to make Clarisse wait and listen to reason. Dalton moved into the center of the doorway. Rick joined him.

Clarisse knew what they were doing but donned her backpack anyway. She took along another sterile suit. When she met them at the door, and they didn't budge, she said the one thing she knew would get them out of her way.

"If you don't let me go, I won't develop the vaccine." She made the threat in an ominous and level tone. She meant it. "I'll leave here and go off on my own."

Dalton put a hand on her shoulder. "What can you do for her, Clarisse? She's been exposed. You, of all people, know what that means."

"There's only one thing I can do for her now, and that's give her the working trial. It needs time to develop the antibodies, but so does the virus. Hopefully she inherited some of Sam's immunity. If I get the vaccine to her now, she might have a fighting chance. Otherwise, she won't. Now, move."

She made that demand, looking Rick in the eye rather than Dalton. Rick not only moved right away but offered to go with her.

Dalton interrupted him. "No, they need you here, Rick. Please go ahead and tell Graham that Clarisse and I are on the way."

"No," Clarisse protested. "You can't go, Dalton. Your sons need you. All the preppers need you."

"Clarisse, I'm coming with you. Rick will tell them. They can minimize the risk. I can't let anything happen to you. Please don't take any more chances than necessary. We need you," and then, in a lower tone, added, "*I* need you."

She saw the pain this admission caused him. Despite his grief, maybe even because of it, Dalton needed to keep her close to him now. She was not alone in her fears for Addy, and he'd never leave her to face such a possible loss without him by her side.

"They're coming," Macy announced, out of breath, in the doorway as she and McCann had finally put the frozen deer carcass away in the greenhouse and walked in from the front door to the bunkroom.

"Why are you letting them come here?" McCann asked for the second time as the rest of them sat silent. He wondered what the preppers' arrival meant and why they took such a chance. There was nothing anyone could do to save the girl at this point, he figured; she was going to die no matter what anyone tried to do. From McCann's experience, once they were exposed the noncarriers always died, despite medical attention.

So why did I fight so hard to keep her alive after her near drowning? McCann couldn't answer his own question. He'd known exposure to any of them meant death to the little girl, but instinct, he supposed, had driven him. A life was in danger. His automatic response had been to save it.

"Rick said Clarisse has something they think might save her. We have to give them room, so we don't risk exposing them, even though they are wearing those suits. Graham, what do we do?" Macy asked. "Stay in the bunkroom?"

McCann couldn't believe this. One of them had threatened him with a gun and, worse, would have killed a little kid just for stepping across a small river. He whirled toward Graham. "You don't seriously trust them, do you?"

Sam didn't give Graham an opportunity to respond. "*I* trust them. Dalton's a good man, and Clarisse is a scientist. If she's got something to help my daughter, they're welcome to bring it." He returned his attention to Addy as Tala and Marcy brought more hot containers wrapped in towels to replace the ones that had cooled.

"We trust them, McCann," Graham said. "They have more reason to fear us than we do them. They don't have the virus. They never have had. If they've decided to come here, they are the ones in danger. We will all remain in the bunkroom while they're here, and let them help Addy in any way they can."

McCann huffed, but he trusted Graham, and if the man said yes, then he would comply. In his short time with these people he had already come to care for them. Especially Macy; he didn't want anything to happen to her. He knew Graham was right about the preppers' tremendous risk coming here, despite their biohazard suits. They must feel like they were walking through the valley of death. Their willingness to do so certainly said something of their character if coming was only to help save this little girl who would die in three to five days' time anyway.

~ ~ ~

Clarisse rushed over to Addy, and Dalton took one look at Graham sitting at the far end of the bunkroom on a dining room chair with his injured leg propped up on another. "Where's Mark?" he asked.

Marcy pointed down at him, where he lay on his bunk. Dalton took one look at his young cousin, used the back of his gloved hand to wipe condensation off his face screen, and strode in to survey the damage. "What in the hell happened to you people?"

"Oh, you know. Tangled with the locals," Graham said with a shrug.

Dalton used his gloved hand to stroke the bruising on Mark's face.

"I'm all right, Dalton." Mark's voice held little power.

"Like hell. *Look* at you, Primo! You're a mess," Dalton said, staring at Mark's neck. "You look like someone tried to slit your throat."

"Yeah. That was Sam. So I wouldn't suffocate. Marcy, show him my straw."

"No. And you quit talking," she said. "Dalton, he had to have a field tracheotomy, his neck was swelled so bad. He got beat up by an old woman with a big club."

"Jesus!" Dalton's voice went high.

"Things happen," Mark whispered. "I hear you guys had a fire. What happened there?" he asked, still barely audible.

Dalton nodded. "Yeah, things happen. Um, we lost several." He dropped his gaze. "Kim, too, from smoke inhalation."

Mark's eyes widened, and he tried to sit up. Dalton laid a gentle hand on the boy's shoulder. "No . . . don't, Mark." He wanted to move the conversation along without bringing more attention to his loss.

Disregarding the risk, Dalton said, "I'll get Clarisse to examine you as soon as she's done with Addy." He turned half around. "Your leg looks pretty bad, Graham. Did you wake up a bear or something?"

"Just a pack of wild dogs. McCann, here, shot them for me." Graham's eyes misted over for a moment. "Dalton, I'm sorry to hear about Kim. I do know what that's like."

"Yeah," Dalton acknowledged. "I know you do."

"How are your boys?" Graham asked.

"They're as expected, man. They're young. They don't understand yet. Hell, I don't get it yet. I fell asleep in the spare partition, the next thing I knew . . . Steven . . ." He shook his head as the memories from the prior night flooded in. "It's hard, man." He turned and went back to the living room. He didn't want to talk about it.

Clarisse looked up at him, tears she couldn't wipe away streaking her face inside the hood of her suit. She understood his awkwardness and, to move things along, she offered a diversion. "I gave her the first injection," she said. "Now all we can do is hope."

"First injection?"

"Yes. I've developed a vaccine. We hope to be administering vaccinations in another week."

Clarisse stroked her gloved hand down the side of Addy's pale face and slid her wet hair back. Tendrils of it had just begun to dry. "With Dalton's permission, Addy just got the first one."

"You mean, you won't be susceptible to the virus anymore?" Tala asked.

"That's right. It will be another month, but I'll test everyone, and if they have sufficient antibodies, then, we will be basically like you—carriers."

Everyone digested this in awed silence. Graham was the first to speak. "That's amazing news!"

Dalton only nodded. "Time will tell." He wasn't ready yet to accept anything good. This all seemed like some sick dream he hoped would wake up from soon.

Sam said, "Dalton, Clarisse told me. About Kim. I'm . . . sorry, man."

"Yeah." Dalton looked downward; it was the only way to divert attention from his own pain. He was grateful to Clarisse when she stood and moved off to take care of Graham's and Mark's wounds.

"Well, this looks a little infected," she said, and everyone's attention turned to Graham. "But, for the size of the wound, I'd say you were lucky." She began pulling items out of her bag. Graham sucked in his breath a time or two as Clarisse cleaned up the wound and added a topical antibiotic. "Whoever sewed you up did a great job, considering. You must have lost a lot of blood."

"It was our new resident, McCann. He's come in quite handy since he got here."

"Your injury, our fire, Addy's misadventure. That's quite a string of unlucky events," Dalton commented.

"Yeah, but that's not all. First, the hunting trip ran into some trouble with someone who, unfortunately, was a little too far gone in this world to deal with the living. Then, I went into town to find something I thought I'd need and got myself attacked in the process, only to be saved by McCann."

Clarisse listened to the men talk as she examined the hole in Mark's trachea. She finished closing it; it had started to seal up on its own, but needed a little help. She applied new bandages. He would have scarring, but the swelling was sufficiently down.

Then she checked on Ennis, who slept through their ongoing conversations. His pulse was steady, and she listened to his heart and lungs. She nodded and smiled at Tala, who looked at her questioningly to confirm that the meds were doing their work.

Finally she turned her attention to Sam, who only let her take his daughter from his arms long enough for her to check out the knife slash on his chest and make sure the back of his head was only bruised, not caved in. Right now the only thing that could be done for Graham, Mark, and Sam was to let them rest. They should all be in bed to let their bodies do the work needed to heal them, along with the aid of antibiotics, in Graham's case. Sam just needed a lot of rest and the reassurance Addy was safe, for now.

Clarisse could only hope that Addy would not come down with the virus at all. Only a few days would tell them for certain. Having done everything that she could do, Clarisse hugged Addy one last time and told Tala to call her several times a day with updates. With a last good-bye, Dalton led Clarisse out of the cabin and back to their own side of the Skagit River, where they had many other crises to deal with.

Sweat poured off Graham's forehead as Tala mopped it with a cool, damp towel. It had been a long night for the both of them. Once again, Macy arrived with a pail full of clean snow.

Tala smiled at her. "That should be enough for now."

"Is he going to be okay?" Macy sounded scared. The hand she placed on Tala's shoulder had a tremor.

Tala gave her a reassuring pat on the arm. "Yes, I think so. He's over the worst part. The meds are kicking in now. So, you go get some sleep for now. I'll need you to take over for me in the morning."

Macy walked away quietly and climbed into her bunk with Sheriff by her side. She gazed over at McCann, sleeping with his hat over his eyes. He snored, finally getting the sleep he'd needed for so long. As her own eyes closed, she prayed to God that Graham would pull through. She was afraid to go on without him. He had become more to her than even her own father had ever been, though Graham was much younger than her own dad. They all needed him in their lives—even McCann, though he wasn't aware of it yet.

~ ~ ~

Tala held Graham's hand while she sat by his side. She glanced around the room where they now had no beds to spare. Everyone was in a state of sleep or dreaming, and she would stay up through the night for them. Graham's fever had broken, and she now waited to see if he might wake up and open his eyes or ask for water.

As soon as the preppers had left the day before, Tala and McCann had put Graham back to bed. His fever spiked again. The few times he was conscious, they hadn't spoken about his trip into town. She searched his pockets for Ennis's meds and found them along with the others. She gave the pain meds to Ennis, and then set the others on Graham's side table. He'd see them when he was well again, and then they'd have the necessary discussion.

Soon, though, Tala had to watch in horror as Addy fought the first signs of the virus they all recognized from past loved ones lost. She held her hand over the new life that grew within her, having second thoughts about Graham's wishes. Would it be kinder to terminate this child?

Tala stared off into space across the light of the lamp on the radio table. They had come so far, living in the ways of the past. No one knew about tomorrow yet; no one had time to worry about it. They were all too busy relearning the lore of yesterday in order to survive.

"Tala," Graham said, startling her. "Where's my jacket?"

"I . . . put it away."

"And the pills from the pockets?" he asked, his voice low.

She wasn't ready for this. She feared seeing Addy fight the virus, a battle Tala was pretty sure Addy would lose despite Clarisse's vaccine. Would she still have the strength to argue with him when he asked her to take the pills that would destroy her unborn baby?

Tala shifted her glance to the box on the tableside.

He stared at her deeply while she retrieved what he wanted her to take. He held his hand out for the box and turned the foil packs out into his hand. He began popping the pills out one by one into his hand, creating a mini pyramid. He reached for her hand, dropped them all in and closed her fingers over them. He gazed at her and reached up a hand to brush away the tears streaming down her cheeks. "Get rid of these," he whispered.

She saw fear in his eyes, but a resolve too. She said nothing, only nodded, and went to the woodstove, where she tossed the handful within. She went back to Graham, and he reached for her hand once more and pulled her to him on the bunk. "We'll give life a chance," he said, and then kissed her.

Tala placed her head on his chest to listen to his heartbeat as he held her and stroked her long hair by candlelight. He wiped her tears away again, and laid his hand over the place where the new life grew within her like a promise.

As daylight broke, Graham inched away from Tala on the single bed they'd somehow managed to share during the night. He gazed down at her sleeping peacefully, knowing the child she carried was their creation. He marveled at the mercies he had somehow managed to attain when so many had lost everything.

As he hobbled on his one good leg while buttoning his shirt for the day, he looked around at the growing residents of Graham's camp. They were over capacity now, and he wanted to check on the two that were on his mind the most: Addy and Ennis.

After he made his way over to the living room and checked the child's forehead for fever, he stood shaking his head. Her little lungs labored and it seemed she would only become closer to losing the battle as the day went on. Graham thought she might have two, maybe three days left. He couldn't help but gauge these things after having cared for so many before and losing those he loved. Her one free hand lay open; even while she fought for breath, she looked like a small, accepting angel.

Sam, of course, held her other hand tucked in his larger one as he slept by her. His other hand held that of the little boy who had pulled her from an icy death, only to suffer the guilt of sealing her fate through his heroism.

The whole situation sucked, and Graham suspected that when the girl passed, Bang would need saving too. Graham rubbed the boy's head lightly and went to see his old friend Ennis, who'd wandered into the living room and sat in his chair at some point during the night. Graham placed another log gingerly into the woodstove, like so many times before, to keep the old man warm. Ennis had an arrow lying in his lap, whittled down straight with his pocketknife in his hands, and his eyes were closed.

Two days later, Graham nudged Sam. "Sam. Sam. It's my turn to watch over her. You go get some real sleep." Sam had only left Addy's side once between coffee refills.

"No, no. I'm not leaving her."

"You're exhausted. Please, go lie down on my bunk just for an hour or two. I swear I'll wake you up if anything changes," Graham promised.

"No." Exhaustion slurred Sam's words. "I'll stay'n sleep 'side her. You . . . keep watch. Okay?"

Graham conceded, and brought him a pillow and blanket so Sam might at least fall asleep in a little more comfort. Graham eased himself into a nearby chair with the aid of a cane Ennis had fashioned from a sturdy branch.

Now they held vigil together over the dying child. It had been touch and go many times. They'd even put tubes down her throat to keep her airway open. Clarisse had been back and forth each day, with McCann escorting her on horseback. They'd brought one of the bunks into the living room for Addy, pushing furniture aside to make room.

Clarisse said that while Addy's treacherous fever had begun to come down, she'd slipped into some kind of coma. As she tried to explain it to them, Addy's body had been ravaged by the virus, and Clarisse theorized that the vaccine, and whatever immunity she might have inherited from Sam, could be waging a war inside her. It would take a toll, though in what form was anyone's guess. At worst, Clarisse explained through tears, Addy might sustain severe brain damage. At best, she would have a very long recovery and, possibly, come through physically crippled. Only time would tell.

~ ~ ~

The night before, Graham had finally managed to get Clarisse to take a break, and McCann had taken her back to Dalton. She was so tired when they arrived, she hadn't the energy to move. Dalton met McCann at the river bend and slid Clarisse's nearly unconscious form into his own arms. Then, instead of taking her to her tent, he'd carried her into his new quarters where he laid her down on his own bed so he could at least keep her safe in her sleep. He'd lost interest in what the others in camp might think of the arrangement.

The prepper camp was back to functioning fully after Reuben and Rick had retrieved the contingency supply trucks and set everything up again. They buried their dead and, after the loss of their spring seedlings, were scrambling to start fresh as the snow finally began to melt and it was clear spring was setting in.

Somehow Graham had fallen asleep in his vigil during the night. Ennis sat in the opposite chair sleeping while he held the little girl's hand. Graham grunted as he got up and went to the window, opening the curtains. The room was bathed in a spring sunrise, and it lessened the sense of doom they'd all been under for so long.

He stared out the open window as the birds chirped and sang their songs while flitting between the trees. He glanced behind him at Addy, whose labored breathing he didn't hear any longer.

"Oh, no," he whispered with sudden dread. He went to her side, afraid to touch her again. He reached out his hand once and stopped, then decided he had to know. He touched her neck and felt warmth. She fluttered her eyes open, and the sweetest thing Graham had ever witnessed happened before him. She smiled.

"Sam! Sam, wake up!" Graham bumped his sleeping form but refused to take his eyes off Addy.

"What?" Sam said, jerking up, eyes wide with apprehension.

Graham nodded his head toward the child. "Someone wants to see you."

Sam leapt to her side. "Addy? Baby?" Sam whispered hoarsely.

"Daddy!" Addy said.

Sam dissolved into tearful gratitude.

Soon laughter and cheers rang throughout the cabin. Tala and the others ran into the living room to finally witness some small victory over the China Pandemic.

While jubilation held everyone in its joyful thrall, Graham noticed an odd stillness in Ennis's body. He made his way around Addy's bed and lowered himself beside the old man's chair. "Ennis," he said. "Oh, Ennis."

Macy noticed. She gasped, "Oh no!" and joined him.

Graham didn't have to check Ennis's pulse. He knew the peaceful look of death, but he picked up Ennis's wrist to be sure. "Damn, Ennis, you didn't even say good-bye." Graham cried and held the old man's body to him. Graham couldn't hold back the sob rising high in his chest, emerging on a harsh utterance of the old man's name.

Macy moaned, "No! Not yet!"

One month later, spring bloomed in full. The welcome sun shone and wildflowers blossomed. Though it was still cold enough for jackets, the members of Graham's camp shed their winter coats to make the journey across the new footbridge built over the Skagit River into prepper territory.

Dalton and Clarisse, who no longer wore their biohazard suits, greeted them. "Hey, I never thought this would happen. Did you?" Graham asked as he shook Dalton's bare hand. "You're sure it's okay?"

"Yes, yes," Clarisse responded to the question. "I've tested everyone twice. We're no longer susceptible to the virus." She held out her arms when she saw Addy coming across the bridge.

Addy broke into a run when she caught sight of her. Clarisse hugged her tightly and, when she pulled away, finally she smiled at the girl and held up her hand to sign, I LOVE YOU, then touched the top of Addy's nose, making her smile. Addy signed the sentiment back, her little fingers forming the words. She'd survived the virus, but without her hearing, which everyone thought a small price to pay for her life. Clarisse had given them some hope that the hearing might return someday, but they had all begun to learn sign language anyway.

Tala presented the wagon full of vegetable starts that Bang had pulled the long distance for them. It was their gift to the preppers who had lost their starts in the fire, along with precious lives.

"Thank you," Dalton said.

Mark made his way through the crowd to greet his cousin. Dalton hugged him for the first time since before the China Pandemic had hit. Mark was nearly as tall, and he was filling in fast and would pass Dalton up soon.

Bang hung back, shyly, and Graham pulled him along using the excuse he needed assistance with his cane. Macy pulled McCann along, because he still wasn't terribly trusting of these new people and wanted to have a running start and enough time to get Macy out of there fast if the need arose.

The whole group stood and talked with Dalton and Clarisse for a few minutes before Dalton began to lead the way to their camp where an enticing aroma awaited them. Sam held a backpack over his shoulder because this would be a one-way trip for him and Addy, though they were always welcome at Graham's camp. Sam wanted Addy to be able to visit with Clarisse whenever she wanted to; their relationship had become one of mother and daughter, and Sam was grateful for that. He would never deny his daughter a chance at a second mother, especially one who had risked her own life to save Addy's.

Once they reached the inner compound, they were greeted by the entire prepper community. Rick held out his arms and yelled, "Twin Two!"

"Macy!" she huffed, and walked over to him to shake his hand, but he would not have it. He hugged her instead, and she shook her head with an embarrassed grin. Tala had made a cake, a rare treat for the twins' sixteenth birthday.

After their celebratory meal of barbecue turkey and dressing made with wild green onions and canned yams, sans the marshmallows, they sang "Happy Birthday" to the twins and toasted their many achievements, which were great, and paid homage to their lost ones, those they would always remember.

Together, the twins cut the cake into over thirty tiny portions.

It was the best cake any of them could ever remember.

To be among the first to learn about new releases, announcements and special projects, please contact Author A. R. Shaw at www.AuthorARShaw.com.

Please consider writing a review for *The Cascade Preppers* on Amazon. Even a quick word about your experience can be helpful to prospective readers.

The author welcomes any comments, feedback or questions.

A. R. Shaw is the author of *The China Pandemic, The Cascade Preppers, The Last Infidels,* and *Deception on Durham Road,* a Kindle Worlds commissioned novella based on characters of author Steven Konkoly's series The Perseid Collapse.

Website and Blog: AuthorARShaw
Twitter: @ARShawAuthor
Facebook: ARShaw Author

A. R. Shaw, born in south Texas, served in the U.S. Air Force Reserve from 1987 through 1991 as a communications radio operator, where she was stationed at the Military Auxiliary Radio System (MARS) Station at Kelly Air Force Base, Texas.

Her first novel, *The China Pandemic* (2013), climbed to number 1 in the dystopian and post-apocalyptic (SHTF) genres in May 2014 and was hailed as "eerily plausible" and with characters that are "amazingly detailed." Shaw continues to write the Graham's Resolution series.

Shaw lives with her family in eastern Washington State where, after the deep snow of winter finally gives way to the glorious rays of summer, she treks northeast to spend her days writing alongside the beautiful Skagit River.

Acknowledgments

No author completes a novel without the tremendous help from friends old and new. Here is a list of those whose brave soul's aided in this series' creation.

Keri Knutson – Cover artist

Brian Bendlin – Editor extraordinaire

Gil Gruson – Radio Expert & Beta reader

Chris Barber – US Army soldier

John Barber – Trauma Surgeon

Mary Katherine Woods – Surgical Nurse

Thomas Shaw – Engineer & Beta reader and my HH

Ryan Chamberlin – Doctor & Beta reader

Steven Bird – Weapons Specialist, author & Beta reader

CDC – Patient with my many questions

Amos Barber – Hunting expert and my Dad

Ron Chappell – Blurb help

Gus O'Donnell – Second opinion on Blurb help

Sari Sandford and her father in Alaska – Ice fishing

Eric & Diana Tibesar – Cigars and smoking

Adam Shaw – Geology expert and my son

Will Moore – Police Officer & K9 expert

Steven Konkoly – Author & Sounding board

G. Michael Hopf – Also Author & Sounding board

Oakley – Constant companion and my insight into Sheriff

Wendy Shaw – My constant sounding board and walking dictionary as well as my daughter

CPSIA information can be obtained at www.ICGtesting.com
Printed in the USA
LVOW07s2259060116

469486LV00021B/1519/P